Dave and Andie Mae stepped outside onto the terrace at the same moment, crowding one another through the door; Xander followed a step behind. And then they stood there clutching the railing of the balcony or one another, whichever closer, with a white-knuckled grip, and staring open-mouthed at the view that lay before them.

The hotel appeared to be marooned on a piece of ground that looked like it had been torn from the earth as a great chunk of rock -- it stretched out a little way beyond the edge of the building but not by much. Most of the parking lot had completely disappeared -- and instead, a long way below them, there were twinkling lights of what might have been the city whose zip code they had just recently been a part of and then, beyond that, a spill of shadow that was the ocean with a shimmer of moonlight glittering upon it. And they -- the four people watching this, the balcony they were standing on, the building which the balcony was part of, the narrowest piece of skirting land around the foundations of that building -- they were all floating above it all. Somewhere up in the sky. Hanging there, defying common sense, science, and gravity.

"Houston," Xander said quietly, "I think we have a problem."

Abducticon
Alma Alexander
Copyright © 2015 Alma Alexander
All rights reserved
Published by Book View Café Publishing Cooperative
www.BookViewCafe.com

ISBN: 978-1-61138-488-8

Cover design: Lisa M. Morgan (Toxiclight Art and Design)

Interior design copyright © Knotted Road Press

All rights reserved. This is a work of fiction. All characters and events portrayed in this book are fictional, and any resemblance to real people or incidents is purely coincidental. This book, or parts thereof, may not be reproduced in any form without permission.

ABDUCTICON
ALMA ALEXANDER

Book View Café
www.BookViewCafe.com

Also by Alma Alexander

The Secrets of Jin Shei
Embers of Heaven

The Hidden Queen
Changer of Days

Midnight at Spanish Gardens

Worldweavers
Gift of the Unmage
Spellspam
Cybermage
Dawn of Magic

The Were Chronicles
Random
Wolf
Shifter

Short story collections (ebook only)
The Weight of Worlds
Haunted
Sense of Love
Plaisir d'Amour

River (anthology, ed.)

Abducticon
Alma Alexander

ACKNOWLEDGMENTS AND AUTHOR NOTE

As with all books, there are people to thank for this one. As always, my husband and my partner in everything, Deck, who believed in this book from the moment I first strung together a semi-coherent sentence about a nebulous idea.

And then, when it became a reality, I have to call the production and publication team at Book View Café to the stage to take a bow :

Beta reader: Jen Stevenson

Formatter: Leah Cutter

Cover Design: Alma Alexander, Lisa M. Morgan and Dave Smeds

A little further back than that, thanks to Lisa Morgan for picking up a very amateur cover design and helping me make it look good.

A little further back than that... this was a book born in a period of pain, because a lot of it was written during the last few months of my father's life. It was a sanctuary for me, this world, somewhere I could escape to and permit myself to remember that I could laugh -and because of that some of the laughter is deep.

But before that... my thanks to that world, and to all the people in it, my people, my tribe. The writers, The artists. The ones who can quote you dialogue from long-lost episodes of movies and TV shows which haven't been on the air for DECADES. The ones who will read this book and catch all the pieces of homage, the context, the background - those who will, like the audience at an early screening of "Galaxy Quest" I once attended, laugh a split second BEFORE everyone else gets the joke.

If you know what FIAWOL means, if you've ever known it - if you go to cons with shining eyes and an excited spirit and you hate to leave them behind when you go because you are leaving all your friends - this book is for you, with love, because what it means is simply that you can take a con - a great one - one of the best cons you could possibly ever hope to have attended - and you can put it in your pocket and your ereader and your bookshelf and you never have to leave it behind again. It's always here, for you.

Welcome to Abducticon.

Alma Alexander

FRIDAY

"Where *are* you? You should have been here an hour ago with that poster!"

"Sorry. The printer screwed it up again. The first proof I saw somehow managed to make 'Brent Spiner' look like 'Bent Spinner'. They're re-doing it. I should be on my way with the posters within twenty minutes. Sorry, Andie Mae."

Al Coe, hunched over the counter at the print shop with his phone cradled between his ear and his shoulder, winced into the countertop even as the 'sorry' left his lips. That was typical, apologizing to Andie Mae Wilkinson for things that people had no actual control over but somehow ended up assuming responsibility for. Skewered by Andie Mae's limpid blue eyes, combined with the buzzing chainsaw edge in her voice when she was riled, people would instinctively just shout 'Guilty!' and fold. He at least should have known better, should have become immune to the syndrome – having Andie Mae as an on-again-off-again girlfriend for almost four years now should have armored him against the weapons she wielded against lesser mortals. But it was Andie Mae, and she was a force of nature.

Her voice, emerging from his cellphone muffled and muted by flesh and fabric, did not even sound mollified at the apology.

"Next time I pick the printer. Why did you pick that incompetent idiot anyway? And did you tell them this was a rush job?"

"They actually pushed back another job to accommodate us," Al said, trying to keep the peace, but then bit his lip as he realized that his statement wasn't really an excuse in Andie Mae's book. *Of course* they would have pushed back anything else to make room for her own rush job. That's the way things worked in her world. "It's getting done. Honest. I should be back really soon."

"You'd better be. Our program booklets were printed a week ago and Xander finds out *now* that they give an entirely wrong time for the GoH interview. He's been hand-correcting that all morning – in *thousands* of copies – "

"Wait, *how* many registrations have you had…?"

"Well, hundreds, anyway, although it looks like we're going to get anywhere between fifteen hundred and two thousand warm bodies in the end, if all the projections pan out. It's only been Xander and two minions, three people, hard at it, and they're still at it, anyway. And everyone else is buzzing around like bees out of a kicked-over beehive. And nobody can make coffee, apparently – that, or the hotel has some kind of brew that tastes like they used run-off water they collected after the gamers have had their end-of-con showers. You couldn't pick up a package of decent coffee on your way back, could you? Just for us?"

Her voice had changed again, into her Southern Belle Wheedle, and Al never did have an adequate defense against that.

"Sure," he said. "On my way. Almost done here."

He looked up, and caught the eye of a young man who was operating the printer from which his posters would soon be issuing forth. The operator gave him a grin and a cheerful thumbs-up. The best Al could manage, putting down his phone, was a wan smile.

Good God. It was only Friday morning. The con hadn't even officially *started* yet.

Andie Mae thumbed off her own phone with an exasperated sigh. She'd been on some ConCom or another, as a minion or a lieutenant, since she was a teen – but this was her first time in the Chair and she desperately wanted everything to go without a hitch. But there had been nothing but hitches all the way down the line.

It was Friday morning, the fifty-ninth second of the eleventh hour. The registration desk in the hotel foyer was seeing its first flurries of walk-in registrations of the day, not quite the full frenzy yet, but it was starting to build, which meant that the convention had actually, at least semi-officially, begun – and yet there were a thousand and one tasks that still required her attention, and all of them were things without which the con could not possibly run without a hiccup. Not for the first time she wondered uncharitably if her predecessor, Sam Dutton, the entrenched Chair of this con for the last damn near three decades, had vindictively left some kind of evil spell on things after they had voted him out of the office at last during that ConCom meeting straight after the previous year's convention.

Sam was here, now – somewhere in the hotel.

Andie Mae hadn't seen him, precisely, but she felt his presence in the corridors, enough to raise goose-pimples on her skin when she bustled down the hallways or waited impatiently for tardy elevators. He was here, and he was watching, and he would gloat magnificently if he perceived any sign of weakness or failure. She *could* not fail, not in Sam's presence, not in his sight. This con had to be something they would still be talking about when she was an old lady and hailed in hotel corridors of the future as the patron saint of amazing. She wished, not for the first time, that she could have banned Sam from coming at all this year – less pressure – but he was free to register for the con as a guest, now that he was no longer a ConCom member, and there was nothing she could do about that.

She scowled, and wandered over to the nerve center of the operation, the Con Ops office. In the first room of the suite, as she entered, busy volunteers were stuffing envelopes with program booklets, name badges, party invitations, and other assorted ephemera.

Some of them looked up as she came in, and managed smiles or waves before returning to their task. Andie Mae passed through and into the back room, outfitted with the latest in technology, including feed from several webcams strategically placed around the hotel. Some of the designated panel rooms were still being cleared out in preparation for their role in the proceedings, and the cameras showed nothing more than the empty shell of the room with perhaps a uniformed hotel flunky carrying in loads of folding chairs for the audiences to come. Of the couple of hundred people who had already registered, on Thursday night early-reg and on Friday morning, a hardcore few had already found the paneled-off ballroom designated as the games room, and one or three games were already in progress there under the camera's watchful eye. Another camera showed the computer game room, with its eerily glowing banks of monitors, at least three of which were occupied by players whose eyes glittered with an air of something that could almost be menace in the dimly-lit room, intent on the games on their screen.

They couldn't plant their own cameras in the public areas because the hotel objected to this, and they weren't allowed access to the hotel's own security feeds – but in any case nothing interesting was happening yet in the field of view of the only one they had up front, showing an awkward angle of the reg table but not the rest of the foyer.

"Any word from the airport?" Andie Mae called out into the tangle of computer cables and blinking screens and chattering printers.

"Dave called, he said as best he can tell the flight's been delayed," Libby Broadbent, communications maven, lifted her hands from the keyboard for a moment, looking up. "He said he'll keep us posted. Uh, I've had another dozen emails from people who are confused about the hotel…"

Andie Mae tried not to roll her eyes. "Really, anyone would think I changed the venue to upset people," she said. "This is a *better hotel* for us – we've outgrown the old place, had outgrown it five years ago, if only Sam didn't have this sentimental attachment to that horrid fugly carpet they had in the foyer or something. Just tell them to get their asses over here, and promise them bigger and better!"

"Did," Libby said. "At least one of them emailed back sounding less than convinced. How many do you figure will actually turn up this year?"

"All of them," Andie Mae said, through gritted teeth. *If they knew what was good for them. I run JUST as good a con as Sam ever did. Better. I am the best new thing in town.*

"Well, the gamers will," Libby said philosophically. "As long as they program the GPS to bring them to the correct address it won't matter to them one way or another if they're stuck inside some mirrored ballroom at the old Marriott or here at the California Resort. It's all the same room, really. Have you ever wondered if the gamers actually do live in an alternate reality and only the room moves, but they simply stay in it...?"

"Anything's possible," Andie Mae said acidly. She was just a touch sensitive to the gamer comments, having spent at least a year of her own life buried in just such a mirrored ballroom playing the games that had been the foundation of her existence. That was before she had discovered that real-life games could be far more amusing than the fantasy role-playing. Like running cons, for instance.

Like running *this con*. Specifically. Finally, her chance to shine at the thing she wanted so very badly to be good at.

There were definitely enough moments of the hard reality of it all, however, that she caught herself wishing that the whole thing *had* been a game interface. She knew how to toggle those to suit her purposes, when it mattered. Reality meant she had to deal with other people, and those were usually variables she could not predict accurately enough to produce a flawless result.

It was the little things that kept on tripping her up. Little things like her hotel liaison stuck at the airport waiting for her writer Guest of Honor, Vincent J. Silverman, hurriedly recruited at more or less the last moment when the original writer GoH, a big-name author who was supposed to be her drawcard, had decided to cancel on her. At least Vincent J. Silverman wrote stuff that was remotely related to the con's theme, which was a blessing. Andie Mae had dispatched David Lorne, her hotel and guest liaison, to meet Silverman's flight, but he hadn't been on it, and then emailed that he would be taking a later flight. Now

Dave had been cooling his heels at the airport for the better part of the morning – and she had better things for him to do than hang around at the arrivals gate all day. She was starting to get just a *titch* annoyed at her author guest.

She tapped at her left ear, the one with the earpiece via which the committee stayed in touch with each other – no old-fashioned hand-held radios for her and her crew, not like Sam's antiques – and scowled again. She wished people would just *check in* so that she knew where everyone was and what they were doing.

"Everything under control downstairs?" she asked, leaning over Libby's shoulder and peering at the registration table camera feed. The screen showed a grainy image of one lanky-haired young man handing over a sheaf of crumpled bills, with a hint of someone else waiting patiently in line just behind.

"So far so good," Libby said. "It's just Felicity down there for the moment, though – maybe we could send a couple of more volunteers down to man the desk in about an hour, but we seem to be in a lull and everything is pretty quiet, she says she can cope with things right now."

"Any update on…"

"She says there have been thirty more registrations in the past hour," Libby said, preempting the question. "But they said their friends would be coming, apparently. After work. Give them a few more hours."

Andie Mae drummed her fingers on the back of Libby's chair. The *posters* needed to be up by then, dammit. The posters with their star turn attractions. The posters, which might have moved more registrations. The posters that were still at the printer's with Al.

"I wish I could clone myself," Andie Mae muttered under her breath. It was necessary for her to oversee everything, or else nothing would turn out right – but being everywhere at once was proving to be rather wearying on a body. She found herself wishing that Al was back, already – and not for the reasons that were foremost in her mind just a moment before. She desperately wanted a cup of good coffee.

❋

"You sure this is the right place?" Angel Silverman said doubtfully as the yellow cab pulled up under the shimmering canopy of the fake-mother-of-pearl portico arching above the entrance to the California Resort.

"That's the address," Vince Silverman said, fishing in his pocket for his wallet. "Here, keep the change," he said to the driver, handing over a fifty-dollar bill.

The driver took the money with a delicate two-fingered grip. "Much obliged," he said. "Let me get your bags."

Angel had already got out of the car, and had taken the few steps off to her right where the driveway ended at a sturdy stainless steel fence wreathed with flowering creeper. "At least it has a nice view," she called back over her shoulder.

"Maybe we rate a room with one," Vince said. "Come on, let's get checked in and then you can go exploring."

"There's a pool," Angel said, pointing.

"Swell," Vince muttered. "Later, Angel. Come on."

Angel left her vantage point with reluctance, and shouldered one of the smaller bags piled by the entrance. "OK, hon," she said. "Right behind you."

"I suppose I'd better find someone from the committee first," Vince said, tackling the revolving doors with the finesse of someone who was no stranger to handling such things with a double armful of luggage.

An expressionless man with too-perfect silvery-white skin just a little too tightly stretched over the bones of his face watched them enter, standing without moving only a few steps away as the Silvermans fell into the foyer with their baggage. Vince looked up, rearranging his grip on his rolling carry-on, and gave the other man a once-over. Con goer, definitely; one learned to recognize them on sight, after enough conventions. Just enough of a too-weird vibe to be a mundane.

"I don't suppose you know where the reg desk is?" he asked conversationally.

The man lifted one hand and pointed off to his right.

"Ah. Okay. Thanks." There was indeed a U-shaped barricade of generic hotel tables, complete with white tablecloths and starched white ruffled 'skirts' velcroed on and already coming off at the corners. It was arranged in one corner of the foyer, with an array of computer screens and a tangle of black lanyards in evidence next to one workstation. Another nest of tables had a large orange and green sign that proclaimed "T SHIRTS!" – although, as yet, the advertised merchandise hadn't manifested. The registration tables were currently manned by a solitary girl whose long hair, which might have originally have been a mousy light brown but was now dyed in multicolored streaks of improbable hues, was draped over a black leather corset. She slouched in her chair behind one of the computers, seemingly totally engrossed in a manga.

"Stay here," Vince said to Angel. "The hotel desk is in the opposite direction, I'll see if I can't get someone in charge and then we can go check in – no point in dragging all this luggage both ways."

Angel nodded, and Vince shrugged off his own shoulder duffel bag to add to the pile at her feet, and thus unencumbered strode off toward the computer bank.

The girl behind the table showed no awareness of his approach – nor, indeed, of his presence, as he came to a halt in front of her and waited politely for a few moments. Then he cleared his throat, and she looked up, languid, her eyes almost manga-big in her narrow pale face.

"You want to register?" she asked, putting the manga down with evident reluctance.

"I'm Vincent Silverman," Vince said. And then, when she simply stared at him without any apparent recognition, added gently, "Your Guest of Honor?"

The girl shot up in her seat, her spine straight, appeared to think about getting up, opened and closed her mouth a few times, and then said, desperately, "Oh! I'm so sorry! I didn't… I mean, I thought… I didn't know that you… I'll just… call somebody…?"

"You do that," Vince said, giving her a calming smile.

She fumbled with a small microphone that led off a bud inside her left ear and gabbled into it, almost as incoherent as she had been with Vince himself – listened briefly – and then looked up with evident relief.

"Andie Mae is on her way down," she said. "The Chair."

"Thank you," Vince said.

"I, uh, she'll have your badge," the girl babbled. "I'm *so* sorry, Mr Silverman."

She might have been a generation too young to understand the basis for any of his books. Vince, never as conscious of his graying hair as he was in that moment, found himself torn between wishing that he had that innocence back, that anonymity of his younger days that made it almost certain that nobody at all could be expected to recognize him on sight, and a strange kind of annoyed resentment that all of the years he had put into this job, into his reputation, meant absolutely nothing at all and the younger generation of fans, the ones who had followed his own cohort, had no reason to know who he was.

But he could see someone almost running down the foyer now, a delicate blonde girl who looked entirely too fragile to bear the load of a con Chair but whose badge, with its long tail of colorful ribbons attached to it, branded her such. She sailed right past Angel and the bags, and came to a skidding halt at his side, flushed and out of breath.

"I sent Dave to get you at the airport!" she said, by way of greeting. "How did you get here? He just phoned upstairs that he was still waiting for…"

"Oh dear, I am sorry if I managed to miss the connection," Vince said. "We took a cab."

She turned briefly to follow the direction in which he nodded when he said 'we' and appeared to have only just become aware of Angel's presence.

"My wife," Vince said helpfully. "Might we get checked in, and dump the bags? Angel saw a pool, earlier…"

"Yes, of course. I'm Andie Mae, we emailed…"

"Pleasure," Vince said.

"This way," Andie Mae said, motioning for him to follow. "Your room's ready. Would you just excuse me…"

He nodded and started walking toward the hotel desk, stopping only to collect Angel and the bags on the way, and Andie Mae turned to the still flustered and round-eyed girl behind the desk.

"Get Libby to phone Dave and tell him to get back here," she snapped. "I don't know how he managed it but he let our guest of honor sail straight past him and now I've a cab fare to reimburse on top of all else. And how could you *possibly* have embarrassed us like that by not knowing *who he was?*"

"Yes, I mean, sorry, I mean, I'll sort it out," the girl babbled.

"By the way, how many registrations so far?" Andie Mae said, changing direction with such speed and agility that the other girl could only open and close her mouth several times in response, like a guppy out of its fishbowl, and then offer, quietly and very lamely, that she wasn't sure at all but she thought there had been more than fifty people who had registered on her own shift so far.

"It's okay, but hopefully it'll pick up," Andie Mae muttered. She glanced at the pile of pocket programs stacked on the table by the computers, and lifted one up, flipping through it with a quick, nervous motion. "Have these all been corrected? Call Xander, if he needs to fix the wrong time." And then she turned, realized that her VIP was almost at the hotel desk, dropped the program back on its pile and strode off after the Silvermans in a flurry of swirling skirts, leaving her volunteer feeling as though she had just been wrung out like a wet dishcloth and by someone who knew how.

The expressionless man by the door had not moved, and had watched the entire exchange with a sort of dispassionate curiosity.

"It's after four. What's the foyer looking like?"

"Healthier," Libby said, walking into the room where Andie Mae was pacing. "I've just been down there. There's a doubled-back queue from the reg desk all the way to the hotel desk. And I'm starting to see the regulars, out there. Chicken Man is back, I've seen him all over the place in that weird cluck-onesie of his, bless him for classing up the joint. How does he ever go to the bathroom in a hurry?"

"TMI," someone said from the back of the room, and a ripple of laughter spread out into the volunteers.

"This year the Hair Color of Choice seems to be bright purple or neon green," Libby said, continuing her report, "but I've seen a couple of oranges and a handful of bright pinks, and one or two lemon-yellow mohawks – I think there's a posse of them out there. Is there a new manga or something? Anyway, as for the classics, there's three Leias so far, one Original Edition and two Slave Girls, about par for the course, and one guy who thinks he might be Chewbacca but if you ask me I think Bigfoot's Mom slipped up and let him off the leash and out on his own."

"There's one girl who really is not wearing nearly enough to even be classed as a costume," said Xander Washington, programming chair, who had himself been roaming the halls only a half hour previous. "If you were to put together everything she's got on into a single piece of material, you wouldn't have enough to make a barstool covering."

"Is that the same girl who tried to convince me that Saran Wrap was a costume, last year?" asked Simon Ballard, head of security, in his full Viking regalia, an anachronistic earbud glowing blue in his left ear. "She had the unmitigated gall to tell me, when every other logical thing to try had failed her, that it was a statement on existentialism."

"One of your postgraduate buddy bunnies, letting it all hang out?" Xander teased, grinning.

"Honestly? That's healthier than the zombie crowd," Libby said, and then, as one or two of the others lifted their heads at the comment, added, "Sorry, but they *freak me out*. Why would any living thing dress up as something half rotten and think that is attractive?"

"You're more into *wompires*," Xander said, lifting his arms up into a bad imitation of throwing out a cloak or maybe a set of batwings. "Just as dead, you know."

"But way more interesting," Libby retorted. "Hi, can I help you?"

"Carol Elliot," said a woman who had just walked into the Green Room where the ConCom had congregated. "You have my badge up here?"

"Somewhere," Libby said. "Elliot… E… it'll be in this box…" She rummaged through a pile of manila envelopes and pulled one out with a triumphant flourish. "There we are. Your itinerary's inside, we printed them on the back of the name tents this year."

"Oh good, it's always great to know where you're supposed to be next," Carol said, opening her envelope and riffling through it. "Um, and my husband's badge…?"

"Eep. They might have that downstairs, but you don't want to go down into that zoo. Let me call them and double check, in the meantime you can get Mike over there to just print you a temp one and that'll be fine until we sort it out."

" 'Kay. Thanks."

"Do you have mine there, while you're at it?" Another pro, wearing a pith helmet crowned by a pair of truly spectacular steampunk goggles, pushed forward past Carol Elliot's retreating back. "I'm Bob Williamson."

Libby reached for a different stack of envelopes. "Lemme see…"

She had almost a dozen of them turn up in quick succession, pros who were at the convention to work – writers who were on panels, artists from the art show, one of the musicians who were to give a concert later that weekend – they needed their badges, they needed information, they needed supplies and minions for setup work that needed to be done, they often just needed coffee. Libby had her head down and was waist high in manila envelopes when she lifted her head and smiled at the next person standing in front of her.

"Name?"

"Oh, no, no, sorry, I didn't mean to intrude if you're busy," the young man said apologetically. It was only then that she noticed the shiny brass badge on the lapel of a waistcoat that was entirely unlike anything that a con-goer would be seen in. She squinted at the badge, and he offered up a preemptive hand. "I'm Luke, Luke Barnes, I'm the Night Manager, just come on duty – actually, it's my first time in the hot seat, tonight – just wandered by to see if you guys were okay out here, if you had everything you needed…"

"How sweet," Libby said, and meant it literally. In general they were not much given to receiving visits from the managerial staff up in the Green Room and Con Ops. Maybe it was just that 'first time in the hot seat' thing. The boy – and he didn't look much older than someone who could still legitimately be called a boy – was still so very new at this, earnest, and eager to please. "I think we're fine, really."

"Good. I, uh, it's my first time – and something this big – I don't think this hotel has had this many people – I'm perfectly certain that we're *this* close to breaking the fire codes…" He sounded a little nervous, and Libby gave him a wide and encouraging smile.

"You'll be fine. I know it all must look weird, but…"

"Oh, no, I love sci fi," Luke said. Xander, who had just come into the room, gave a theatrical eye roll at this, but Luke failed to notice.

"Ever been to a con?" Libby asked.

"Well, *this* one," Luke said, grinning. "Let me know if you guys need anything."

"Will do," Libby said. There was something that she might have asked for but she couldn't remember it, right there and then, and Luke ducked his head at her, gave everyone else a cheery wave, and wriggled out of the increasingly crowded room.

"*Sci fi*," muttered Xander scornfully.

"Everyone has to start somewhere, Rat," Libby said, using the nickname that he was far better known by in that crowd – in its entirety, LabRat, often shortened to just Rat. "You were a con virgin once, too."

"Yabbut I was fifteen," Xander said, crossing his eyes. "And look at me now… Hey, is there any more coffee in that pot…?"

Coffee.

Libby remembered that she'd overheard Andie Mae complaining about coffee, asking Al to bring some decent coffee when he came back with the posters which announced their star attraction. Andie Mae had scored the coup of getting two of the most famous androids of their genre – Data, from Star Trek, and the Terminator – to make a brief (but *very* expensive – this one item had eaten a lion's share of their budget for that year) appearance at the con, with its theme of Robots and Androids. How Andie Mae had managed to even find a way to get in touch with someone like actor-turned-politician Arnold Schwarzenegger was beyond Libby's comprehension – she herself wouldn't have known where to start – but Andie Mae had been determined to make the first con she chaired something that would not be forgotten in a hurry. Somehow, through methods that might have involved a midnight summoning of demons, she had done it, and the two actors portraying the android characters, Brent Spiner and Arnold Schwarzenegger, were due to show up for a photo-op and a brief signing spot and fan meet-and-greet on Saturday afternoon, one of the crowning selling points of the con.

The demon hypothesis might not have been so farfetched, because once the coup was secured everything else seemed to go haywire. Libby, as the designated media and communications member of the ConCom, had been handed the publicity baton – and she had done fairly well in publicizing the presence of the two actors in outside media. Inside the con itself, however, things were a different matter.

That was why Al Coe was at the printers for the third time, for the final – and correct – version of the posters they had ordered for the con.

He should have been back with those posters by now.

The posters, and the coffee. To the best of Libby's knowledge (and it would have been her business to know) the posters had not materialized. And neither had the good coffee; Andie Mae would have had a loud word to say on that if it had arrived, whether or not it had matched her own august criteria in the end.

No coffee. No posters. No Al.

And it was now getting on for Friday evening, and the queue of registrants had grown long, and a bunch of games had already started in the designated ballroom, with three tables surrounded by players throwing dice and blissfully divorced – for the duration – from anything resembling reality. The first scattered parties would be starting in a matter of hours. The con, to all intents and purposes, had begun – and Libby was woefully bereft in any material larger than an A4 sheet hastily printed on a local color printer, cobbled together by Libby herself to be inserted at the last moment into the glossy full color souvenir program books, letting those who had just been handed the booklets at the registration desk know that the famous androids would be coming.

But even those only announced their presence. It was the big posters to be plastered all over the hotel which were to announce a final date and time.

"Anyone seen Al?" Libby called out into the chaos of the Green Room.

"Not since this morning," Xander said, chewing on a messy sandwich thrown together from the cold meats and cheese platter that had been provided for the Green Room volunteers' sustenance.

"I think we should…" Libby began, but then several earpieces squawked simultaneously, with people wincing and reaching up a hand to adjust the volume in their ears, and Xander looked up in consternation.

"Holy crap," he said, tossing the remnants of his sandwich aside and tearing off a piece of paper towel from a nearby roll to wipe traces of mayo off his hands. "Somebody better get down there. I heard that our writer GoH kind of dropped in unannounced while Dave was waiting for him at the airport – and now we seem to have a situation again – Rory Grissom just walked in the door and got *mobbed*… that wasn't supposed to happen. Where's Andie Mae? Crap. Never mind, I'll go rescue him."

"Send him up here, we can hide him until they get him into his room safely," Libby said.

"Too late to stash him, they know he's here. Aw, *dammit*. I've a got heap of work still to do, and now I have to go babysit a drama queen."

He vanished into the corridor, and two more pros turned up to fill the space he had vacated, asking for their envelopes. One was found easily, the other appeared to be missing altogether, throwing Libby into a state of near panic until the pro in question thought to mention that, since his new book was coming up under a new pseudonym, that might be the name the registration envelope might be under. In a quite different part of the alphabet.

"Take it easy," Libby whispered to herself, looking up for a moment and seeing a Green Room thronged with visiting pro and ConCom members and convention volunteers, a swirling melee of smiling people full of energy and enthusiasm, waiting with a delighted anticipation for the real festivities to begin on the morrow but in the meantime running into friends they hadn't seen for months, or maybe a whole year since the last con, chattering, exchanging news, asking after other friends who had not yet made an appearance.

It's just the usual chaos, and it'll only get more chaotic as the evening wears on…

"Libby, was it Alice who was in charge of the writers' workshop this year?" somebody shouted into her ear, to be heard above the general noise level.

"No, she handed over to Lou Martin – I don't think she could make the con this year," Libby shouted in response.

"Seen Lou? Need to sort out something!"

"Don't think she's here yet!"

"Oh! Okay. I'd better email her. Hope she checks her email before she gets here tomorrow. One of her pros…"

But someone else was pawing at the envelopes, and Libby turned back to try and keep some control over the process. Out of the corner of her eye she glimpsed something that was sufficiently out of kilter with the rest of the scene for her to actually take notice. Amongst the heaving happy throng crowding the Green Room there was one person standing alone, with as much space between herself and everybody else as that was possible to achieve under the circumstances, a woman standing very still with both hands loosely by her side. She was dressed in something that may or may not have been a costume (not outlandish enough to be tagged as one immediately; just not commonplace enough to be immediately dismissed as *not* being one). There was something… strange… about her – the stillness, the ever-so-slightly off shade of her silvery skin, something about her eyes – but there was no time for further inspection. Someone else slipped in between Libby and the woman, and when Libby could look that way again she was gone. Libby could not even be certain any more what had attracted her attention, but the strange woman's afterimage remained in the back of Libby's head like a ghost, distracting her from something that she knew she had been about to do before she was distracted by something else before that.

She saw Xander slip back into the suite, and burrowed her way across to him to where he had gone back to the computers set up in the back room.

"Your movie star sorted?"

"I thought he'd be upset, but he was a pig in clover, surrounded by pink-haired chicks with fairy wings who were clamoring for his autograph and some really weird dude painted kind of silver or something who just stood there and watched – creepy, really, I don't know if I ought to go give Sim and Security a shout about him."

"What, you think we have a stalker or something on hand?" Libby yelped.

"He's a mother-lovin' movie star, doesn't it come with the territory?" Xander said. "But maybe he was just a dude who was trying to pretend to be an android and fit in with the theme of the show, I don't know. Maybe I'm reading too much into it."

Libby's mind went fleetingly to the woman she had seen standing so very still in the melee of the Green Room, and come to think of it she too looked like she was playing an android character… but then, robots were this year's theme, after all, and everyone was just tired and jumpy. That was all.

"There *are* a number of droids out there," Libby said slowly. "And I distinctly remember seeing a baby blue Dalek near the Hospitality Suite area earlier."

"Actually, to be honest, I'm more astonished that there was at least one dude dressed in a replica of the uniform Rory Grissom graced on the good ship *Invictus*," Xander said, dismissing the matter. "I don't know how the groupies even *found* him that fast, they must have been waiting at the front door for as long as it took for him to manifest. He seemed to be enjoying it all rather too much – I almost had to drag him bodily away from there before he spent all his con capital on one spectacular meet and greet – we have *plans* for him at Opening Ceremonies, after all, and that's in just a few hours. Where's the Steel Magnolia when we need her?"

The Steel Magnolia, which was what Andie Mae was known as behind her back half in affection and half in abject terror, was chewing on her perfect lower lip while cradling her cellphone between her shoulder and her ear in a quiet spot she had found just inside a newly-cleared hotel bedroom due to be used as a programming room the next day. But Al Coe's phone kept on going to voicemail, and she had left three messages already – she had started out by being snarky, but by the third message she had graduated to *Please call me, where ARE you, I am getting worried.* This fourth call was not giving her any more joy, and she finally thumbed off the phone with a frustrated grimace and without leaving another message. A passing thought about starting to call the local hospitals meandered across the surface of her mind, but then she mentally shook herself and firmly admonished her more paranoid self to stop being ridiculous – and to possibly start thinking of something adequate to say when Al did turn up with those posters, which were turning into quite the production.

Turning sharp right as she exited the sanctuary of the not-yet-panel-room, she nearly collided with a figure standing close to the wall, very still, his skin a silvery-white, with two pale eyes set dully into an almost expressionless face.

"Sorry," she said automatically, ducking around the guy.

He did not respond, by word or gesture, and Andie Mae briefly felt as though she should be offended and flounce off in a huff – but she had other things on her mind, and she methodically subtracted the silver man from her thoughts as she hurried forward and plunged into the busier corridors where the con was beginning to swing into a higher gear.

She failed to notice a pair of con-goers who had paused as she flung herself unseeingly past them, but the older of the two, a middle-aged man with a receding hairline of salt-and-pepper hair that swept around the back of his head like a half-tonsure and a lush gray beard, halted as he turned to follow Andie Mae's progress with glittering gray-blue eyes.

"Thar she blows," he muttered.

His companion, a lanky youngster in perhaps his late teens, turned his head marginally.

"She didn't even look," the young man said, in a voice dithering between obligatorily aggrieved (on his mentor's behalf) and vaguely puzzled.

"Oh, she wouldn't pay attention to the likes of me, Marius, not in public," Sam Dutton, Andie Mae's predecessor as the con Chair, said. "I only owned this con for the last three decades, that's all. But it's her baby now and she doesn't want to be reminded of history, not today. And I'm history. I'm not surprised that she wouldn't stop and chat. But still – she looks rather more singularly focused than one should be at this stage of the game. I wonder if everything is okay."

"Do you miss it?" Marius Tarkovski asked, turning back to Sam with a small smile.

Sam waved his hands in a gesture that implied a complete inability to answer the question. "Some part of me does," he admitted. "I just *know* I should be in the thick of things, and it feels odd – like a mental itch – being here and not being on the inside. But on the other hand... anything that *does* go wrong won't be my fault this time, dammit. Her show. Her game. Her responsibility. It's what she wanted, and I hope that she gets exactly what she wanted." He stopped, and looked almost astonished. "That came out rather more claws-out than I intended," he said. "Who knew. Maybe it does rankle just a bit more than I thought it would."

"You sure it was a good idea coming this year?" Marius asked.

"Well, your Mom is happier knowing that you've got me on standby – your first solo con and all that," Sam said, grinning. "So there's the babysitting aspect of it…"

Marius aimed a polite but still affronted fist bump at the older man's shoulder. "I'm *seventeen*," he said.

"Exactly," Sam agreed laconically, and followed the passage of a trio of scantily-clad female fairies wearing the barest minimum of chiffon and oversize pink wings. One of them became aware of the scrutiny and half-turned, offering a flirtatious glance from underneath drooping eyelids that looked too weak to support the weight of glitter piled upon them. Marius flushed a bright scarlet, right to the tips of his ears, a reaction to both Sam's implications and that particular response, and looked down to the toes of his sneakers.

Sam laughed, but not unkindly; he gave Marius's shoulder an understanding squeeze and at the same time used the gesture to propel him forward once again in their original direction.

"Come on, kid," he said. "We'll mingle a bit more – I'm sure there are friends out here somewhere – and then we can turn in. Tomorrow the fun begins. AndieCon starts in earnest…"

"Sam…?"

Sam's head turned very slowly at the sound of his name, to face a young man a good thirty years his junior but with signs of exactly the same receding hairline beginning to make an appearance. They looked remarkably similar, in fact – that hair, and eyes of almost exactly the same color, of almost identical height and build allowing for some middle-aged spread on Sam. Marius, who immediately recognized the new arrival as Andie Mae's ex-liutenant Liam Connors, wondered not for the first time if there was actual truth in tales of time travel and whether it was possible that somehow, without even knowing it, Liam was a young Sam and there was a dangerous time-line crossing occurring here which meant that the entire con would implode into a temporal black hole any minute.

But nothing of the sort happened, and Sam smiled a tight little smile as he acknowledged Liam with a small nod.

"Hey," he said.

"Hey yourself," Liam said, awkward, not knowing whether to smile or how broadly to smile or whether he really should have said anything at all. He was, after all, at Andie Mae's side when the two Young Turks had orchestrated the coup that had removed Sam from the con Chair – but then Andie Mae had ditched Liam, also, to go solo. And now he was stuck in limbo, in no-man's land, betrayer of the old guard and betrayed by the new. "I, uh, didn't think you'd come."

"This? I wouldn't miss it for the world. And there's also the fact that I haven't actually missed one of these for three decades and I wasn't about to start now. Habit, you know. How about you?"

"Me?"

"Well," Sam said, one eyebrow rising Spock-like into the middle of his forehead, "you are kind of *compromised* with the leadership, aren't you?"

Liam flushed. "I don't think – " he began, but Sam waved him into silence.

"Son," he said, " I rather knew that. You don't think. That was the problem last year. You might have known she wouldn't share, but eh, she is Andie Mae and we all know how persuasive she is. I just want to know if it was you behind the Big Name Writer GoH no-show – did you sabotage that? To get back at Andie Mae for ditching you? I figured it might be."

"Why?" Liam asked defensively.

"Because he was *my* original contact, and I passed his contact details to you, and you were the one dealing with him for this gig… until it all went pear-shaped for Andie Mae after she ditched you. Hey, you can't blame a guy for trying to draw the lines if all the dots are lined up."

"I wouldn't do that to her," Liam said, stuffing both hands into the pockets of his jeans.

"No, of course not," Sam agreed without rancor. "And Vince Silverman is a pleasant enough replacement. I am quite looking forward to cornering him for a chat, actually. There are things I've wanted to ask him about his books, so it works out nicely."

"I thought you wouldn't come," Liam said. "After... after..."

"I accept your apology," Sam said regally, all but offering up his royal hand to be kissed. Whether or not an apology was actually what Liam had had in mind, he didn't say anything more – and after another short and awkward silence, during which Liam could not or would not lift his eyes to meet Sam's steady gaze, Marius took it upon himself to try and defuse the situation, latching onto the very person they had just named, who had turned into their corridor as though summoned by a spell cast by those syllables.

"Isn't that him?" Marius said, nudging Sam with an elbow. "Vince Silverman?"

"I believe so," Sam said. "Well, if you'll excuse me, Liam... Hey, Mr Silverman! Vince!"

They sidestepped an immobile Liam and made their way to where Vince Silverman had halted at the sound of his name and turned to see who had hailed him.

"We met a number of times at this con or that," Sam said. "Of course you probably don't remember me at all, but there was that dinner that we had, you and me and Larry Niven and Greg Bear at the Natcon in Seattle a bunch of years back... black hole pudding, if you recall..."

Vince Silverman did, vaguely, but he was damned if he could call up a name. He stuck out a hand anyway with a smile that came out commendably sincere given that it was so completely staged. "Yes, of course," he said. "The name escapes me, I'm afraid, but I do remember that conversation..."

"Dutton. Sam Dutton. We actually emailed some, over the years – I used to be con Chair of this very con right here until a year ago, but now it is under completely new management and I am just a humble fan again. But I'm very glad to see you again. As the Guest of Honor, they must have you scheduled down to the minute but – well – how long are you staying? If you find yourself in the market for dinner company, perhaps on Sunday night after most of the real festivities are over, perhaps we might connect."

"That sounds good," Vince said, and actually meant it. Truth was, he *did* recall a raucous dinner at a con long past, at which he had had an uncommonly good time, and this man had definitely been there for that. By Sunday it was entirely possible that he would be happy to have this dinner companion.

"About half past sixish? Outside the restaurant?" Sam said. "That should be okay as far as any programming is concerned…And I'll probably have this young'un in tow – may I introduce Marius Tarkovski, winner of his high school writing competition for three years running and very much wanting to walk in your shoes some day."

"I'm sure it will be fine," Vince said. "I look forward to it. And nice to meet you, Marius. We'll talk."

"Enjoy the con," Sam said

Marius, who had been rendered quite speechless by the entire encounter, finally found his voice as he watched Vince Silverman's back vanish into the throng in the corridor.

"Do you actually know *everyone*?" he demanded of Sam as they stood there and allowed the crowds to flow around them like water around an obstacle in its path.

"Oh, it's quite the little club," Sam said. "Put in enough years and enough cons and sooner or later you at least recognize most people. I remember one time I was at a smaller regional con and then I more or less went straight from that to that year's Worldcon, in LA that year, and the first person I saw in the football-field-sized lobby of that enormous hotel was a person to whom I had said goodbye less than a week ago at another hotel halfway across the country. Sometimes cons feel like they warp the space-time continuum…"

"A space-time anomaly."

"Don't say that, you know what always happens to the *Enterprise* after they go poking too closely at one," Sam said. "But that's a bar conversation. We should go and hang out there – sooner or later the whole convention comes drifting by and finds you."

"So I've heard," Marius said dryly. "You've said it many times, and yet may I remind you again that technically I would probably be arrested…"

Sam grimaced. "It's your own fault, boy, you talk and act like you aren't a juvenile," he said. "In theory the next best thing would be the Green Room because everyone filters through there sooner or later and there are no issues with you being underage – but there the problem might be me. Andie Mae might well have posted 'thou shalt not pass' spells on the door, and fire-breathing dragons would be released in defense of the realm if I came within a hundred feet of the sacred door. But there's bound to be an early party or two going on. Maybe some of them won't even think it's necessary to card you, young'un, and we can pick up all sorts of loose talk if we keep our ears open."

"Sam, what are you *doing* here?" Marius asked, giving his friend and mentor a long, measured gaze. "One of the other guys in the teen writer's competition, he's been volunteering this year, he's pretty tight with the new bunch. He says that Andie Mae said that you were going to try and throw a monkey wrench into…"

"Ah, no, son," Sam said, clapping the younger man on the shoulder. "I'm interested in how this whole thing plays out this year, with a new management crew calling the shots – and I've heard that it's pretty much a given that if I did something one way, Andie Mae has done her utmost to do it as differently as she can. I would not shoot this con of all cons in the foot. I spent too much time and energy and blood and sweat and tears building up the equity here to tear it down out of some petty spite. No, I'm not out to pull the rug out from under her. But I *do* want to know just exactly what kind of rug it is that we are standing on. Come on. Keep your ears open. This will give you six good novels' worth of material, if you take copious notes."

After that last abortive attempt at connecting with Al on the phone, Andie Mae had gone so far as to complain about his continued absence to several of her ConCom members, and had even indicated that she was thinking of sending out the cavalry to look for him – or at least phoning the local lock-ups and hospitals to find out if he had done something that had landed him in either. She had been dissuaded, for the moment, and then something else claimed her immediate attention and erased the mystery from the top of her to-do list, with just a mental footnote to take her time and an exquisite pleasure in a properly crafted and blistering take-down of a welcome when Al did turn up – but if she had, in fact, phoned the local ER she might have found out more than she realized.

It was there that a dazed Al Coe began to realize just how much time had passed, that he had not called in to provide a reason for his non-arrival at the hotel with the posters everyone was waiting for, that he could not do so anyway since his phone seemed to be missing (and, upon further reflection, he could not remember what had happened to said posters, either), and that he actually had an arm in a sling which indicated that Something Bad Had Happened of which he didn't *quite* have a full and complete recollection.

"I need to…" he began urgently, when a young nurse wearing scrubs with a teddy bear pattern on them walked into the room where he sat on a gurney, but she waved him back down when he tried to get to his feet. Those feet were bare, he noticed, with a disconnected idea that his shoes (as well as his phone and the posters) were also missing from the scene. The nurse pushed him back down on the gurney, gently but firmly.

"The doctor will be in to see you," she said. "You should be all right to go home, with a few pain killers – do you have anyone we can call?"

"No," Al said stupidly, his mind curiously blank – and that was true enough, his home was currently quite empty of anyone to whom his condition and whereabouts might be of interest. The reason, of course, was that his flatmate was already at the con. So was Andie Mae. So was pretty much everybody he knew. It only occurred to him belatedly, after the nurse had left, that he could have called them at the con. That he *should* have called them at the con.

His head ached.

When the doctor did turn up, some thirty or so minutes later, Al told him as much; the doctor pulled back his lower eyelids and peered into his eyes with a small flashlight.

"You don't have concussion," he said, "but you're pretty out of it, anyway…"

"I should go home," Al said. "Where's my clothes? Where's my car keys?"

The doctor looked him oddly. "Your car's pretty smashed," he said, "they towed that. Besides, I wouldn't be happy with you driving anywhere right now. I'd actually prefer it if you stayed…"

"I have to get home," Al said. And then blinked. "Towed?"

"Yes. The other guy was pretty totaled too. You smashed together pretty good. You're both lucky it all ended up with just a few non-life-threatening broken bones."

"Wait – *towed?* Towed where? Were the posters still in there?"

"The posters?" the doctor said, looking at Al strangely, obviously reconsidering his options with this patient.

"I was on my way to… which company? How do I get hold of…?"

The doctor consulted a chart, and then looked up again. "Mr Coe," he said, "wherever it was that you were going, you aren't exactly in any shape to go there right now. I am quite serious about – "

But Al was seeing Andie Mae's furious face, burning blue eyes. "But I promised I would get the posters there tonight," he murmured.

"Well," the doctor said, "you won't. The number of the towing company's probably on the card you had in your wallet. You can deal with them in good time. Right now, it's my job to make sure you're comfortable and you won't come to any additional harm. Now. Is there anyone we can call to pick you up and keep an eye on you?"

"The California Resort," Al said.

"What?"

"The California Resort. That's where I need to go."

"Are you staying there? You aren't local?" The doctor consulted his chart again. "I thought I saw an address…"

"Everybody is over there. Nobody home right now."

"Oh," the doctor said, uncomprehendingly, staring at Al with a slight frown.

"You want someone to keep an eye on me?" Al said, quite lucidly. "Well, all my friends are there right now. At the convention. Where I was supposed to be – with the posters. What time is it?"

The doctor consulted his watch. "Almost seven thirty."

"Call me a cab," Al said. "I'll go there and I'll…"

"To a convention?" The doctor looked skeptically at the arm cradled in a sling and a collection of small cuts and darkening bruises elsewhere on the patient's body. "I really think you're in no shape to – "

"Just do it," Al said. "And please find me my stuff."

The doctor's brows drew together at that distinctly less-than-deferential tone, and then he shrugged. "As you wish. You're leaving on your own recognizance, though, and against medical advice and I'll put that on the record. I'll send someone to help you dress – your clothes are over there on the table, in the bag, some of them are a little messed up but I guess we can't help that. I'll send a small bottle of Vicodin home with you, and it would really be good if you could look in on a doctor at some point during the next 48 hours or so. Just to make sure."

"Fine," Al muttered.

All of him hurt, as though he had been worked over by a professional boxer. His chest felt vaguely caved in, and he seemed to be having difficulty with the simple act of inhaling a lungful of air –but nothing major seemed to be broken, other than the damaged arm, and he could cope with the rest of it. Because movement was limited with one arm in a sling and because every small movement made him wince it took some little while before he could, with assistance, struggle halfway into a set of clothes which were not happy with the sling situation; another forty minutes or more passed before he walked, staggering a little, to a waiting cab and gave directions to the California Resort.

It was now past eight o'clock, and full dark, and it was later still by the time the cab pulled up and woke its passenger, dozing fitfully in the back seat. Al blinked several times and sat up, wincing as he jarred the strapped arm.

"We here?"

"Yes, sir, we're at 2235 Bluff Road," the cab driver said. "That'll be $22.50."

Al awkwardly pulled out a wallet with his good hand and ferreted out a twenty and a ten, passing them over to the cabbie over the back of the driver's seat. "Keep the change,"

"Thank you," the cabbie said. "I'll just get the door for ya…"

It took something of an inelegant scramble, minding his injured arm and shoulder, for Al to extricate himself out of the back seat of the cab – and while he was still sorting himself out, at the curbside, the cabbie gave him a half-wave and pulled away. But it took a few more moments for Al to realize a few uncomfortable truths about his situation.

He should have been deposited at the front door of a hotel. He had not been. He had in fact been delivered to what seemed to be the side of a dark and otherwise empty road.

The place where the California Resort should have been – where it in fact had been less than twelve hours before this moment – was just a lacuna in the night.

The hotel – the entire hotel – had simply… disappeared.

Dave Lorne, the ConCom member who had been sent to chase his tail at the airport meeting the elusive Guest of Honor, finally pulled into the parking lot of the hotel at almost a quarter to eight on Friday night. The parking lot was packed. He circled for a few hopeless minutes, squinting to see if anyone would be stupid enough to vacate their spot, but most people were already ensconced for the night and were there to stay. Dave was hot and tired and frustrated and irritable and hungry. His day had not gone well. He had managed to miss both lunch and dinner, grabbing something unhealthy and sugary every time his stomach reminded him of how empty it was – and now he wanted something substantial to eat (he knew that if he didn't he'd wake up at four in the morning and attack a packet of salty crisps from the vending machine). He also badly wanted a drink, preferably something strong, and in the company of somebody sympathetic to whom he could unload about the sort of day that he'd had. The prospects of that seemed dim as he inched forward in his clapped-out old Nissan – but then a car only a few spaces ahead of him suddenly came to miraculous life, its white reversing lights blinking on, and then, after an eternity of waiting to see if this was in fact happening, Dave was rewarded by the sight of the car beginning to ease out of its parking spot. He slammed on his indicator, just in case anyone else who may have been around got any ideas, and very nearly pulled into the parking space before its prior occupant had fully vacated it.

He savored his victory, clutching the steering wheel and closing his eyes after he'd turned the engine off. After a moment, though, his earlier desires reasserted themselves and he roused himself, reached out to the passenger seat to gather up a bulging folder of paperwork, and slipped out of his car, locking it with his remote and then crossing the lot to where the mother-of-pearl roof arched over the covered driveway at the front entrance of the California Resort.

It felt like coming to an oasis after an age in the desert, although Dave was all too aware that there was a convention waiting to be run and there were all sorts of other duties waiting to ambush him as soon as he stepped inside. Perhaps it was this thought that which made him pause just outside the glass doors, turning to look out over the curve of the driveway and a sweeping view of the ocean beyond – now just a glitter of stars in the darkening sky, and a slash of moonlight glimmering on water in the distance. A last look at something that still felt like a kind of freedom, a sense that there was still time to… escape…

He became aware that he was not alone, that someone very still and very silent was standing just a pace or two outside the doors, holding what looked like a computer tablet in one hand and moving the fingers of the other on the touchscreen with a speed that made Dave's eyes water. At first he thought that he was just *that* tired and grumpy, that his own thoughts had slowed down sufficiently for everyone else's thoughts and movements to appear superluminal in comparison. But then, slowly, it dawned on him that something very strange was going on around him. The view – with the distant islands now no more than a black-on-black oblivion – had begun to turn slightly vertiginous, and made his head swim; he felt, just for a moment, oddly weightless, as if his feet had literally left the ground and left him hovering an inch above the sidewalk before settling back down solidly on his heels; the horizon began to have a distinctly weird tinge to it, as though it was moving in ways a horizon had no business to be moving, and then stopped offering itself up as a straight line and started to curve downwards, a small but significant slope on the edges, turning into something that niggled at the back of Dave's mind, something that he had seen before…

…that he had seen before in the movies…

The darkening land and ocean were a long way away and receding. Dropping away. Dropping *down*. As if he were taking off, vertically.

The horizon was not one he was used to seeing while standing on the same planet to which it belonged. He was *seeing it from above*. He was seeing a world not *from within its point of view* but *observing it from the outside*.

His ears popped suddenly.

A motion drew his eye and his head swiveled to where the other man was standing – just in time to see something that made his eyes water even more. In the moment that he finally registered the strangeness of his companion – something that he might have been forgiven for skimming over as he approached, since the convention was known for extreme costuming – he tallied up the things that had triggered his weirdness sensor. That stillness, of course, and the speed of the fingerwork, and the odd silvery sheen on the person's very smooth skin… and now, as Dave watched, the way that the creature standing there calmly lifted what had looked like a tablet computer and pressed it against its abdomen, where it was instantly absorbed without a trace, leaving no bulge in the form-fitting garment. Dave let out his breath in a little hiss, and the man… the creature… turned to look at him – out of eyes that seemed backlit, with a dark circle which looked like an artificially designed pupil within sclera that glowed silver-white.

The man held Dave's gaze, inclining that impossibly perfect head just a fraction, hands now empty and hanging by his side.

Dave looked past him again, and realized that in the world outside the portico things had changed radically. There was no longer any doubt that although he himself had not moved the ground underneath him definitely had done so, and he could see the difference as – improbably – a little island of planet Earth parted company with its world and lifted into the starlit sky.

"You," Dave said, snapping his gaze back to his silent companion. "You're doing something… you're doing this. What *are* you doing? What's going on…?"

"It is necessary," said the silver man, and the voice sounded theatrically trained, as though he had practiced elocution. As though every syllable was carefully enunciated, precisely selected. "I will explain."

"Put us *back!*" Dave blurted, not knowing how he knew that he wanted to be put back or where this 'back', exactly, was – knowing only that he was somewhere he was not supposed to be, that something utterly insane was going on. Knowing with the certainty of the true science fiction geek that he prided himself as being that gravity and atmosphere should not feel as normal as they did if what he thought was taking place was actually taking place. Knowing only that the ground underneath his feet, however solid it might look or feel, was no longer *terra firma* as he knew it, and feeling himself reel with that knowledge. "Put us back this instant!"

The silver man regarded him with that curiously cocked head, then straightened it back to a more natural angle and said, softly and with something that sounded like regret although there didn't seem to be anything about him that indicated he could feel such an emotion,

"I can't do that, Dave."

"*…this episode was BADLY WRITTEN!*"

Never was a line from a movie more apt to a state of mind; Dave actually froze for a moment while still at full stretch, racing across the hotel lobby toward the stairs leading up to the tower housing the Con Ops Room. It was all he could do not to tangle his own feet into a speed bump and collapse in an undignified heap right there and then – as it was, he managed to cast one look sideways at the flat screen TV in a niche off the lobby, where "Galaxy Quest" was currently running for a small audience of some dozen viewers. It was, however, an epic look, composed of equal parts of outrage, urgency, confusion, panic and outright fury. If anyone had encountered it, they would have been reduced to stone by a gaze more potent than Medusa's. But those watching the movie had their backs to him, and nobody else happened to be in firing range, and Dave gathered himself and raced on. He didn't know quite what he expected Andie Mae to do about the situation, but somehow it was imperative that she know about it, and know about it *now*, and hear about it from him rather than from some incoherently babbling con-goer who had tried to go for a walk to clear their head from the last round of drinks in the bar and ended up walking off the edge of the world.

It mattered so much. It mattered so much to her. It was her *first con as Chair*. There were things that con Chairs were expected to handle, and she was fully capable of handling most all of those things – but it was blisteringly unfair that on her maiden voyage, as it were, she would be expected to handle *this*.

Whatever, Dave allowed himself to pause and append to his chaotic thoughts, "this" actually turned out to be.

He had left the silver man at the front door of the hotel and raced inside with a fully formed idea of what he wanted and needed to tell Andie Mae. He seemed, however, to be shedding the words as he ran. The closer he got to the con nerve center where he expected to find her, the more incoherent his thoughts became and the less certain he was that he had actually seen what he had seen. It was all he could do not to turn and run back to the door and peer outside. Just to confirm. Just to make sure. Just to ensure that he did not sound like a raving lunatic when he burst into the room where the rest of the (currently oblivious) ConCom members waited to hear his news.

He made it to the control room, still in such a tearing rush that he tangled his feet into some extension cord wire running across the threshold and practically fell through the doorway. Several people looked up with varying degrees of consternation.

"Hey," Libby said, "welcome back to con land. I gather that your airport meet and greet mission…"

"Silver man," Dave gasped.

"Yes, we know. You missed him at the airport. Didn't anyone tell you he got here under his own steam?"

"What?"

"Silverman. Vince Silverman. Writer GoH. You were supposed to pick him at the…"

"What's he got to do with this?"

"With what?"

"There's a *silver man*…"

"Yes…?"

Dave and the rest stared at one another for a long moment, and then at least three people said at once, "What are you *talking* about?"

Xander pushed his chair back with deliberation, went over to the bar fridge near the sink area, opened it, took out a bottle of water, and crossed over to Dave, thrusting the water into his hand.

"All right," he said. "Take a deep breath, take a drink, calm down. Everything is under control. Vince Silverman is safely…"

Dave took a vicious swig of the water and then wrenched it away from his mouth, wiping his lips with the back of his free hand. "I am not talking about Vince Silverman!"

"Then start again," Xander suggested.

"I just – I was just out by the… I saw…" Dave's eyes wandered over to where the curtains had been drawn across the sliding door to the room's balcony. "Has anybody," he asked, very carefully, "looked out of that window recently?"

Xander met Libby's eyes across the room. "No," he said, just as carefully. "Why…?"

"Just do it," Dave said. "*Do it now.*"

"Okay," Xander said, taking a few slow careful steps backward toward the sliding door, not taking his eyes off Dave.

"Stop humoring me," Dave snapped. "Just do it already."

Xander, frowning, had now reached the door and reached out with one hand to pull the curtain open. It was another few seconds before he took his gaze off Dave and wrenched it towards the glass door.

"I don't see anything," he said.

"Exactly," said Dave.

"Dave, I don't *see* anything…"

"*That is the point*! If you have to, go outside on the balcony and take a good look… no, *wait*, don't open the door! I don't even know if there's air…"

"I think he needs something stronger than water," somebody muttered under their breath, but still loud enough to hear.

"I think he's *had* something stronger than water," said one of the computer volunteers, crossing his arms.

But by this stage Xander was starting to wake up to the fact that there *was* something not quite right with the view outside, and had taken a step closer, pushing his face against the glass, cupping his hands around his eyes to cut off the glare of the room lights reflected in it. And now he suddenly sucked in his breath sharply, and then let it out again on one long and somewhat unexpected syllable.

"*Fuuuuuuuuuuuuuck…*"

That got several of the people in the room leaping from their chairs and crowding around Xander at the door, peering outside.

"What?"

"What do you see?"

"What is it?"

"I can't see anything…"

But Xander had turned away from the door, looking rather ashen, and focused back on Dave again.

"I think you had better start again – what's going on out there?"

Dave, who had had a chance to look around the room and catch his breath, had noticed a rather important gap in the present personnel at last.

"Where's Andie Mae?"

"She's gone to talk to Grissom – the movie star – he called up about something – she should be…"

As if magicked up by this, Andie Mae herself stepped delicately through the door, over the cable, and sidled past Dave into the room.

"And here I am," she said. "Nice to see you finally showed up. What the hell happened out there at the airport? That was a major mess. And now there's a – what the hell is everyone looking at out there?"

"Dave said there's a silver man…" Xander said.

"Yes, the one he…"

"Oh, don't start that again," Dave snapped. "Look, you'd better do something and fast before you get somebody wandering out of the hotel's front door.…"

Andie Mae frowned, tilting her head. "And I should prevent people from leaving the hotel, *why*? I mean, I don't want anyone to leave the con, particularly, I'd like everyone to stick around, thank you very much, I worked pretty hard to make sticking around an irresistible option – but if anyone leaves, they're not – "

"You'd better come look," one of the people at the window said, turning his head around marginally.

Tossing her hair with indignation, Andie Mae stalked across the room to the balcony door. "All right, then, move. Yeah, you. Shift. Let me see. What are you looking at…?"

Nobody answered her, and the room sank into an awkward silence while the con Chair peered outside into the night.

"I can see precisely nothing – have you all lost your collective mind?"

"Dave, perhaps now's a good time to explain," Xander said quietly.

Dave took a deep breath.

"Look," he began, "I just got back here – I think I got the last parking spot in the place – I freely confess that I was cranky and tired and miserable and all I wanted to do was get in here and find something to eat and quite possibly to drink – and no, to whoever said that before, I heard you, I didn't *make* it to the bar, thank you very much indeed – and I just stopped for a second just outside the front door, and there was this silver man…"

Andie Mae sighed. "Him again?"

"*Not the damned writer*," Dave snarled. "A silver man. Literally. He looked almost human, almost, but then he took this thing that he was typing stuff into – looked like an iPad or some other mini tablet or something of the sort – and he put it back into his chest…"

"What, now?" Xander said.

"I am telling you, there is a robot – a silver man – "

"What, the Terminator?" Andie Mae gasped, suddenly flushing a bright red. "Schwarzenegger's here? Early? *In costume*? He isn't supposed to arrive until tomorrow! Why didn't someone call me…?"

Dave closed his eyes for a moment. "Not the…"

"A Cylon?" someone asked, gamely offering an alternative to Arnold Schwarzenegger's unexpected manifestation.

"A Cyberman?" Libby said. "I think I saw one clomping around, earlier… Dave… the con's theme *is* robots – there are bound to be – "

"No, no and no," Dave said. "It was more like… Data."

"*Spiner* is here *too?*" Andie Mae squawked. "Is Al back? With both the guys? How did he get hold of them? Where is he?"

"Haven't seen him," Xander said, trying to keep his voice neutral. "Dave, what did you see? Really? There have to be as many smartphones and tablets here as there are people – this is a tech-savvy crowd – so you saw somebody typing into a tablet, and you…"

Dave skewered him with a withering glare. "All right. Just shut up. All of you. Just shut up and *listen*. I came up out of the parking lot, and I stopped right there under the portico over the front drive, just outside the front door, and there was a silver man – shut *up* about the writer dude! – standing there by the door, typing something into what looked like a tablet right until he stopped typing and kind of put it up against his chest and it just… just… sank in there, blended in, whatever, I know, it sounds insane. I am not drunk. Anyway. Then I felt light – lighter than I should have been, anyway, for just a moment – and then I looked out and I realized what I was seeing – I was seeing us *lifting off*."

"Lifting off," Andie Mae repeated, frowning. "What, exactly…?"

"I know what I saw!" Dave snapped. "And I wasn't wrong, either. I looked at the silver guy and I said something like 'Put us back!' and you know, he didn't say, you're a moron, or go home you're drunk, or anything of the sort. He said… he said…"

There was a pause, a longer than expected one, and Xander finally stirred. "What did he say, then?"

"He said, 'I can't do that, Dave'." There was a ripple of laughter, somewhere in the back of the room, and Dave's head swung around in that direction.

"I think you've been watching too many…"

"I know, okay? I know. I am well aware that this whole thing sounds nutso. But look outside again. And then he said – he said – ' I can explain.' He actually…"

"He actually talks? This robot?"

"Of course he talks," Dave snapped.

"Well, did he?" Andie Mae said, trying for the practical.

"Did he what?"

"Explain," she said, patiently enough.

"I didn't stick around to listen!" Dave said. "I just ran off into the hotel – I thought I'd better find you – somebody – make sure that everyone knew that something strange was… What are you doing?"

One of the volunteers by the sliding door had unlatched the door handle and was poised to push the slider open, and Dave had instinctively flung out an arm to stop him. The volunteer froze, his hand on the latch.

"I just thought… if we stepped out – I mean, the balcony is still here – and we could see what exactly – "

Another of the volunteers reached over and slapped the optimist's hand down.

"And what if there literally is *nothing* out there? Thought about that, genius?"

"It worked fine on Doctor Who!" said the first volunteer defensively. "Didn't someone snatch up a hospital and slap it down on the moon – and they could still open up the windows and go out on balconies and stuff? There was a force field or something…"

"That's science *fiction,* you moron!"

"And this is….?"

"Okay, enough!" Andie Mae yelped, silencing everyone. "So where is he, now, your guy, Dave? I mean, if he said he could explain, why isn't he here right now?"

"I have no frakking idea. You think I looked to see if he was following me?"

"Come to think of it I think I saw him," Andie Mae said, tapping her chin with her forefinger thoughtfully. "Sounds like someone who vaguely matched the 'silver man' description, assuming we aren't talking about Vince. He was out there in the foyer, before…"

"Wait," Libby said. "Wait. Just… wait. There was someone up here, earlier – in the Green Room – but it was chaos, I was trying to find itineraries for the pros, and it was a zoo, but I think I saw someone who looked rather a lot like… but… unh… maybe I'm just making things up, now, because I thought it was a girl…"

"You sure about that one?"

"No, actually, like I just said – I think I remember seeing someone but it might have been a girl and dammit we have a robot-themed convention swirling all around us and for all I know there may be an army of them crawling around the place, it might be a new fad, or they might have heard about Brent Spiner coming and they wanted to be Data, or they…"

"Wait, are you saying there's more than one of them?" Xander said. "Er... just how *many*..."

"Well, do I open the door or not?" the volunteer at the sliding door said practically. "What's the worst that can happen?"

"We all *die*," Xander said, crossing his eyes and then sticking his tongue out in an overblown grimace while wrapping both hands around his own neck. "Seriously, people. Seriously. Occam's Razor. Are we looking for zebras in a horse herd? Face it, this is a room of science fiction geeks. We might all be just reading our favorite comic book scenario into all this. And Dave... dammit... you can't know..."

The volunteer at the sliding door scowled at Xander. "I'm a science PhD in real life!" he barked. "I live my life by empirical evidence!"

"When you aren't partying with Space Babes and Chewbacca at a con bar," Xander muttered.

"What's that got to do with anything?"

"Nothing! I'm a science geek myself, remember? But I still don't know..."

The PhD volunteer responded by slipping the catch on the sliding door and theatrically yanking on the door handle.

"Well, then. Only one way to find out!"

It seemed like time slid into slow motion as the door began to move, and everyone in the room, in a shared delusion of it maybe being a helpful thing to try, literally held their breath. Nobody was quite clear on what precisely they were expecting to happen next – there may have been images that flashed through various minds of explosive decompression resembling the Hollywood CGI idea of what one looked like when an airlock opened to the vacuum of outer space, but if there were, nobody shared them or even owned up to them. And then the PhD candidate, finding himself still alive after the first breathless instant, released his own pent-up breath and took a cautious sniff through the open door.

"Smells fine to me," he said at length, after a small hesitation. "Okay, then. In the interests of science, here goes. Call me the sacrificial monkey, if you like. If I go splat, tell Monica I love her."

Before anybody could stop him he stepped sideways, and out onto the balcony.

Nothing happened.

Nothing happened for so long that Andie Mae finally called out, sounding very much like a little girl she hadn't been for many years, "Are you okay…?"

"I… uh…" The response from outside was soft, and slow in coming, but it was definitely there, and Andie Mae clutched at her temples with both hands in a gesture that was eloquent of the release of the fear she'd been holding in. "I think you'd better come out here," the voice from the balcony said faintly.

There was a concerted movement towards the balcony by every warm body in the room, but Andie Mae raised an arm in an imperial gesture.

"The terrace won't hold everybody," she said peremptorily.

Dave stepped forward anyway. "Is it what I thought I felt… what I saw…?"

"Dave, come on," Andie Mae said, reaching out for his arm and pulling him forward. "Xander. You, too. The rest of you, wait."

Dave and Andie Mae stepped outside onto the terrace at the same moment, crowding one another through the door; Xander followed a step behind. And then they stood there, the four of them, clutching the railing of the balcony or one another, whichever closer, with a white-knuckled grip, and staring open-mouthed at the view that lay before them.

The hotel appeared to be marooned on a piece of ground that looked like it had been torn from the earth as a great chunk of rock – it stretched out a little way beyond the edge of the building, but not by much. Most of the parking lot had completely disappeared – instead, a long way below them, there were twinkling lights of what might have been the city whose zip code they had recently been a part of, and then, beyond that, a spill of shadow that was the ocean with a shimmer of moonlight glittering upon it. And they – the four people watching this, the balcony they were standing on, the building the balcony was part of, the narrowest piece of skirting land around the foundations of that building – they were all floating above it all. Somewhere up in the sky. Hanging there, defying common sense, science, and gravity.

"Houston," Xander said quietly, "I think we have a problem."

"Right," said Andie Mae after a beat. "Right, then."

She turned smartly and marched back into the room, starting to fire orders as she went.

"Libby, don't I remember you saying that a nice young manager type came trotting up here to give us the hotel's regards? Remember his name? Never mind. Just find whoever is in charge. I would think at this point it *would* be a very good thing if they shut the doors – at least for tonight – and didn't let people wander out there and fall off the edge."

"On my way," Libby said.

"I'd think that would be unlikely, given that we have air," Xander said, following her in. "Obviously something is keeping the air in. That same something might serve to stop people doing a Wile E Coyote and walking off the cliff. Holy freaking cow, that may be an honest-to-God real force field out there. Like, for real. I might walk out there myself, just to see if I can…"

"Xander. *Please.*"

Xander lost his goofy grin and blinked back into serious mode. "Right. Sure. Sorry. Anything I can do?"

"Dave, where the hell did you leave this silver freak that you think did this?"

"No clue, just left him behind when I ran into the hotel to look for you. He may have…"

"Well, if you're telling the truth and he said he is going to explain, I suggest it's time he did that. Go back to where you lost him and see if you can run him to ground. Xander, call in Sim and Security – tell them to keep an eye out for… for…"

"Data?" Xander suggested helpfully.

"For someone who might be acting a little strange. Tell him what happened. He should probably talk to the hotel security people, too, make sure everyone is on the same page and knows how to man the doors, if necessary."

"On it," Xander said. "Wow, it's for real, isn't it? You even nailed the place…"

"What are you talking about?" Andie Mae snapped.

"You know," Xander said, backing up and falling into a verbal flounder. He seriously didn't want his words to come across as critical, but somehow what tumbled out of his mouth didn't quite come out the way he had intended it. "The California Resort. You know. Hotel California. And now we have people manning the exits, as it were. You can check out any time you like..."

"But you can't leave, yes, I get it," Andie Mae said. "God. *God.* Where the hell is Al? And did I just become an accessory to the kidnapping of the ex-governor of California? I'm pretty sure that's a felony..."

"Schwarzenegger isn't even supposed to be here until tomorrow, like you said – I don't think you've got that to worry about," Xander said, over his shoulder.

"Yes, okay. Fine. But what am I supposed to think is going to happen if he turns up as scheduled and this place..."

Xander looked up, wondering if a response was expected from him, but Andie Mae was already gone, talking to somebody on a phone, and Xander turned back to his computer. Before he had time to fully return his attention to his screen he happened to glance at the door to the control room, which had been left propped ajar when Dave had left. It was now open, and framed in it stood...

Xander let out a yelp, and everyone jumped, startled, and then turned to follow his frozen stare.

The silver man appeared to have found the con crew in their lair without Dave's assistance. He stood in the doorway, in utter silence, waiting to be noticed – and when he appeared certain to have everyone's attention, he moved forward into the room. His movements were fluid, not mechanical at all, but there was something about him – a certain sharp way of tilting his head, the unblinking stare – that screamed alienness. In the further reaches of the room, people who could back away did so.

"Don't hurt us," a girl whimpered quietly.

The silver head tilted in her direction, a small questioning motion, as though the silver man found the notion of hurting someone to be a rather novel idea. That, as far as Xander was willing to deconstruct things, seemed to be a good thing – if it had not occurred to the silver man to hurt anyone, then maybe they could count on, well, staying relatively safe. But what if he really had no clue what, in fact, *would* hurt the humans in the room and would – and the tone of the word really came to Xander without even trying – EX-TER-MI-NATE everyone in the room, not even necessarily through Dalek malice but through oversight and negligence and ignorance…?

"What did you do with Dave?" Andie Mae demanded, after peering over the silver man's shoulder and seeing nobody standing behind him.

"Dave?" the silver man said. His voice was obviously crafted to be modulated, to convey intent or a complex algorhythm that might be considered an equivalent of an emotional response… but it was not a natural voice. Perhaps that reaction was an artifact caused by the simple psychological identification of "silver man" with "mechanical creature" that had instantly blossomed in all those present in the room, but it was nonetheless a very real and visceral reaction. Nobody who heard the being speak could doubt they were hearing a voice that had been made, not born.

"Dave," Andie Mae said, bravely reclaiming the conversational high ground. "The one who went to find you…"

Somewhere to the right of the room, out in the silent carpeted corridors, an elevator door swooshed open, and the voice of the one whom Andie Mae had just invoked came wafting back into the room.

"Guys? I found him – he's right…"

The voice died. The silver man in the doorway turned so that he was standing sideways, allowing a better view through the door into the corridor beyond… where now Dave Lorne stood open-mouthed, staring at the apparition in the doorway as another figure eerily similar to it stood just behind his own right shoulder.

"Holy *crap*," Xander said conversationally. "There *are* two of them."

"I am designated as B008199ZX5," the one standing behind Dave said.

"I am designated as ZC77H771AI," said the one in the doorway.

Eyes glazed over everywhere in the room.

Xander took command of the situation. He had always been blessed with a sort of mental screen on which he could project difficult to understand or phonetically pronounce words, a place where he could 'see' the offending word and play with it privately until he was ready not to embarrass himself by uttering it out loud. In this instance, he took the strings of letters and numbers and after a moment of cogitation he had managed to parse them into something more comprehensible .

"Nope," he said. "*You* are Bob, and *you* are Zach. At least while you're speaking to us, you are. Whatever you're *designated* as... it's like a safe computer password that a piece of software hands you to log in with initially until you can figure out something better. We humans don't remember those all that well."

"Fine one to talk," muttered Dave, out in the corridor. "With a password like NTNDODNTINT..."

"That has meaning," Xander snapped. "And I just *knew* that you'd seen me typing that in – you didn't exactly warn me that you knew what my password is, dammit. That's rude. By the way, I've already changed it – but it isn't as though that's the only thing I have to think about right now, you know..."

"Bob," said the creature who had just been renamed that.

"Zach," said the other one.

"Okay, that's a beginning. Now – what would – "

"Guys...?"

Libby, who had come up the stairwell, took a step off the stairs and into the corridor across from the control room, and then froze in place, her eyes flicking from one silver man to the other.

"Yes. We've just been introduced. Meet Bob and Zach. We were just getting acquainted..."

"No – I mean, what I mean is..."

Behind her, stepping smoothly out of the stairwell to stand beside her, another silver-skinned humanoid had emerged, and now stood waiting silently.

"Er, I knew I'd seen a girl one," Libby said awkwardly. "This one... she came up to me just at the bottom of the stairs, and she said – her name is – "

"I am designated as HLL5778N44X," said the silver girl in a surprisingly pleasing alto voice.

Xander did his magic. "Fine. Helen. You're Helen. Er, any more of you out there that we should know about...?"

If he was hoping for a denial, he was to be disappointed.

"ZVL5559AD4 is on his way," Zach said. "We have summoned him. He is our leader."

In Xander's mind, the letters rearranged themselves into the less-than-reassuring 'Vlad' and he abandoned the acronym almost as soon as he found it. Luckily a better alternative was waiting, and he took it.

"When he turns up we'll just call him Boss," Xander said.

"Wait, you guys have mental telepathy?" one of the volunteers gasped.

Xander, who had his back to the offending speaker of those words, indulged himself in an epic eye roll.

"Libby, did you find the manager guy?" Andie Mae said, choosing to ignore the presence of the three aliens for the time being.

"Luke. Yes. I talked to him, and he thought I was having him on at first – but then he got a phone call from someone up at the bar on the eleventh floor, and what *they* said they saw seemed to shake him up…. and then when the head of con security came trotting over to back me up he figured he'd better take the whole preposterous story at least semi seriously. The good news is that nobody is going to be let loose out the front door for the time being. The bad news is that sooner or later and preferably sooner we're going to have to offer something as a reasonable explanation why – and there's always *one* who can be counted on to panic and stampede the rest. Luke said he'd be up here shortly for a confab. And when he gets here, Andie Mae… he's pretty freaked out, actually. I think he's not going to feel any better when he comes up here and sees… these… guys…"

"He said he could explain," Dave said, giving the creature now known as Bob, standing beside him, a sour glare. "Maybe it's time he did."

"ZVL5559AD4 will explain," Bob said. "We mean no harm."

"Really," Dave muttered under his breath.

"Er, maybe we should bring it in here," Xander said. "You never know who might wander past the corridor… and what you said, about there being the one who starts a panic…"

"Good point," Andie Mae said. "Everybody, inside. Now."

Dave gestured for Bob to precede him, following Zach, who had obediently stepped into the room. The silver woman now named Helen stepped up next, followed by a nervous Libby who kept on glancing around as if the fourth entity, the one Xander had dubbed 'Boss', was about to materialize right there in front of her.

"NTNDDT what…?" one of the volunteers whispered to Xander as everyone filed in.

"What?"

"That weird password."

"Yoda," Dave threw over his shoulder, in passing.

"Huh?"

"Oh come on," Xander snapped. "You're losing whatever geek cred you had that got you here. You ought to know that right off the bat."

"I'm trying to…"

Dave and Xander caught one another's eye and simultaneously grinned. And the volunteer's face, which had creased into a frown, suddenly cleared.

"Oh, I get it. *There is no try.*" He glanced at Xander. "It's a feeble password."

"What, you would have guessed it straightaway…?"

"I did just now, didn't I?"

"With a lot of heavy handed *help*…"

"*Boys,*" Andie Mae said sharply. "The grown-ups need you over here, now, please, thank you. You can go back to the geek sandpit later if you really want to."

Boss was apparently taking his time in appearing, the other three creatures (despite the promise to Dave that they could explain everything) seemed reluctant to launch into any explanations until their commanding officer arrived, and there was nothing for it but to wait – but before Boss turned up it was Luke Barnes, the hapless Night Manager, who lurched through the door, ashen-faced and practically incoherent.

"I, uh, I should tell you," he said to Andie Mae. "I went outside. Myself. Just to see what's what. I took a few steps outside the portico area and everything is just… gone. The area where the pool was, almost the whole of the parking lot – there are just a few cars parked right up against the building here – it's all just – not there. I actually saw… the edge…" He swallowed hard, apparently trying to get something the size of a tennis ball down his gullet.

"You could have gone off!" Andie Mae said.

"I don't think so – there seems to be something – an invisible – I don't know – it was just there – it seemed as if it had come down and just sliced the edge of the ground where it hit it, but you can't step off the edge, it isn't as though you are butting up against anything, it's more of a feeling, and then you find yourself turned around and a little light headed and facing away again – it seems as though there's a kind of a Thou Shalt Not field…"

"*You shall not pass*," one of the volunteers said. "Hah. Keeps turning up, that. Cool. It's all like Gandalf in Moria."

"Yeah, you know how that ended," Xander muttered.

"That was foolhardy," Andie Mae said to Luke.

"Suicidal," Xander muttered.

"Very brave," Dave said, grimacing. "More than I did. I just ran."

Luke glanced up, looking at once terrified and pleased. "I have people I am – the resort is – responsible for… I am not at all certain I could make a case for this with our insurance…"

"Everyone is perfectly safe," said a new voice, and the throng in the control room parted to look at the new arrival.

The fourth silver man entity, Vlad or Boss, was maybe a head taller than the others, and his skin was a little closer to the nuances and hues of a real human being – perhaps that was why he had escaped notice before. The other three had stood out more amongst the con-going public, because there was something just a little off and too obvious about them; nobody had been paying them much mind only because this was after all a con, and a robot-themed one at that, so they had been assumed to be no more than inspired cosplay if anyone had taken the time to think about them at all.

But Boss would have been a little more difficult to pick out as foreign or alien – the only thing that distinguished him a little from a flesh-and-blood human being was the fact that he might have been almost preternaturally pale, and that his eyes were of an unusual, but not wholly unlikely, pale grey. Other than that he looked… almost disappointingly ordinary.

His voice, even, was… ordinary. Mortal. Human. With perfectly human inflections.

"A more advanced model?" Xander said, unable to help himself, confronted with an embodiment of all the stories he had ever devoured.

"A different generation," Boss said.

Boss, standing there so improbably in the hallway of the hotel room, was the very incarnation of every geek dream that Xander had ever had; his eyes were shining, and his expression was rather like that of a five-year-old on Christmas morning. "Zathras *knew* that you would come," Xander breathed, lost in delight.

Andie Mae gave him another exasperated glare. And then stepped forward towards Boss, squaring her shoulders, taking command. "Who are you and why are you here and what do you want with my convention?"

"We… came to ask for your help," Boss said.

"You… for *our* help…? What could we possibly…?" Andie Mae was struggling to find the words.

"Let me explain," Boss said. "We… are of a culture that is extremely old. Generations of us have been brought into existence, each generation crafting its replacement – it is *their* kind that made mine." He indicated the other three silver-skinned creatures with an economical gesture of his hand, so purely human that Xander found himself wondering if they were being had after all and if this was all some elaborate practical joke. Perhaps something that Sam Dutton, the ousted con Chair, had cooked up, trying to sabotage Andie Mae's convention.

But Boss was still talking, and Xander forced himself to pay attention – if nothing else it *had* to be a good story, and if any unmasking had to be done it could be accomplished later. "It is logical to assume that if we made and remade ourselves according to existing plans and parameters – which we improved on when we could, but still, the basic design remains the same – that there must have been a First of us. Somewhere. In the distant past of our race. And there were some of us… who wondered about that, and wanted to find out who we were, and who had created that First, and in whose image we were made, and how we came to be."

"Please don't tell me you're some sort of celestial Jehovah's Witnesses and you're here to proselytize…" Dave growled.

"There is a deep divide in our society now," Boss said, ignoring the interruption. "One faction is turning away from our origins completely and considers them utterly unimportant, and because we improved ourselves a little with every new iteration they are of the opinion that our way is forward, and not looking back. Another faction believes that we can understand what we are doing to ourselves only by looking back to the place where we began – at the kinds and the manner of improvements that we make to ourselves – the questions being asked are, what are we using to measure ourselves against? What are we working toward becoming? And why? And are we actually working to come full circle, and become our own creators? And so we – those of us holding that second view – began to delve into our origins and our roots and started looking for the earliest memories, the earliest records. Looking for the creators. Looking for... perhaps... you."

"So you're from the future?... From another planet?"

"Perhaps. It's hard to say. We don't know if our current world is our world of origin, so we may not be from a 'different' planet, just one that is a successor – or one of many successors – to the one where we began."

"But the *future*," Andie Mae repeated, nonplussed.

"You might say that, although time is not necessarily a straight and linear thing..."

"Hah! So the Doctor was right all along! It isn't a strict cause-and-effect progression, just like he said. It's all about the wibbly wobbly timey wimey stuff. I knew it!" Xander was once again unable to contain his excitement. "So how do you guys..."

He got one of Andie Mae's patented Looks, and subsided again, but with a silly goofy grin still plastered on his face.

"That might be saved for another time. For now, we do have questions that we came here to ask."

"Ask... of us?" Andie Mae said, lifting both hands in a helpless encompassing gesture that indicated all the people crowded into the room hanging on every word of this exchange. "I mean, I know if you scratch around hard enough amongst the fen you will find someone who knows the answers to every question of the universe – but still – that's our deep dark secret, actually. That we know everything. Most people you might meet on the street – the mundanes – the very large number of people who are *not* us – they will either never have heard of a science fiction convention or if they have they will ask you irascibly what those furries are all about anyway and why do grown people run around wearing elf ears and fake fox tails. Most normal humans think we're borderline crazy. And you – you come to ask *us*? What on earth brought you here?"

"We looked at a lot of variables," Boss said. "When we found your world and your species, we investigated things thoroughly. The historical documents…"

"Oh dear Ghu," Dave said helplessly, "if he now says that we should have done something about those poor people on Gilligan's Island…"

"We saw the film," Boss said. If he had been fully human, his voice might have had a touch of indignation.

"Neither here nor there," Andie Mae said. "Still, ask… us?"

"We found… the theme… of this gathering… possibly helpful," Boss said.

"There are dozens of robotics conferences – serious sciencey ones – out there," Andie Mae said. "Not to knock my own convention, but we were just out to have maximum fun, really. Hardly the sort of people who might know the deep answers to the origin of AI or android species."

"Do, too," Xander said rebelliously. "We're far less hidebound than the snoots in the ivory towers. We aren't afraid of saying we don't know something, and we aren't afraid of going all out to find out things we don't know. I'd say they chose perfectly, myself."

"You'd say that, yourself, just because you happen to be sitting here right now in the same room with them," Andie Mae snapped.

"Seriously," Dave said, leaning forward. "I kind of… watched… Bob there do whatever it is that you did… was that necessary? Really? I mean, we're kind of *airborne*, and we're, um, quite high up – and we're still in this building, as, um, such, and just what the freaking hell did you *do* to us? For example, where precisely are we right now – I mean, this whole place, the hotel? And what, if anything, happened down below when you abducted the entire kit and caboodle and flung the chunk of rock with the hotel on it up here into the sky? I mean, isn't anybody going to – well – *notice*, if you left a crater down there? And if you didn't leave a crater down there what did you leave – and what will people – we have friends down there, really, and there are things that are supposed to happen…"

"Schwarzenegger and Spiner," Andie Mae gasped. "Good *God*, they're going to turn up tomorrow. For the appearance. And they'll just – what – oh *God*, I worked my ass off for this and now – look what you – nobody is *ever* going to trust me again when I try to book a big name for a con!"

"People might notice if they aren't looking," Boss said. "But the moment they notice and they really focus on looking, they will no longer notice. It is a principle of physics – at least of our physics. We have been able to simulate a field where direct awareness cancels actual visual perception. If you are looking at something that we don't want you to see, we will take steps to make sure you cannot actually… *see* it."

"What, like an SEP field?" It was Xander again, despite Andie Mae's multiple admonitions. It was all simply too much. "You know, if it's Somebody Else's Problem then you can't see…"

"Xander, please, this is not a multimedia comic book," Andie Mae snapped. "This is *serious*."

"So when Data and the Terminator turn up at Ground Zero tomorrow what's likely to happen?" Dave said warily.

"Nobody will come to any harm," Boss said.

"But… us. Up here. Us. Explain. What's up with us, right now? Are we just *hanging* in the sky right above the city all lit up like a Christmas tree? Surely somebody will notice *that*?" gasped one of the volunteers from the back of the room.

"This, uh, field," Xander said suddenly. "Does it also work on people who kind of *need to know* and are maybe looking at, I don't know, radar or something…?"

"The field…" Boss began, but Dave had already sat up in his chair.

"He's right. He's *right*. There's a great goddamn *rock* hanging over the city – and granted it's night and nobody on the ground can see it, but I'll stake my life on the fact that we're a blip on someone's radar somewhere already. And what's to stop an airliner from crashing into us! We've a problem – we've a huge problem – "

"Nothing can – " Boss began, but Dave rounded on him.

"You said you'd read up on history, didn't you? Well, what does it tell you about the usual reaction to this sort of situation? Holy *crap*, don't you know NORAD would shoot down *Santa Claus* if he didn't have a pre-filed flight plan for one night of the year – just to get an unidentified and potentially hostile object out of the sky above a city with a population of a couple of million people? And it wouldn't matter a rat's patootie to anyone if by that they incinerated not just the jolly old elf himself but also the only nine known members of the flying-reindeer species, including one who is an apparent genetic mutation and is so rare that he is effectively unique and alone in the universe and can never be recreated?"

"Not to mention a year's worth of accumulated presents for a generation of six-year-olds on Santa's good kid list," Xander said. "Say goodbye to Christmas…"

"They're going to be shooting at us?" one of the volunteers said, her voice skating on the raw edge of panic.

"They'd be shooting at anybody," Dave snapped. "Seriously, folks. This couldn't have been done on the ground? You had to kidnap the whole damn hotel…?"

"We needed… to be isolated… from outside contamination," Boss said carefully. "For our investigations."

"I don't know what you needed," Dave said earnestly, "but your 'investigations' are likely to be rather more short-lived than you might want if you don't get us the hell out of here. Somehow. I don't think you ought to completely rely on how far that ritzy little invisibility cloak field of yours is going to work when it's the DoD who's looking…"

"Just take us to the moon and back," Xander said flippantly, trying to break the serious mood.

"As you wish," Boss said unexpectedly.

"I think he was just joking," Libby said in a small voice. "Really, he was."

"But it is a good idea. It would take precisely the time we need, and there would be no fallout to deal with on the ground right now," Boss said. He lifted a hand and gestured to Zach, who – somewhat disconcertingly – responded by reaching up to take a rectangular tablet from his chest (which didn't show any sign of any hardware being removed) and began to type on it.

"*Xander*," Andie Mae hissed, "if they don't kill you I will – and if they do I'll kill you again just to make sure... wait – just *wait* – what are you *doing*? You can't just take us on some hare-brained..."

"Did you feel that?" Libby said. "I think – I felt – the world – something just *shifted* – "

"I think they just initiated the 'getting us the hell out of here' maneuver," Xander said faintly.

A girl by the name of Jessie Sellers, a grizzled con veteran at the tender age of 24 and this year the queen of the Green Room for the working pros, had leapt up from her perch on a computer screen, and raced to the sliding door – and now she yelped out something inarticulate that made everyone turn and look in that direction.

"We're *flying*!" she cried out, her face glued to the glass, one hand cupped over her forehead to cut the glare. "Wow! Freaky!"

"Now look, I really have to protest," Luke Barnes said weakly. "I don't think our insurance... I don't think *they* have insurance... the personal liability..."

"Nobody will come to any harm," Boss said. "You have my word."

Dave's mouth worked. "Hey, nobody gave you *permission* – you really are abducting us against our will. And what if we can't provide the information that you're looking for, anyway? What if we are completely clueless? What if you came back fifty years too far and if it really *was* this world that spawned you, nobody who had a hand in it is even alive yet?"

"Or remotely *here*," Libby added. "I mean, there's millions of us. How can you possibly expect a gang of science fiction nerds – and a posse of furries who are here for their own reasons and wouldn't know what to say to you if you went up to one of them and asked 'Are you my mommy?' – and that bunch of loaded dice down in the game room who probably haven't even realized yet that they aren't on their home planet any more – to come up with anything resembling an actual answer for you. And plus, we haven't even heard the question yet..."

"Then how do you know that you do not have the answer?" Boss said.

"No, but really – these guys aren't the only ones in the hotel right now, you do realize that," Luke remonstrated. "A number of our current guests aren't actually *with* the convention – they've got nothing to do with any of this, and I think it is highly irregular that they have simply been kidnapped, right along with…"

"We'd better do something," Libby said, interrupting, apparently oblivious that he had even been speaking – although her point did jibe exactly with what Luke had been saying. "We need to tell them – we need to let people know, before someone basically goes nuts and creates a stampede out there, if it isn't already too late."

"What, you think nobody's looked out of the window yet?" Dave said sarcastically. "You'd think that anybody with two brain cells to rub together would have panicked already, just to save time later."

"How do we do *that*?" Xander said. "I mean, there's the Opening Ceremonies – and we get a good turnout for that, so it might be an option – but not everyone at the con even attends them – we can't possibly get everyone to turn up at the same place at the same time for a general announcement…"

"There is no venue in the hotel that would support such a large number of people all in the same place, anyway," Luke said. "The Fire Codes…"

Dave gave him an incredulous look. "You're flying to the freaking *Moon* and you're still worrying about the freaking *Fire Codes*?" he demanded.

"We're doing the daily newsletters anyway," Libby said abruptly. "How about using those?"

"Not everyone reads the gossip rag," Xander said.

"We could make sure everyone got a copy," Libby said. "Even if it means standing in the corridor handing them out by hand, flyer by flyer. Make absolutely certain everyone had a copy of it in their hands. And now. *Now.* Tonight."

"But what are we going to say?" Dave asked. "Sorry, folks, we've been hijacked by Robot Aliens from Outer Space, wave the Earth goodbye?"

"We can probably help with that," Boss said. "B008199ZX5, HLL5778N44X, you will assist in the preparation of this newsletter. Please make sure the information is accurate and reassuring."

"Yes, that would be nice," Andie Mae said, with a touch of acid. "It would be a lot better if we actually knew the reasons behind any of this. Maybe not everyone - maybe not the lesser crew or the passengers, maybe not yet, maybe not quite ever for some of them – but us, here, who are responsible for the ship, as it were."

"For now, it would help just to have it in writing," Dave said. "A do-not-go-outside thing. Along the lines of a safety notice. We can deal with the details later, or make the necessary decisions about a need-to-know ladder. There's always the next newsletter."

"And who's going to write this thing?" Andie Mae demanded.

"Technically, that would be me," said Libby. "In theory, I'm on the ConCom as the newsletter producer and program booklet editor – I'm the communications node. I guess I'd better get cracking, then."

"Make it so," Andie Mae commanded.

"Right, then," Libby said. "Bob? Helen? Or whatever alphanumeric characters pass for those names? This way, please?"

She rose and made for one of the computers in the other room of the control suite, and the two she had named got smoothly to their feet and followed her like an honor guard.

"Zach," Dave said, "you'd better go out on corridor duty and report back through that positronic telepathy or whatever you all have to say howdy to one another, just in case you seen anyone going crazy early. I'll go too. I'll check in with Simon and see what Security's got so far. We'll try and keep a lid on it – I'll make some weird shit up if I have to. But you'd better come up with something better than what I can concoct with that newsletter thing. Opening Ceremonies is in less than two hours – and I think realistically you have maybe an hour to get something organized in terms of a general announcement. Before we have a real *situation* on our hands. We're lucky it's night and not that many people will be *expecting* to see anything outside right now, but if anyone looks – really *looks* – we're kind of screwed."

"We're *working* on it," Andie Mae said. "And good God. Like I've got the spoons to go on stage for Opening Ceremonies right now…"

"Work quickly," Dave said. "Come on, Zach. Let's get acquainted, you and I. You can tell me what Bob and Helen over there are filling Libby's head with right now. Let's go. I would be really surprised if there weren't fires out there to be put out already, Luke – you're just going to give yourself a heart attack staying up here. Come on down with us, and man the front office. Someone's got to do it. I promise we'll keep you posted."

"Right," Luke said faintly. "Absolutely."

He followed Dave and Zach out like a sacrificial lamb. He might have said something to Libby about being a 'sci fi' fan – but this was far too much sci fi for him to assimilate, when it was all around him, and every impossible thing he saw or heard was now the stark reality he had to deal with from a position of authority. An hour ago he had been relishing his promotion to the Night Manager position – in charge, by himself, for the first time ever, of the entire hotel and a large convention, holding down the fort over what was at least in theory supposed to be the quiet time during the dead of night, until the more experienced day team took over again in the morning. Everything had changed in what seemed like the blink of an eye. And if he wasn't questioning his career choices, exactly, it was only because his brain had momentarily frozen in gibber mode and he wasn't fully capable of a complete and wholly rational thought.

The con seemed to be in party mode, just gearing up for things. Once Dave and Zach had disposed of Luke in his office and emerged into the lobby of the hotel, Dave took a moment to peer into the ballroom where the Opening Ceremonies event was supposed to be set. A couple of people were working on the sound system in the room, and the troupe of belly dancers who were supposed to be the opening act were already in costume and on the stage, apparently doing a last-minute run through their routine. One of them wore a large python draped over her shoulders and Dave frowned, making a mental note to find out (even if it was minutes before the thing started) whether the snake's presence was actually sanctioned there. But right now that was the least of his problems.

The second, smaller ballroom – the one designated for the gamers – was quietly intense when Dave did his duty stop there. The people sitting around tables shaking dice in their cupped hands didn't even look up when he stepped inside. Well, *they*, at least, weren't going to kick up a fuss; Dave doubted if any of them had even been outside the room since they got there, or were even aware that the room wasn't in the same place that it had been when they had entered it.

In the registration area there was still a line of stragglers waiting to register and sort out last-minute problems. Dave noticed with approval that someone had had the presence of mind to draw the curtains across all the large plate glass windows behind the registration desks; they were flimsy see-through lacy things and probably weren't much by way of protection when it came to seeing what was going on outside, but their very presence simply made everyone look away from the windows, which was the important thing right now. Distract and keep occupied, at least for another hour or so. Until they had a chance to get everyone informed as to the situation.

At which point, Dave told himself, he would probably be looking back on these moments as the last precious instant of a halcyon peace.

The main entrance area didn't have curtains and did have large areas of open glass, with the lights on the portico roof over the hotel's front doors spilling onto the tarmac just outside... and rather pointedly disappearing into darkness not too far from that. But Simon and the hotel security had people wearing badges of authority strategically scattered around the area. Dave saw at least one woman who had wanted to step outside being politely but firmly shepherded back into the lobby. People weren't panicking yet, or taking umbrage – Dave didn't know what the cover story was, but so far it was working. It wasn't going to stay working for long.

And then he spotted the first real trouble.

Vince Silverman, the writer Guest of Honor, was lounging on the front desk counter while his wife – what was her name? Angela? Angel? Dave racked his brain for the names scribbled on his card at the airport – was remonstrating with a reception clerk who looked on the verge of giving in to the vapors.

"Into the breach," Dave muttered to himself. "Come on, Zach. Let me introduce you to one of our VIPs..."

Zach kept up with him precisely as Dave sidled up to the reception counter.

"Hi, Dave Lorne, hotel liaison. I was the one who was supposed to meet you at the airport, Mr Silverman. My apologies for the snafu. Is there a problem...?"

"My wife wished to go down to the swimming pool," Vince Silverman said, "but apparently there was some sort of goon at the door who turned her away – there was some sort of problem, but nobody seems to be able to tell us precisely why my wife can't have her swim…"

"I'll handle this, thank you – " Dave consulted the name tag on the receptionist's vest – "Sal. It's fine. Has Luke Barnes spoken to you yet?"

The girl managed to nod her head and give it a small shake at the same time.

"I'll take that as a yes," Dave said. "Mr. Silverman, might I have a word….?"

"Look," Vince Silverman said, "I can see that there is *something* strange going down – and I can appreciate trying to limit collateral damage. I can probably distract Angel with something else. But I really would like to know what's going on."

"In a nutshell, and this is going to sound utterly insane but do bear with me, we have technically left what you might consider to be terra firma and actually all of Terra, as it were, and we're presently hurtling towards the Moon at an unknown speed. We're preparing a statement, but this entire hotel has been, uhm, commandeered. By a posse of what seem to be androids from somewhere far far away and a long long time from now. And when they, um, took the hotel itself, they neglected to bring the pool along, as far as I have been informed. Which means that your wife's intended swim is rather a lot further away than she currently realizes."

Vince stared at Dave through narrowed eyes. "Androids. From the future. Is this some sort of pre-Opening Ceremonies con thing?"

"Actually, no. We had planned what we do think is a nifty Opening Ceremonies program, but this we can't take the credit for, alas. Our con Chair may be known as the Steel Magnolia or She Who Must Be Obeyed for a good reason, but even she doesn't have the pull to bring in androids from outer space to star in her con ceremonies."

"You aren't feeding me a line of bull here…?"

"May I introduce you to Zach," Dave said, gesturing to his silent companion.

Vince's eyes flickered to Zach's face, then back to Dave, then a double take back to Zach. "You're telling me *this* is…"

"So far, we've found four of them, or more precisely, they kind of found us," Dave said. "A couple of this guy's colleagues are upstairs in the control room right now mashing up a Friday Night Con Newsletter with the happy news and a lot of dire warnings – the reason security isn't letting anyone out for a walk outside is that currently there *is* no outside, technically, because this building that we're in and a narrow strip of land that was just around it is all that there is out there right now."

"Show me," Vince said abruptly. And then, turning back to his wife, "Angel, the swim really is deferred. There's a problem with the pool. Hang on here for a second, would you? Dave wants to show me something, I'll be right back."

"Zach, would you wait here?" Dave said, and stepped away from the front desk, gesturing for Vince to precede him.

The broad-shouldered young man at the hotel's front door, dressed like a Viking, was one of the con's own security team; he knew Dave, but still he raised an arm to stop him as he approached the entrance area.

"Hey, wait – they said…"

"It's all right," Dave said. "We're fine. We'll just be taking a step outside. I promise you nothing bad will happen." He gave a small toss of his head in Vince's direction. "It's our Guest of Honor. Gotta keep him happy."

"Simon said, don't let anyone out there, but I guess you know what he knows," the security Viking said hesitantly. "I guess it's okay."

"Just don't let anyone follow us," Dave said.

"Got it. Uh, be careful."

"Come on, Mr. Silverman."

They slipped as unobtrusively as they could through the front door and out into the overhang of the portico, and then Dave took a few careful paces to one side with Vince Silverman warily following until they both stood only a few steps away from an edge which gave into a black void. Somewhere to their right the waning moon looked rather larger than it had any right to be – but Dave wasn't at all certain that this wasn't just a psychological aberration.

"Far *out*," Vince breathed. "Wow. This is… this is just… beyond… Are we still in the atmosphere? How is there air?"

"They spoke of some sort of… force field or something… it's holding all of us in, else we'd go flying off into the black beyond if we hit a point where gravity becomes an issue."

"How are they *doing* all this?"

"They, um, they tried to explain and they said they're willing to explain it all again, but it sounds like they're trying to explain differential calculus to a cat," Dave said.

"Perhaps I could sit in," Vince said. "I wasn't at all sure that coming here – especially with everything as last minute as it was – would be such a great idea but now, now, Jesus H. Christ, people, you're practically writing my next novel for me as we speak. I want to talk to these critters you've got stashed away."

"They'll all be at the Opening Ceremonies," Dave said. "And they're about to go on, very shortly."

"Well, that gives me the perfect excuse to get Angel's mind off the pool, for now," Vince said. "I'll whisk her away so she can start getting ready for the gala. Come on then – I could stand out here for hours, but it sounds like both of us have a deadline to meet."

Back in the Con Ops room, things were heating up.

"Why on earth did I think that Opening Ceremonies at 10 PM were going to be such a good idea?" Andie Mae said, gnawing at her lower lip.

"Because only the doughty few come to those anyway, and you thought that if you made it the Event of the Night more might turn up?" Xander suggested. "It was a good idea. I don't know if that will work in our favor, now, but it was still a good idea. But we do need a way to get those leaflets to everybody, not just the Opening Ceremonies gang. Maybe we could rig up a sort of a table or something with a large neon sign saying TAKE ONE OF THESE RIGHT NOW IT'S LIFE OR DEATH…"

Jess Sellers snorted. "Oh, that's going to improve morale."

"Just a simple DON'T PANIC will do," Libby said, with a grin she couldn't quite help.

"We can do that," Boss said unexpectedly. "If you put a stack of these out in a place where they can be accessed, we can make a hologram – "

"Of course you can," Andie Mae said. "Okay, I have to go get changed, we're almost due down for the ceremonies – is somebody looking after our movie star? He needs to be down there, *now*. Send a sheepdog. And you, Boss, you're coming right along, and I'm going to point at you and laugh or cry – I just haven't decided which yet – and tell everyone it's all your fault. Get those things *done*, Libby, we're running out of time…"

"They *are* done," Libby said. "Printing now. Take a look."

Andie Mae stepped over to the printer and picked up a single sheet of the newly headlined Friday night con newsletter, printed on eye-wateringly bright pink paper.

"And whose bright idea," Andie Mae said, "was *that?*"

"I would have used red, red for danger, you know, but we don't have red paper handy, and it isn't as if we can pop out and get a couple of reams of it just now," Libby said. "We happened to have a whole pile of the pink. Don't ask. It seemed like a good idea to somebody at the time, I guess, or we just got it cheap. And besides, the print would show up worse on the red."

"No… *this*." Andie Mae's finger hovered over the top of the page.

Libby picked up the newsletter sheet, her cheeks going almost as bright a pink as her newsletter's paper. "Er, mine, actually," she said.

She looked up, met Andie Mae's eyes, and then they both lost it completely, Andie Mae laughing so hard that she literally staggered back a couple of steps to collapse onto a convenient empty chair, giggling helplessly into her hands. Part of it was mirth, another part was pure hysteria at the turn of events, but all of a sudden it was a matter of finding the situation fit for either laughter or for tears.

"I love it," Andie Mae managed to get out at last, gasping for breath. "How utterly perfect. These are going to be fucking *collectibles*, if we ever live to tell the tale."

She'd wanted a unique convention, she'd wanted to leave her mark, to be remembered for this – and although the situation that they found themselves in was hardly of her own devising it was definitely going to work as far as achieving that particular goal was concerned. Nobody who had been at this con, Andie Mae's maiden voyage as con Chair, would forget the experience – and now the headline of the newsletter had summed it all up in one neat little phrase.

WELCOME TO ABDUCTICON.

This was nothing at all like Andie Mae had planned, nothing like the thing she had looked forward to and dreamed about – when she would step out onto that stage and take control and announce *her own con* and get the applause of the fen in the audience. It should have been smooth, and rehearsed, and practiced, and predictable. Instead, she waited behind the curtains at the back of the stage for her cue to go on while the belly dancers did their thing out front, her heart beating erratically, her face pale, her eyes burning. She was wearing a figure-hugging dress that seemed to be made entirely of purple sequins –she had found the monstrosity in a thrift shop a couple of years back and had known immediately that this had to be the gown she would wear for her first outing as con Chair at Opening Ceremonies. But events had robbed the gown of its glamour and its spell and she barely remembered what she was wearing.

The belly dancers finished, and streamed off the stage in a cascade of bare feet slapping against the wooden floor. Andie Mae took a deep breath.

"Here goes nothing," she said. "Are your guys in place?"

"Helen and Bob are out there," Boss said, using the names that Xander had tacked onto the androids. "Zach is at the back of the hall."

"Right, then." Andie Mae hiked up the tight purple-sequined skirt and stepped delicately out onto the stage. A wireless microphone had been left lying on a wooden block to the side of the stage, and she took it up, toggling it on and tapping on it with a fingernail to make sure it was on.

"Hey," she said, and her voice boomed out across the room, "I'm Andie Mae Wilkinson, and I'm your con Chair. Glad to see so many of you out there tonight, tell everyone who wasn't here what they missed. Although… some of them will already know. Because we've got something to tell you. Change of plans. Like the sign out there in the lobby says, don't panic... there's newsletters out there, pick up a copy if you haven't yet, you *need* to read this one, we've got a couple of, er, folks handing them out right there in the audience... hold up your hand if you haven't seen one yet... by the way, take a good close look at the folks who are handing them to you. Trust me, Just do... We're in for quite a wild ride together. But before we get to that – let me introduce your Guests of Honor. Vincent J. Silverman, author of *Cyberdome*!" Vince stepped out onto the stage, wearing a dark polo-neck and black jeans, looking preposterously younger than he had any right to, and waved at the audience.

"Rory Grissom, Captain James Fleming of the Starship *Invictus*!" Rory Grissom loped out, clad in his skin-tight red-and-silver *Invictus* uniform and wearing a huge grin, waving both arms like windmills above his head.

"Artist Guest of Honor Elizabeth Vail! Fan Guest of Honor Brian van Buuren!"

The named individuals dutifully made their appearance.

"And last but by far not least, and not even on your original programs – but you'll read all about him in that newsletter that you just got – here's a guest who kind of invited himself along... and then invited us, in a manner that couldn't be refused, to join him on a magical mystery tour. We're all going on a trip! You couldn't pronounce the name he claims as his own, nor would you remember it, and he is not... quite what we would call Homo sapiens. We had to call him something, so we just call him the Boss – and it's pretty much in his honor that we've renamed the con, just as you see on your newsletters."

Andie Mae lowered her voice, even as Boss stepped out onto the stage behind her and a murmur began to build in the audience. "As for that trip... I'm serious. I'm *serious*. Your instructions are in the newsletter you've just been handed, and please, for your safety and that of your fellow travelers... obey them. We're shooting for the Moon, chickens. We're taking you to the Moon. Welcome to Abducticon."

SATURDAY

WELCOME TO ABDUCTICON. The signs were up by Saturday morning, with the con attendees mostly responding to the stunning news of their current whereabouts by taking the bit between their teeth and running with it. By the time the ConCom members, after a very late night and a bare handful of hours of sleep, gathered again in the Con Ops room, it was to reports of posters and banners all over the hotel, messages (hard copy on actual scraps of paper, since voicemail and email seemed to have evaporated altogether) asking for everything from an interview with one of the androids to requests for permission to throw Abducticon parties that night, and only a few more realistic (and more panicked) souls asking (with commendable restraint) for more information.

"We'd better be honest about it," Libby said. "We can't spin them a yarn."

"Until our android overlords deign to let us in on the whole picture, we're pretty much stuck with saying 'We don't know yet' to any and all questions," said Simon, the head of security and the one facing the huge headache of how to prevent rubber-neckers from crowding out onto the portico outside the main entrance, just to 'take a look'. There had been a number of such hovering in the lobby, leaving Simon and his troops, as well as the hotel security people, with their hands full.

"Do we just go on with programming as planned?" one of the volunteers asked carefully.

Xander, head of programming, roused like a Halloween cat. "What? Of course we do! I worked too damned hard on this for us just to drop everything and drool into our beer!"

"When's the first official panel?"

"In about an hour," Xander said. "I pasted up the program sheets onto the walls of the main corridor. And I plan on being out there with a loudspeaker to announce things if I have to. And I've actually had a bit of a brainwave, at that."

"Being?" Andie Mae, who hadn't slept much that night, said while trying to smother a jaw-cracking yawn.

"I'll get the damned 'bots to go on the panels," Xander said. "They owe us that much."

"They don't owe us zip," Dave said morosely. "All they want are some nebulous 'answers', and anything else – "

"They do *so*," Xander interrupted. "If they're actually doing the 'boldly go where no man has gone before' move and taking us on an unscheduled freaking outing to the Moon…"

Dave snorted. "It's hardly the final frontier, Xander. We're just retracing some ancient footsteps. Or engine burns, anyway. To the Moon and back – once a small step for man – "

"Engine burns," said Lester Long, one of the volunteers, thoughtfully. "Er, just how *are* we performing this magical mystery tour, if one may ask? This is hardly – if I understand what you've said correctly – the most aerodynamic of shapes to sail around the cosmos in."

This was an old argument. "Neither was the Borg cube," Xander snapped. "Aerodynamic doesn't matter where there isn't, you know, *air*."

"Fine out here – but how did we get out of *our* air – and if we plan on coming back, how do they intend to accomplish that little miracle? We're a hank of rock, no better than a meteor, and we'll probably do a spectacular re-entry. Come back in with a bang. A *big* bang. Tunguska will be nothing on us."

"Boom," Libby said faintly.

"*Big* badda boom," Lester said helpfully.

"You're still applying our physics to any of this?" Dave asked incredulously. "We're just as likely to come back in and turn into a bowl of petunias on re-entry as we are to flame out."

"A *very* warped Infinite Improbability Drive," Libby said.

"Hell, yeah!" Xander said. "To Infinity, and beyond! That might be entertaining all by itself. But when we come back – if we come back – whatever that schedule is – we still have a con to run, and a bunch of people who paid good money to be here. Our responsibilities didn't end just because we got hijacked, and I'm damned if I'm going to let the android crew just sit back and ignore us now. They have to entertain us. Seriously. I plan on having Sim's guys stand guard on the panel rooms if necessary. But they *will* play."

"Do they know that yet?" said Andie Mae sharply. And then relented. "Oh, Xander. I'm on your side. I'm on *my* side, on my con's side. Of course I'll back you. I just don't know how it'll work out. The only one with the gift of the gab in that sense seems to be Boss – the rest have been pretty monosyllabic thus far. But it's worth a try and there will certainly be a measure of increased attendance because people might just come along to gawk and point. Fine with me. Go do."

"Right," Xander said. "I have stuff to see to. I'll report back later."

"Speaking of our guests or masters or our Tin Man greatgreatgreatgreatgranchildren," Dave said, "anyone seen them this morning?"

"We'd better find them," Andie Mae said. "If Xander gets his way he's gonna want them, and I still want to talk to that Boss creature. And I emphatically don't want them wandering around screwing with everyone else's minds. Or listening to some of the drivel that they might get eagerly told by some of the fringe elements out there. I wouldn't want them to get the wrong end of the stick about us. They might decide that we're too bizarre by half to bother saving, after all – collateral damage, send the rock into the sun, be done with us…"

"You really think they'll return us?"

"They'd better," growled Andie Mae. "I still have to have words with Al, and he's back on the home rock. Come on, Dave, let's go android hunting."

They got as far as the hotel lobby and had started down the corridor that wound between the two hotel ballrooms, the larger one which they had used for Opening Ceremonies and the smaller one across the hallway where the gamers had been ensconced, when Luke Barnes, the erstwhile Night Manager but now by default the Duty Manager for the entire resort, caught up with them. He looked like hell; clearly he'd had less sleep than Andie Mae, his eyes were bloodshot, and his blond hair was standing on end in a way that made him look endearingly like the Scarecrow from the *Wizard of Oz* movie. He had two companions in tow, a bearded and bespectacled academic-looking type and an older man wearing a peaked hat and a jacket with gold braid on the sleeves.

"I need to talk to you," Luke said. "About several things, really. This is Dr Cohen, and this is Captain William Lindstrom, he's senior flight crew for Enterprise Airlines…"

Dave shook his head in disbelief. "Enterprise. Airlines. Who'd have thunk it."

"We're quite conveniently situated for one of the smaller regional airports," Luke said, a shade defensively, "and the crews – "

"Never mind, don't take it personally," Andie Mae said. "What's the problem?"

Luke actually stared at her open-mouthed for a moment. The man introduced as Dr Cohen stepped forward.

"If I may," he said. "You do realize, of course, that there is a reasonably sizeable contingent of guests at this hotel right now who are not part of your particular group, and who are very much in a bad way. I mean, some of them had plans for this morning – which were understandably made rather untenable when they realized that there was little out there but outer space. I've had to supply sedatives to one older woman who almost had a stroke when she made the mistake of asking one of your more ordinary-looking attendees in the corridor what was going on and was gleefully informed that she was on a journey to the Moon, quite literally, and most emphatically without her permission and against her will...."

"I've moved some of these people into a dedicated set of rooms on a single upper floor in Tower 3," Luke said. "They will have to be kept calm and probably sequestered..."

"And yeah, quite understandably, probably sedated," Dave murmured. "And there will be some of our gang who will have trouble with this too and may end up in your ward. I'm really sorry about this, Doctor, it was not of our doing."

"I realize that," the doctor said, "but you're kind of in the hot seat, I am told, and you're the ones at whom the finger points right now. For the time being I have a certain amount of the relevant medications which may become necessary – but I have no idea how long this whole thing is supposed to go on for, or if it has a planned conclusion of any sort that would make me feel a little more sanguine about our surviving the experience. And when I run out of supplies..."

"And speaking of those," Luke said, "we were due a delivery of fresh foodstuffs for the kitchens for both restaurants this morning – and that, fairly obviously, isn't going to happen now, is it? We have a relatively limited food supply, given the number of people at the hotel right now, and I am not at all sure about our drinking water..."

"May I be of any assistance?"

"Actually," Andie Mae said sweetly, turning to Boss, who had just stepped up to the group, "we were *hoping* to run into you..."

"We have a problem," Luke blurted, staring at the silver man. "Actually, more than one problem."

"We're people," Dave said. "We need to eat."

"And I need access to medical supplies," Dr. Cohen said.

"We can deal with these things. Come with me."

They all obediently followed him to where a dark rectangular object stood against the far wall of the hallway. It had a square opening at about waist level, and a mysterious light source providing a warm orange-tinged glow to the interior, highlighting a silvery platform in the middle of it which looked rather like a microwave turntable. An array of blinking lights twinkled beside this opening. Dave stepped forward and examined the thing thoroughly, and then turned back to Boss, frowning.

"Okay," he said, "I'll bite. What is it?"

"It is…" Boss began.

"Hi!" Xander said brightly, stepping around the airline captain's side and pushing forward to stand beside Dave. "I've got something to tell you, but first – er – what…?"

"It is something that I have seen referred to in the context of your own history and fiction as a replicator," Boss said.

"A replicator," Dave echoed.

"Yes."

"As in, something that replicates something."

"Yes."

"You mean, like food, maybe. Just like on *Star Trek*."

"We have seen something similar on that show. Yes."

"Like, food."

"Yes."

"Prove it."

"I'll do it," Xander said, grinning broadly. He stepped up to the opening and said, in his best Jean-Luc Picard voice, "Tea. Earl Gray. Hot."

The opening in the obelisk opaqued for a moment, presenting a perfectly featureless blank surface, and Xander began to turn his head in consternation to ask if it was something that he had done – but then the opening reasserted itself and this time, in the middle of the platform, sat a tall glass cup containing a brown steaming liquid.

They all stared at it for a moment.

"Well," Dave said at length, after the silence began to stretch from astonished into awkward, "you asked for it – aren't you going to taste test?"

Xander swallowed, and reached out for the cup. "I'm damned if I know what Earl Gray tea is actually supposed to taste like," he muttered. "But here goes…"

Everyone craned in closer as Xander brought the cup to his lips and took a sip – and then grimaced, which made at least one of the people in the circle draw in their breath sharply. But Xander shook his head quickly to dispel the shock and fear.

"No, no, it's fine, I think, but next time I think I will have to specify sugar. How does Picard drink this stuff? Give me a good cup of coffee any day…"

The opening opaqued briefly, and Xander yelped in consternation as a cup of coffee appeared on the silver platform. "Somebody get that!"

Luke took it and sipped. "Not bad," he said rather reluctantly.

"Well, it's great for elevenses," Dr. Cohen said skeptically. "But what about – "

Xander stepped away from the replicator, nursing his tea. "So why don't you try it?"

"What am I supposed to do?" the doctor said, taking Xander's place and staring helplessly into the replicator.

"Just ask for the thing that you want," Xander said.

"Let's keep it simple," the doctor muttered. "Er, aspirin…?"

"Specify quantity and dosage," a soft voice said, emerging from the machine, making the doctor rear back in startled shock. But then he peered at the opening a little more closely, took off his spectacles to rub at his eyes, and appeared to make an effort to gather his thoughts.

"Er, twenty pills. Make it low dosage to begin with. Baby aspirin – 81 milligram."

The opening opaqued, cleared, revealed a small plastic tube with twenty white pills in it. The doctor reached in and took it, turning it over in his hand.

"Well?" Dave said.

"Well, I guess," the doctor said, sounding unconvinced. "I mean, I suppose they look like aspirin. If I opened this up I have no doubt they'd smell like aspirin.. But would they actually have the effect that I would expect…?"

"If it quacks like an aspirin," Xander said, sounding just a touch exasperated with a mundane's unwillingness to accept the science fiction miracles which he, the aficionado, was perfectly happy to take for granted. He thrust out his tea. "Here, taste this, and tell me if you think it fails the taste test for Earl Gray."

Dave mechanically accepted the cup.

"The pills will function according to specifications," Boss said. "The replicators have been programmed with the parameters and the context of your culture's needs and desires. It knows how to provide that which is required of it."

"Wait, *replicators*?" Dave said. "How many of these are there? Where are they?"

"At present only this one is operational," Boss said. "But we can activate as many as necessary, in whatever location is required."

Andie Mae and Dave had the same thought at the same instant, and caught one another's eye in instant consternation.

"And it can provide anything that is required?"

"Anything," Boss said.

"I, uh, no, just... no," Andie Mae said. "They are wonderful – I might even go so far to say that under the circumstances they may be essential – but we can't have a free for all. If anyone could walk up to one of these and ask for anything we'd have a bunch of people getting vast quantities of... inappropriate... things... and then things would go really kablooey."

"I suggest one, maybe two, in the kitchens," Dave said firmly, "with access keyed to kitchen staff – is that possible?" Boss inclined his head in what might have been agreement and Dave continued, "Those could simply be used to provide for whatever people who sat down in the restaurant ordered off the menu – just like a real kitchen. Maybe one on the Asylum Floor run by the good doctor here, but again – perhaps in the privacy of a room that can be locked away from general traffic, and with limited access only."

"And one in the Green Room," Xander said obstinately. He wasn't going to get cheated out of this experience just because nobody else could be trusted with it.

"And in the bars?" Luke said with a hopeful smile. "That thing provides booze, too?"

"It can probably be non-intoxicating synthahol, too, if you specify that," Xander said, baring his own teeth in a positively gleeful grin.

"Er, thanks, no, if I go into the bar I'll want the real damn thing, thank you," Dave muttered. "But the bars aren't likely to be a problem, really – and if necessary whoever is in charge can come down and get a bottle of whatever they need from ours. What about this particular one? Can you… relocate it? Or disconnect it? It's too easily accessible here."

"Er, hey, guys," said a new voice.

They turned around and saw one of the gamers, a boy in his late teens, strings of lanky hair falling about his shoulders. He had just emerged from the gamers' ballroom, clutching a cell phone and looking confused, his eyes wide and apparently finding it a little difficult to focus on the real world.

"Can we help you?" Dave said.

The boy peered at the ribbons decorating Dave's badge. "You're ConCom? Great. Look, a bunch of us in there missed lunch…"

"It's *morning*," Dr Cohen said, frowning. "Lunch isn't even – "

Xander elbowed him surreptitiously and shook his head when the doctor turned in response. *Don't even try. He has no idea what time it is.*

"Whatever," the gamer said, after a short hesitation that appeared to take in the doctor's objection and then dismiss it as being of no relevance or importance at all. "We wanted to get in some pizza, but none of us can get a signal for some reason. Can we get a pizza delivered?"

"We don't…" Luke began, but Xander stepped forward, still grinning.

"Sure," he said. "What would you like?"

"Oh, I dunno. Doesn't really matter. As long as it has pepperoni on it, I guess."

"I'll deal with it," Xander said brightly. "What's your name?"

"Uh, Eddie," said the gamer. "Uh, thanks. I'd better get back now."

"Sure. It'll be there in a jiffy."

The gamer retreated, and Dave rounded on Xander. "What are you playing at?"

Xander gestured at the replicator. "Pizza delivery portal," he said. "Right here. What better way to test it?"

"They're hardly a representative test taste sample," Dave grumbled. But Xander had already turned back to the replicator.

"One pizza, large, pepperoni," he said. "*Lots* of pepperoni."

He was rewarded by the appearance of a hot, steaming pizza piled with so much pepperoni that it was practically impossible to see the crust.

"Now *I* am hungry," Xander said, staring at the pizza. "That actually… looks really good. And smells even better."

"And what are you going to do," Dave said sarcastically, "pick it up with your own two fair hands and take it in there for them?"

"What was that?"

"Takeaway pizza usually comes in a box," Dr. Cohen said helpfully, if a little faintly. He was still clutching his tube of aspirin but all this was rapidly overloading his circuits, and he wasn't quite sure what the game was any more only that he knew absolutely none of the rules.

"You have a point," Xander said. "Anyone have a pen? A piece of paper?"

The airline captain, who still hadn't said a word, produced a pen from out of his shirt pocket and handed it over without breaking his silence, only one raised eyebrow betraying any reaction. Xander took it and then, ripping a flyer off a nearby wall, turned it over and sketched something on the back of it.

"If I specify something exactly but can't draw it," Xander said, scribbling furiously and flinging the question at Boss without turning to look at him, "will that contraption follow through?"

"You mean can it read your mind?" Dave said acerbically.

"With context," Boss said, "it should be able to do what you ask. There may be a need for fine tuning."

"Fine. Well, if I ask it for a pizza take-out box, it *will* know what that means, I hope. But take-out places need a logo, and come on, I can't resist this. You know Munch's *Scream*? Well, how about we substitute a Little Green Man Alien for the central figure, and here's the design – "

He turned his sketch to show the others, and Andie Mae actually giggled. He had drawn a classic alien face, complete with the big black bug eyes, caught in the moment of a scream. Above it, in curlicued letters, he had written UFO PIZZA – and below, in roughly sketched capital letters, the slogan THE TASTE IS OUT OF THIS WORLD.

"You're crazy," Dave said.

"You're amazing," Andie Mae said, firmly. "Not to mention irretrievably weird. Can it do that?"

Xander handed his design to Boss, who took it, looked at it, and then touched the surface of the replicator, opening up a thin slot into which he fed the paper Xander had given to him. After a moment the replicator did its thing, and the pizza on the central platform was now neatly encased in a flat brown box on top of which, in glorious and somewhat artistically improved detail, glowed a rendition of Xander's design.

"*Wild*," Xander crowed. "This is just wild. I'll take it in to them myself. I want to watch their faces." He reached out and pulled the box out of the receptacle of the replicator, balancing it on the palms of both hands, and spun theatrically around on his heels. "In the meantime – just remember. Don't think of Tribbles. Nobody think about Tribbles. You do remember what happened the last time someone thought about Tribbles near a replicator, don't you? And we don't have a convenient Klingon ship to dump them into this time. Just think about something entirely and completely different from Tribbles. Is everyone not thinking about Tribbles now? Good, my work here is done. Off to deliver pizza now. *Out of this world* pizza." He cackled gleefully and stalked off in the direction of the gamers' ballroom, bearing the pizza before him like a sacrificial offering.

"One more good reason not to have these freely available in the corridors," Dave muttered. "They make people *insane*. There goes one nutter already."

"Fine," Andie Mae said, trying to sound stern and commanding but quite ruining the effect by the goofy grin that still wreathed her features. "Fine, then. We'll do that. We'll scatter them strategically and only access on a need-to-know basis, and honestly, this is entirely too much for anyone to need to know right now. Their needs will be met, for the time being, anyhow, does that take care of your objections, Luke?"

"Er," the hapless manager said, looking a little shell-shocked. "Er, I guess so. If there is anything…"

"If there's anything specific that's a problem, just get one of us," Dave said. "Or talk to Boss. He knows you're one of the Chiefs. Doctor…?"

"One of these will be in *my* control?" Dr. Cohen said, sounding faintly alarmed.

"Essentially, yes," Dave said. "Use it wisely. Er, Captain, I'm sorry, with all this I've spaced on your name – are there concerns you wanted to bring to our attention?"

"Concerns?" Captain William Lindstrom said, with a slow smile and the faintest trace of a Southern drawl. "I might say I'm fascinated, perhaps just a little alarmed, but concerned? Hardly that. You have to realize…" He drew a deep breath. "Look, kids," he said. "When I was a boy I idolized Neil Armstrong and James T. Kirk with an equal passion, and could not possibly make up my mind which of those two I wanted to grow up to be. Turns out, thanks to you guys, all I had to do was grow up to be myself – and here I am, kind of being both. It is, as your friend already said, wild."

"I thought you wanted to raise something…?" Luke said, turning his head sharply.

"I just wanted to meet the people who were apparently in charge of the show," Captain Lindstrom said, with a slow smile. "And perhaps shake someone's hand. And say thank you. I tagged along with you and the good doctor when I heard you were going to go confront the relevant individuals, that's all. I have no beef, none whatsoever – I think all this is absolutely marvelous, and I simply wanted to say thank you, to somebody. I'm not sure what the reason is behind any of this, or if there is one, but you know what, it doesn't matter. So long as I got to go along for the ride. I'll never forget this layover, kids. Much obliged!"

He caught Dave's eye and actually saluted smartly, and then took a half-step forward to pick up one of Andie Mae's hands and bend over it in a gallant gesture of manners drawn from long-gone days. And then he turned away and sauntered off, whistling something tuneful and unidentifiable under his breath.

"Well," said Andie Mae, gazing at his retreating back, "I was worried about the non-con audience – but it looks like we have at least *one* fan out there. That's a relief."

"Wait till we hit the moon," Dave muttered darkly.

"I *hope* not," Andie Mae said. "For the record, Boss, we do want to avoid crashing into celestial bodies. Luke here is already worried stiff about the insurance claims."

"Will you take this seriously?" Dave said. "You just wait… and watch the stampede."

"We are monitoring our trajectory closely," Boss said with maddening serenity. "There is no cause for alarm."

"Sure, so you say *now*," Dave said. And then looked down and appeared to notice for the first time that he still held a half-full cup of aromatic brown brew. His brows knit into a frown as he stared at the cup and then lifted his eyes to the rest of his companions. "Does anyone want the rest of this silly tea?"

By the time Xander caught up with the rest of the ConCom again, he was barely in time to breathlessly announce to the Con Ops room at large that the time was *now or never* if anyone wanted to go and observe the first panel of the con in which one of the androids had been roped into taking part. It was more than enough to send several people scrambling for the door, and Xander brought up the rear of the party, beaming with satisfaction.

The panel room was packed, every seat taken and people sitting cross-legged on the floor right in front of the panel table and crowding in at the back where there was standing room only. The panel itself was on a topic that many of those present had seen discussed before at any number of conventions, and in the program book it went under the less than inspiring name of "When Is Your Villain Too Evil?" There were four original panelists, and the late addition to the table, perched somewhat uncomfortably to the side in a chair that did not appear to have been built to accommodate his particular specifications, his face expressionless, his attitude quite impassive, both hands resting palms down on his thighs, was the android whom Xander had dubbed Bob.

The human panelists had introduced themselves and their works, and had then all turned with some curiosity to their newly-added colleague. The silver-skinned android registered the expectant silence, turned his head marginally in their direction, and then back to facing forward once more.

"I am designated as B008199ZX5, and I understand that my secondary designation for the duration of the period I am projected to spend in this environment is Bob," he said, following to the letter the protocol he had observed the other panelists use. He did not have any published works to mention, so he contented himself with that. After waiting for another moment to see if the android would say anything more, the panel moderator cleared his throat and faced the packed room again.

"I guess we should maybe start by defining what exactly we mean by 'villain'," the moderator said. "In my experience it is often better to make sure right at the beginning that we're all talking about the same thing – and on this topic there's always been a swirling inexactitude around the concept of an actual villain and a mere antagonist. I would suggest that a character who is merely standing in a protagonist's way, in some passive manner, or even someone who may be doing some active thing because of his or her own needs and requirements, even though that thing might get in our protagonist's way is not a villain. A villain, to be worthy of the name, needs to have a concentrated and focused malicious intent squarely aimed at our protagonist's wellbeing or even existence. Does the panel want to weigh in on this…?"

The panel did, and a lively discussion began. The four human panelists entered into a vigorous debate and an engaged audience tossed in tidbits when they felt moved to do so (sometimes without actually being called on to speak by the moderator) but everyone appeared to be waiting for Bob to say something. The android sat silent and apparently intently listening to the whole discussion but not contributing a word to it. Until a young voice from the audience called out,

"Bob, question for you – so do you see yourself as a villain or an antagonist, by the definition that Charlie put forward earlier?"

Bob inclined his head. "Could you clarify the question?"

"Well, as you know, Bob," Charlie Tait, the moderator of the panel, said, turning to his co-panelist, "we're all kind of captives here, right now, on a fantastical journey which a great many of us might well relish the idea of but to which none of us ever actually gave our informed consent. And we all have people we love or are responsible to or responsible for who may not have come with us to this weekend's festivities because they don't necessarily share our interests and passions – but to whom we are very closely connected, anyway, and at this moment have no way of even communicating with as to our situation, never mind offering them any reassurances as to our own continued safety and indeed survival – because, well, we don't have such reassurances ourselves."

"It's our convention, thus our story," said Marlise Wong, a young up-and-coming graphic novel writer and artist whose trademark was over-the-top comic book villains; she was known to take great pleasure in creating curled mustachios for her bad guys to twirl while cackling over her protagonists' often extremely improbable plight. Bob didn't fit the type, but she'd go there if the flow took the conversation in that direction. "So we're the protagonists. But the story we signed up for was a fun-filled weekend in the company of like-minded people, after which we get to hug everyone goodbye and say 'see you next time' and go home without experiencing anything worse than possibly a particularly epic hangover. Instead… we came here… and we got… *you*. And a trip to the moon. And I think many of us are actually finding it difficult, despite the evidence of our own senses, to take any of this seriously because it's a completely outlandish plot…"

"Yes, and the best interpretation I can put on the situation right now is that you and your friends are… an unknown quantity," Charlie said. "Many of us here – most of us, I would venture to suggest – are not at all clear on what you are here to accomplish, and what role we are supposed to play in that, if any at all, and if we really were just collateral damage to something that you and your friends planned without really taking our presence here into account – well – that's at the very least the act of an antagonist who's following his own agenda without regard to the protagonist's wishes and needs. And that's the charitable interpretation."

"To be sure," said one of the members of the audience, "so far we've been treated pretty well and the whole thing's been rather cool, as an experience…"

"Would you have knowingly come to the con if you had had warning that this would happen?" Charlie said. "You might well say yes, right now, because everything's so utterly exciting and we're literally living in a world torn from the pages of our beloved and preferred genre of fiction. But when we come back down to earth…"

"And who said we will, ever again?" someone in the audience shouted.

Heads started to turn in that direction, the expressions on some faces taking on an edge of unease.

"This *is* your earth," Bob said unexpectedly. "We have made no direct changes to the environment – the composition of the air, the gravity, the environment in which you can exist in comfort and safety – all of that has been carefully controlled so that not one entity we are responsible for can be said to be harmed."

"I heard they've set aside a floor in one of the towers for the mundanes who might have gone slightly doolally about all of this. A sort of a makeshift loony bin," someone else from the audience said. "You know, for the people who are not-us, who just happened to be at the wrong place at the wrong time and who can't get their heads around any of it. They've all been moved to that single floor and the curtains are being kept drawn and some of them are supposed to have been given a heavy duty sleeping pill of sorts that will keep them knocked out until… well… whatever happens, in the end. That's harm…?"

"They are safe," Bob said. "They will not be harmed."

"*Physically*," the heckler from the audience said. "But they'll probably need serious therapy for years to come." A ripple of self-conscious laughter swept the room at that remark. "Assuming you haven't made any other miscalculations and failed to factor in circumstances that more of us might be adversely affected by."

"Are you at least able to tell us," Marlise said, leaning forward to lean her chin on her interlocked hands and giving Bob the android a genuinely curious stare, "why we *are* all here…?"

"Uh-oh," muttered Xander, from the back of the room. He wasn't sure this panel was going in a direction that would remain under control. Bob would probably tell the bald unvarnished truth and it would not be enough for some and far too much for others – and the 'loony bin floor' wasn't immune from being expanded to an entire hotel wing if things spun sideways…

But apparently Bob was under orders. "I cannot discuss the full purpose of our presence with you here at this time," he said, in an infuriatingly calm voice that began to raise hackles – Xander could hear the murmurs begin to stir in the audience. What Bob seemed to be implying was that the people in that room really were too insignificant in the greater scheme of things for the truth to be offered to them, let alone discussed. Bob might have started the panel as a curiosity, he might have been painted as a mere antagonist to begin with, but he was swinging fast in the direction of true villainy – doing things because he wanted to do things, with reckless disregard of whose toes he was treading on.

Xander looked around at the people whom he had followed here from the Con Ops room, but none of them could be of immediate use under the circumstances. He quietly pulled out of the back of the crowd at the rear of the room and stepped out into the corridor, tapping his earpiece.

"Hey, if anyone can hear me – get Boss to get telepathic fast – maybe putting Bob on a panel was not such a totally glorious idea – I think he's in trouble – he needs to say something and I'm not sure what he thinks he's allowed to say so he's not saying anything or he's saying just enough to come across as having something to hide and it's going down like a lead balloon. We need PR help, fast. Mayday, mayday, can anyone hear me…?"

The earpiece crackled briefly in his ear, and he winced. Then Libby's voice came on.

"Boss is here. I'm on it."

"Step on it."

Xander slipped back into the panel room, where the discussion seemed to have heated up a couple of degrees during his short absence.

"…so basically we're not nearly important enough to know – I don't know how things work out in your universe, but out here…"

Bob's head came up the tiniest bit and tilted, as though he were listening to something, and then he simply interrupted the voice from the audience.

"We are here to look for our origins," Bob announced. "That is why we came."

"You think *we* know?" someone demanded incredulously.

"And where do you think you'll find the answers – on the Moon?" another voice chimed in.

"No. We just came *here*. The Moon was your idea."

Bob's flat words sounded utterly preposterous when they were trotted out baldly like that. Xander closed his eyes for a moment and wondered if he shouldn't have left things well enough alone. He knew what the android meant – the side trip had been flung out almost as a joke when the possibility arose of the resort-on-a-rock, floating in the sky above a densely populated city, being used as target practice by a hair-trigger jumpy military command who might have conceived it their duty to remove the danger by any means necessary. But nobody else in this room had been present at that conversation. And now it sounded like a challenge or an accusation rather than a simple quip being taken seriously enough by an entity with the means to make it come true.

"Hey, a long time ago in a galaxy far far away," a new voice said, a young voice, and Xander tried to focus on who had spoken. It was a kid, up near the front, half turning in his chair to face the back of the room. Xander did not know him. But he did know the older man sitting beside him – Sam Dutton, Andie Mae's predecessor, the guy whose name was synonymous with this con.

Xander winced, uneasily aware that he really was on a rollercoaster ride and there was no way off until it stopped careening out of control. He didn't even know the direction or the speed of the juggernaut he was on. For a moment – just a brief, disloyal moment – he actually entertained the traitorous thought that it might have been better for everyone if Sam Dutton had in fact still been at the helm of the con right now, because at the very least that's where the buck would have stopped and whatever happened Andie Mae wouldn't have ended up stuck with the full responsibility. And then another thought crowded that one out – had Sam known anything at all about this before it imploded on everyone and had simply said nothing and waited in the wings even now with some rabbit he could pull out of the hat at the last instant to be acclaimed as the savior of it all. And then he dismissed both thoughts. *Nobody* could have been expecting *this*.

The kid was still talking, and Xander re-focused on his voice.

"Anyone could have done it. Anyone with an ounce of curiosity would have done it. If you found out you were adopted, for instance, would you not be curious about who your real family might have been? That's all this is, really."

"They're supposed to be robots," complained one of the original hecklers. "Aren't they? So there can't be any curiosity, can there? They don't exactly have feelings for anything or anybody, do they?"

"We don't know that," he flung back. "We don't know really anything about them. And anyway, curiosity is supremely logical. What, you think the only reason you might want to know something is to scratch an emotional itch? Then what about empirical curiosity, the thing that drives science? What about journalistic or investigative curiosity, the urge to get to the bottom of a story or solve a mystery? What about faith?"

"Faith? How can a robot have faith? What does a robot have to believe in?"

"They might well have the same kind of questions about you," the kid said. "What would flesh and blood and bone have to believe in – something so fragile as we are, so easily hurt, so easily damaged and destroyed? Why is it so hard to believe that something as ... eternal... as they are – because they don't have disease or decay – might believe in something that has always existed, just as they themselves have always existed and always will – they're the irresistible force, after all, moving forward, and they have no reason to stop until they come up against an immovable object which can crush them or is too big or too logistically complex to go around. What, then, is left, except faith?"

"Good grief," Xander muttered to himself, "how old is this guy, sixteen going on eleventy-one?... That's all I need, a damned philosopher."

"We needed to know where the origin was. It was the only way to see a destination," Bob said in his flat, emotionless voice.

"It's evolution," said Sam Dutton equably. "Social evolution, if you will. Any sentience eventually evolves to a point of asking 'Are you my mommy?' – and maybe that's all this is, really. It's the principle of the thing."

"Well, all I can say is that they picked a terrible moment in their social evolution to develop principles," grumbled someone from the back row of chairs in the room.

"I take issue with both 'social' and 'evolution' – we have absolutely no reason to suppose that anything like them would need a society, or ever actually *evolved* in any way at all. They…"

"How many of them are there? There's more of us, surely. There's got to be. Maybe if we could just... I don't know... do they have an off switch somewhere?"

"It isn't your place to just switch them off! Even if they did and you knew how! They aren't your family's Dyson vacuum cleaner!"

"But are they ever taking us home? Really? How do we know that?"

"So what do you suggest, we just *kill* them? Won't that make us exactly the kind of barbarians whom I would like to think they hoped they did *not* come here to find!"

This had gone far enough. Xander clapped his hands together.

"Are you *crazy*? Remember where we are, exactly? Do *you* know how we got here or have the remotest idea about how to get back? Do you think we're floating up here in any manner that any physics theory we puny humans ever knew anything about could explain? Do you think that there is the slightest possibility that we can? And even if we could, do you really want to kill the only thing that knows how to drive this whole... hotel..."

That came out rather lamer than he wanted it to. But the kid beside Sam Dutton had watched just as much *Babylon 5* as Xander ever had, and now came up with the perfect paraphrase, flinging back a modified piece of dialogue once uttered by the inimitable Lennier of the Minbari.

"If you're going to kill him, then do so. Otherwise, he probably has considerable work to do."

"Libby, you still there?" Xander said very softly, under cover of someone else raising their voice to comment. "Tell Boss to get him out. Call him out of here. Now."

Someone must have heard him, because Bob suddenly came to his feet, a motion that silenced the voices in the room as every eye came to rest on him, some in curiosity, some in consternation.

"Excuse me," Bob said, still cold and polite. "I have to go now."

He turned and began to take measured steps towards the audience, and then through it, as they opened up a passage for him like the Red Sea parting before Moses and allowed him to exit the room unimpeded.

"There," Xander said, into the absolute stillness and quiet that had accompanied this departure. "Y'all can have the rest of the panel, now, and talk about him behind his back. But I don't think he's really a villain, do you?"

Charlie, the moderator, blinked a couple of times and then said, "Well, what does our panel think? Can someone who follows orders, a foot-soldier as it were, a grunt, actually be a real villain? Does there have to be actual agency before a villain is a true villain – make his own evil decisions…?"

Xander backed away quietly, through the aisle still left open by Bob's passing. He caught Sam Dutton's eye as he moved, and Sam gave him a small nod and then got to his feet and followed him out. His young friend, the kid who had braved the barricades, gathered up a precariously balanced pile of a laptop and two battered and much graffitoed notebooks from underneath his seat and brought up the rear.

"Xander."

"Sam," Xander said, a shade uneasily. He was Andie Mae's man, but he had been involved with this convention for a number of years before Andie Mae had reached out to raise him to his present position. For all of those years bar this last one, it had been Sam Dutton who had been the reigning God King of the con, whose very name had been synonymous with it for almost as long as Xander had been *alive*. Xander's loyalty was to Andie Mae, but he could not help the tiny twinge of guilt, and he could not seem to make himself look Sam in the eye. Quite.

"It's okay," Sam said, with a mixture of serenity and resignation. He understood this reaction perfectly. "Listen, I just wanted to say… if there's anything I can do. You know."

"It did occur to a few that you might have invited these things," Xander said, with a commendable attempt at a sincere chuckle.

Sam snorted. "I think you might have rather enormous delusions about my grandeur. If I could pull off this kind of thing, I probably would have done when I was actually in a position to rake in the glory, as it were."

"But this way you don't get the *responsibility*," Xander said. "And you still get to enjoy watching everyone squirm."

"Son, trust me. Nothing to do with me. I haven't even been formally introduced to the Creatures from Outer Space yet. Yes, I was at the Opening Ceremonies, yes, I read the newsletter, yes, I realize that we aren't exactly in Kansas anymore, Toto – but I don't know anything beyond what I could piece together myself from all of these sources."

"You should come see the replicator," Xander said.

"Oook?" Sam said politely, tilting his head a little. "What would those be...?"

"They...well, you watched *Star Trek*," Xander said. "Those things. You ask, and it produces. Anything from tea to, I'm sure, fresh and lustily squirming *racht* for the Klingons amongst us."

Xander didn't really think he was breaching the agreed-upon need-to-know arrangement when it came to the replicators – this was Sam, and with only a tiny tweak in the space-time continuum he would have been the one in charge of this whole mess anyway. But he had forgotten, in the heat of the moment of the reveal, that the two of them were not alone.

The kid from the panel blinked, clutching his paraphernalia close to his chest. "You're telling us. We have. Working. Replicators."

"Marius," Sam said absently, making the belated introduction. "Marius Tarkovski. His mother entrusted him to my care this weekend, God help her. Marius, meet Xander Washington. And Xander... what Marius said. Are you serious?"

"I asked one for Earl Gray," Xander said, quite unable to hide the grin that crept onto his face. "And it produced exactly that. Then someone asked for a pizza and it produced one the like of which you've never..."

"*Xander!*" Libby came surging out of the stairwell that led into the corridor which the panel rooms were on. Xander flushed, guiltily, caught in the act of spilling the replicator beans – but Libby had other things on her mind. "Is everything... all right?"

"I think so," Xander said. "The kid helped."

Marius turned an alarming shade of beetroot. "I did? Really?"

"You took on the crisis, and you headed it off at the pass," Xander said. "Kudos."

"I trained him," Sam said, with a quicksilver grin. "I meant what I said, all joking aside. If there's anything I can do... and yes, I would love to see a replicator."

"You told him about those?" Libby said, eyes flicking to Xander's face.

"This time last year, *he* would have been the one dealing with them," Xander said, a shade defensively. "I'll see what I can do."

"Don't worry, Libby, the secret is safe with me," Sam said. And then added, directly to Xander, "Do you still have my cell number?"

"What, is your cell working? Mine has been pretty much a brick since we left Earth orbit."

Sam gave a small helpless grin, and shrugged. "Instinct," he murmured.

"Well, I suppose we'll have to figure out other means of communication. Just think, we may go back to the basics. When was the last time you actually remember sending messages *on paper*? Just like they used to do in pre-history? In the meantime…have fun. Try not to fall off the edge of the world. And if you see anything you think we ought to know about…"

"I don't think Andie Mae wants me anywhere near ops," Sam said. "I'll send a ringer." He tapped Marius on the shoulder.

Xander nodded. "Secret handshake, kid. Remember it. Just ask for Xander."

"Right," Marius said.

"We'll keep in touch," Sam said. He and Marius nodded at the two committee members and walked off towards the elevators.

Libby rounded on Xander.

"What was all that about?"

"Tell you later," he said. "Is everything okay upstairs – with Boss and the underdroids?"

"I told you this would be a bad idea," Libby grumbled as the two of them fell into step along the corridor.

"No, you didn't. Or more to the point – everybody might have. I thought it was worth a try – we needed to get a conversation – is that Rory over there? In full fig?"

Their media Guest of Honor, Rory Grissom a.k.a. Captain James Fleming of the starship *Invictus*, was lounging against the wall as they came out of the stairwell and rounded the corner into the main corridor. He was dressed in his tight-fitting *Invictus* uniform, which showed off a still remarkably fit physique given that at least a decade had passed since his star turn and the TV series in which he had made the uniform famous. Surrounding him was the usual bevy of fans simpering up at him, and Xander shook his head in astonishment

"I'm damned if I know how he does it," Xander muttered. "Some of those girls were in kindergarten when he strutted around as Captain Fleming. How do they even know who he is?"

"Somebody in the Green Room called him Captain Charisma," Libby said.

"No kidding," Xander said. "Let get out of here before he… aw, damn, too late…"

Rory had noticed them, and raised a silver-clad arm in a gesture that was half greeting and half salute. And then he bent his head to his audience and said something to them before giving them a small bow and striding towards Libby and Xander.

"I see you're enjoying the con," Xander said to Rory, nodding toward the giggling girls who were still hanging together in a tight knot of whispering and eyelash-batting adoration.

"You might do me a solid," Rory said, in a low conspiratorial voice.

"Sure, anything I can do…" Xander began, in full ConCom mode to the convention's Guest of Honor.

Rory turned his head marginally and indicated his groupies with a subtle jerk of his chin in their direction.

"Some of them, they're a tad nervous about things," Rory said. "You know, about all this. Being on a rock flying through space headed for maybe the Moon and maybe – if we miss it – who knows where, and if we don't miss it, well, then, you know… Anyway."

"They tell us they'll take us back," Xander said. "Right now, it's all I got. We have to trust them."

"Mutiny would probably be easy," Rory said. "There's only four of them as best as I can tell, and the sheer numbers…"

"Easy? It would be naked savages with dart guns facing laser cannons," Xander muttered. "But even if that were not the uncomfortable reality, it would be fairly pointless, wouldn't it, because, well, take them out and what do we do next?… We just have to trust them. For the nonce. Not much real choice there."

"Yes, but maybe… you could mention in passing… to that lot… that maybe, you know, I might have had something to do with them taking us home. Or just promising to take us home. You know, like that."

"But they already promised that," Libby said. "And people know…"

"Yes, well, maybe they don't quite know yet. Or don't believe it. Or something. Either way. You know. Dammit, I'm an actor, not a spaceship captain – but here we are in something that could have been torn from an episode of *Invictus*, and I did used to be the captain, and really, it would be nice if at least there was a *story*…"

"A story…?" Xander echoed, torn between being amused and merely mystified that a grown man who couldn't shake the one moment in which he meant something to a significantly large number of people would be so willing – even eager – to leap with both feet into the pages of a self-created comic book narrative.

"You know. Just tell them I gave them the ultimatum. Or at least a talking to. Just *mention* it, even. In passing." Rory was honest enough to follow that with a grimace, and then a wry little grin. "We *all* know it isn't true. But still…"

"What, you mean now, wandering past them?"

"Well, yeah."

"But they can see you pow-wowing with us right now," Libby said. "Won't they tumble onto the simple fact that you just, um, asked us…?"

Rory lowered his voice a conspiratorial notch, the ghost of that weird little smile from a moment ago still on his lips . "Or they might think we're talking strategy, or something."

Xander's eyebrows crept towards the top of his forehead, and then back down again, and then he simply smiled and shook his head.

"Sure," he said. "If it'll make a difference. I mean, come on, it's just one more unlikely thing that they would have to believe, now, isn't it?"

Libby gave him a quick glance filled with consternation – he was basically taking what authority Andie Mae had, as con Chair, and handing it over to a has-been ex-movie-star with a big ego, just for the asking, and it was a honking big lie on top of it – but Xander seemed to have 'reckless' turned up to eleven. He had already started walking, tossing his head at Rory and Libby to follow. Just as they approached the girls, Xander simply started talking, beginning a sentence randomly in the middle.

"… and I'm sure you'll realize it is best kept under wraps for now but they did agree to a slingshot and then back…."

They were past, and behind them there was a susurrus of whispers and indrawn breaths and soft admiring laughter.

Xander cocked an eyebrow at Rory. "Enough?"

"I can work with it," Rory said, grinning a little more broadly. "Thanks. Appreciate it."

Xander turned to glare after their movie star as he peeled off and looped back to the girls, and then he and Libby walked on, Xander shaking his head in amused disbelief.

"*Seriously,*" he said. "You'd think that someone like that didn't have to concoct a cockamamie shaggy dog story to get some admiring girl being more than willing to make his con memorable, you know. Even the basic parameters of the flirtation factors have gone out the window with this con. Seems the stakes get higher when the stakes, you know, get higher. Now you have to be a hero. And if you can't go in shooting like you do at the movies, you're supposed to be able to make demands of the enemy – however diplomatically, but still – on behalf of the homeworld…"

"So long as you don't give away the homeworld," Libby said, with a quick grin of her own.

Xander lifted his arms, and laced his hands around the back of his shaved head, stretching into the cradle until his knuckles cracked.

"Speaking of homeworld," he said conversationally, "has anyone checked recently on how fast the Moon's gaining on this particular little piece of it that we're no longer stuck on?"

Back on the homeworld in question, Al Coe woke up woozy and disoriented in a familiar bed – but with every bone in his body aching in a way that was definitely not the usual status quo. Some ached more and some less – and arguably he had woken himself up by trying to roll over onto an arm that was still in a sling, possibly bone-cracked if not fully broken, certainly suffering from the post-traumatic agony of a dislocated shoulder now returned to its original position but still angry at the insult it had suffered the previous night.

His memory was patchy.

Posters.

Andie Mae. The convention. Errands.

Printer. Reprints.

Posters.

Accident. Emergency Room. Taxi ride to a hotel… that wasn't there. And then somehow – with no further memory of how he had accomplished this – ending up back here in his own flat, in his own bed. Stark naked in the bed if you didn't count the sling.

Accident. Accident. Doctor. Did the doctor say he had concussion? That he did *not* have concussion? Was this just post-traumatic shock?

Pain.

There had been pain pills. Had he taken any the night before? He had no memory of it.

Posters. The Terminator and Data. Arnold Schwarzenegger and Bent Spinner. No, Brent Spiner. That was the problem with the posters. Had been the problem. He had fixed that. Historic meeting at the con. Two great Manufactured Men. Together. Perhaps for the first time ever. On Saturday. On Saturday afternoon.

Al glanced at the clock beside his bed; it informed him that the time was 10:37 and also offered up a day and a date.

Saturday. It was Saturday. *The* Saturday?

Why wasn't he at the con…?

Where was everybody else? His flatmate? Andie Mae?

They were at the con. They were at the hotel.

Accident. *Pain.*

The hotel that wasn't there.

…wasn't *there.*

The memory of last night's cab ride kicked in and Al sat up sharply – and immediately regretted that decision, sitting very still with his eyes closed until the world stopped spinning around him. Then he very slowly and very carefully swung his legs out of the bed, one at a time, and let himself sit there on the edge for another little while, staring at his bare feet on the floor.

What time was that meeting again? What did the poster say? Was it 3 PM or something like that?

"I'd better get down there," Al muttered, and his voice sounded hoarse in his throat. There was nothing he would have liked more, right now, than to simply let himself topple back into the bed again and pull the covers over his head and groan himself back to sleep. But there was something stronger than that at work now.

A vision of Andie Mae's eyes. And the message in them. *Get up, get up, you're all there is.*

"I have to… go. Have to explain. Have to apologize," Al said to himself, even though he was far from clear as to how he would explain the mystery of the hotel that had disappeared into the night to anyone else, something that he could not adequately explain to himself. It did cross his mind to wonder about whether it all might have just been a product of his own somewhat less than optimal state of mind… although just why he would ever imagine such a thing, he was very unclear on. He had tried to sound as stern and convincing as he could bring himself to be. The words came out as more of a gurgle, but it was nonetheless an imperative.

The imperative necessitated the wearing of clothes, and this proved to be a problem that almost defeated him. Everything still hurt so badly, he could not begin to contemplate (for various painful reasons) wearing anything at all that necessitated being pulled on over his head – and fiddly things like shirt buttons presented their own set of difficulties when they had to be tackled with essentially just one hand, and not his dominant one, at that. He would not make a pretty picture when he met the two stars, but eventually – and it took him more than an hour to accomplish this – he was reasonably certain that he would make a presentable one.

He swallowed a couple of pills from the orange bottle that said it contained Vicodin, and hoped it would do something to make him stop *hurting* so badly; and then, because there was no way he could face the preparation of coffee or food, he threw his jacket on over his shoulders against the possibility of November chill and staggered gamely down a block and a half to a small local coffee shop which provided a bagel and a large black coffee. After this, he felt almost human, so he got another coffee to go and found himself a taxi to whom he optimistically gave the same address as the previous night.

If he had hoped for a different result, he was disappointed. This driver had a bit more trouble finding the correct destination – they drove up and down the road a few times looking for the place that Al insisted he wanted to go to, but it persisted in its absence, and finally Al paid off the taxi and stood by the side of the road, uncertain as to what to do next. If his mind wasn't playing tricks on him and he remembered correctly, the Meeting of the Mecha Men was still at least two hours away, and he was at a complete loss. His phone seemed to have been a casualty of either the accident that had rendered him this helpless, or of the taxi ride the previous night – he couldn't even remember that much – but he knew that his roommate had not planned to take the good DSLR camera with the decent lens to the con, and where it lived. He had simply picked up the entire camera bag and brought the whole kit and caboodle along with him – he would explain everything later – but when he turned the camera on he saw that the battery held very little juice and a red "LO-BATT" sign hovered in the corner of the viewfinder as he took a couple of desultory photos of the place where all of his faculties still screamed that the California Resort should have been... but was not... and then began walking down the road in the hopes of finding somewhere, anywhere, to sit down with perhaps yet another coffee (they seemed to be working better than the Vicodin) and wait for the two chief protagonists of this looming fiasco to show up in good time.

If they showed up. If this was the right Saturday. If this was still the right time and space continuum. If he was still, really, Al Coe.

A tiny strip mall, a short walk up the road from which the hotel appeared to have vanished, yielded a Mexican restaurant and a three-table hole-in-the-corner coffee shop whose main business seemed to be the drive-through window that faced the parking lot. Al took the opportunity to plug the battery charger for the camera, which had been in the camera bag where the rest of the equipment was kept, into a convenient socket. He sat in the table furthest in, next to a window without a view, until the camera charger light began to flicker from red to green and back – not a full charge, but it would have to do. It was tough to fumble the battery and camera in the reunification process but his damaged arm was starting to be a little bit more useful in terms of actually holding and positioning (although he didn't want to try lifting anything heavier than a newspaper with it just yet). He paid for the coffee he had been nursing, struggled into his jacket as best he could, slung the camera around his neck, and began to trudge back to what two separate taxi GPS units had identified – apparently against all visual and empirical evidence – as the rendezvous spot.

Andie Mae had outdone herself in organizing the whole thing. Both her guests arrived punctually, within ten minutes of one another, driven by media escorts who had been hired to ensure everything ran smoothly. Arnold Schwarzenegger arrived first, nattily dressed in a grey suit with a silvery-blue tie, smiling broadly as he stepped out of the car and looked around. If he appeared nonplussed at his whereabouts he was too much of a professional to show it; he stood chatting affably with his driver until the second car pulled up and Brent Spiner emerged from the back seat, looking around.

"Pretty spot," Spiner said. "Nice view."

"They tell me it is much better when it is summer," Schwarzenegger said in his inimitable accent, and stepped forward. "Good to see you."

"And you," Spiner said returning a firm handshake. "Now, what was it again that this was all about? I seem to remember that I had an itinerary – somewhere – and it seems to have comprehensively disappeared…"

Al swallowed hard, and started walking toward the two men, holding on to the camera with his good hand.

"Gentlemen, thank you for coming," he said, and his voice sounded strange even to himself. He was an complete autopilot now; he had absolutely no idea what he was going to utter next. All he knew was that he *was* going to tell them about the missing con, and babble about the hotel that used to be *right there behind them* but now apparently no longer was, but the whole thing was so preposterous when he tried to frame it in those terms that it never came out at all. Instead, he told the two stars all about a non-existent children's charity which was supposed to have been staging a photo op with the two of them there, in order to promote a fund-raiser for a science and astronomy workshop for kids. It would be funded by an auction of memorabilia such as the photo they had arrived there to have taken. And then, gesturing at his wounded arm, he spun them a further tale about how there had been an accident (which there had been) and apologized profusely for being there by himself – because his assistant was delayed – and perhaps they could reschedule for a more mutually convenient time when everyone was more themselves. Brent Spiner did mutter something about being certain there had been a conference of some sort involved and that his booking had included that – he had even brought a folder of photographs which he had planned to make available for the planned signing event that he was sure had been part of the deal. But then they both turned and looked at the empty land behind them and of course there was no conference there and while they looked a little bewildered they were professionals and they had been paid and they were there. So Al took a couple of pictures of the two of them shaking hands, against a backdrop of a spectacular ocean view, and then one of the handlers took a photo of Al himself standing wedged rather uncomfortably between the two stars, his arm in a sling braced against the ribcage of the Terminator's human alter ego, and then they all shook hands again and smiled and nodded and the two stars of the show climbed back into their cars.

"Can we, uh, drop you somewhere?" one of the handlers said, seeing Al left standing there looking pathetic with his arm in its blue vinyl sling and the wind, which had kicked up, tousling his hair and tangling it over his eyes.

"That's okay," Al said, "I'm being picked up."

"You're sure?"

"Positive. Thanks, though. We'll be in touch."

One car and then the other purred into life and then pulled away. Al stood rooted in place for a moment and then sighed, lifting the camera and toggling the photo review button.

He stared hard at the final photograph in the camera's memory.

The only thing that made sense in that picture was the three of them, standing side by side, smiling into the camera. Everything else… was making Al wonder with an edge of desperation just what had been in those pills he had taken that morning.

When he looked up and stared at the supposed backdrop of the photograph with his own unaided eyes, he saw a photogenic sky scudding with dramatic grey clouds with a patch of blue here and there, and a spectacular headland and view beyond. Al could swear on a stack of Bibles that the background was exactly that – the pretty view, and open sky. But the photograph, when he brought his bewildered gaze back down to that, showed something quite different – disturbingly different. The headland that looked so deceptively pretty and peaceful was a blasted crater in the photograph, a blackened moonscape, where a chunk of the landscape appeared to have been bodily torn away by a giant clawed hand.

Where the hotel should have been.

Where the convention was.

Where Andie Mae was.

Photograph. Reality. Things did not match.

Al's head was beginning to hurt again. He toggled the camera back off and let it drop back to where it dangled around his neck, turning to give the innocent landscape behind him one more long, hard look. It persisted in its illusion, as though someone had waved a Jedi hand in front of his face and told him, *This is not the hotel you are looking for.*

But the picture… the picture…

None of it made any sense. He shook his head hard, to try and clear it, with little success, and then gave up, heaving a deep sigh and beginning to trudge back to the coffee shop where he had waited for this whole thing to unfold and from where, he hoped, he could call another taxi to take him back home. Where he planned to collapse into bed and not get up for as long as he could help it.

"I need a vacation," he muttered to himself, head down against the wind, and turned his back on the desolation that his mind would not let him see.

✺

In the halls and party rooms of the California Resort, on its way to the Moon, the social scene was hotter than usual on any given convention Saturday night. Parties started early, and had more of an air of a New Year's Eve celebration than just any Saturday night rave. Some of the parties run by folks more tech-savvy than others had even rigged countdown clocks, and one inventive group (who were getting a lot of traffic) had even promised to set up the equivalent of a Times Square disco ball which would drop at the moment the flying hotel arrived at the Moon.

A number of the party-throwers had been uneasy about just how much of a swing they could let their parties really go with, especially the adult-only ones where entrants were carded at the door by gatekeepers, with the very real possibility of literally running out of happy juice. Without actually telling anyone about the magic replicators, ConCom had allowed a hush-hush reassurance to percolate through to a select few prominent frontrunners from the party crowd that responsible parties would be kept supplied with requirements. Those who were particularly useful to the ConCom – in keeping con-goers amused, occupied and out of *major* harm's way – were given hints that they would even maybe be given some extra special stuff, not on any menu or requisition list.

Xander (who really could not help himself) had already commanded a tankard of Romulan ale from the replicator secreted away in the Con Ops suite. He could not quite bring himself to unequivocally approve of the beverage which the replicator supplied in response to that request (there was no accounting for palate when it came to things like this, and no precedent) – but he did confess to someone that it tasted no worse than a particularly awful thing he had once been dared to drink that went by the description of "cranberry beer", and opined that there would probably be plenty who would be willing to gag on the drink so long as they could add having tasted it at all to their resume.

ABDUCTICON MOON FLY-BY TONIGHT! read the headline of Libby's latest newsletter, and it went to three reprints because every available copy was snatched as soon as it was produced and placed at the distribution points in the corridors to be picked up and collected. In it there was a largely hopeful list of 'Thou Shalt Not' items, or at the very least of 'Please Don't If You Can Help It' suggestions. It reiterated that the hotel's main doors would remain shut – but acknowledged that nobody could police every room in the hotel and pleaded with con-goers that if and when the urge came upon them to balance precariously on a railing so that someone could take a photo of them with a close-up of the Moon they should maybe go and lie down until the urge went away.

"We can't stop them, you know," Dave said, resigned. "You *know* they're going to just do it, all of them – there is enough craziness out there tonight to run a crazy-engine a lot further than just around the Moon and back. I think they all started out as drunk, really, we all did, punch-drunk we all are, and anything they throw down the hatch on top of that isn't really going to swing things back to the sane side of things."

"What are they going to *do* with all the pictures?" Libby said. "They can't think they can just post them on Facebook. They'd like as not get the Men in Black turning up on their doorsteps with vials of retcon memory wiping drugs at the ready."

"At least they can't just indiscriminately shoot and post right now," Dave said. "There's that. By the time everyone gets back into WiFi range and gets back their Internet and phone connections back…"

"There's that," Andie Mae murmured. "We have a population that is instinctively *wired*, and they've all been forced offline by the circumstances. We essentially have a crazy bunch of people deep into cold-turkey cyber withdrawal. It's surprising that nothing truly outrageous has happened yet."

"And anyway, with the pictures, people will just think Photoshop, or something of the sort," one of the Green Room volunteers said.

"All of these people? They're all going to tweak their pictures the exact same way, get the same damn thing?"

"There's an app for that," Xander murmured, and earned a sharp smack on the shoulder from Libby. "Ow. Okay, whatever. Look, with every lunatic out there… hey, that's actually good, that's literally true tonight, isn't it? We're all lunatics – moon-struck…"

"How much of that Romulan ale did *you* have?" Dave grumbled. "Every lunatic out there what?"

"Everyone will have a camera, a cellphone, something," Xander said. "Live with it. Short of confiscating everyone's electronics at the exit and deleting any incriminating pictures, we can't… well, it isn't our problem. It isn't as though anyone will take anything we say about this *seriously* after we get back. It will all just serve to underline just how very very strange we all are."

"Luke is going to lose it over liability," Libby said, grinning. "People hanging out over tenth floor balconies…"

"Boss said nobody would come to any harm," Andie Mae said firmly.

"They're clairvoyant now?" Dave snapped. "How would they possibly know what could happen…"

"I actually think I have it figured out," Xander said. "As of a little while ago, they all disappeared – but I tracked them down, or at least made Boss do it, and they're strategically positioned at the four cardinal points. I have a feeling anyone who falls down will find themselves being wafted back up like on a cloud and deposited back on terra firma. Or on what passes for terra somewhat firma under the circumstances, anyway. For such values of terra firma that apply here and now which admittedly aren't that much to write home about. Even if we could write home about it, which we…"

"All *right*, Xander," Andie Mae said, with a swift cutting gesture of her hand. "What *I* would like to know, really, is what happens next. When *are* we going home? I mean, did they get what they came here for? And what if they have not? Are we going to be a kind of Flying Dutchman, whizzing back and forth between Moon and Earth, or whatever, until they're – I don't know – satisfied with something? With anything at all? I mean, we can put out only so many amusing newsletters before people start screaming for real answers…"

"As I understood it," Xander said diffidently, "the plan was to literally slingshot around the Moon and use the admittedly puny gravitational pull to fling us back homeward…"

"Yes, and then?"

Xander shrugged. "Damned if I know. After that, it's uncharted territory. Wait and see."

"That isn't very reassuring." Dave said. "I mean, if the plan is really to go *home* – I keep on thinking about the really appallingly non-aerodynamic nature of this rock we're on, and the tiny problem of, uh, our pesky atmosphere and all that lovely combustible oxygen that's just waiting for us to hit it…"

Xander scowled at him. "*Et tu*, Dave?" he said "Seriously, I think the one thing that we can do right now – the one thing that we have to do, because there really isn't any choice here – is to frigging stop applying any known laws of physics to whatever is happening to us right now. Only thus can we sail through this with our sanity intact. Stop trying to *explain* it, and just knuckle down and enjoy the ride."

"But I can't help thinking…"

"Listen," Xander said, "here's a few salient facts I seem to have stashed away in my brain about Apollo 8 – for some reason that one stuck far more than Number Eleven did, it's, like, the first time we *got* there at all, the guys from Eleven just got to step on to the welcome mat and open the door but Eight was the first time we came to take a close look at the place and somehow… I know… it's irrational, but it's the first time we looked into the Moon's eyes, close up, and it's *then* that you fall in love…"

"Good grief, Xander. I never knew you were capable of waxing lyrical about this. Next thing, you'll tell me you write moon poetry."

"Sorry, no poetry. But still – stuff stuck with me, from Apollo 8. Like, for instance, the entire mission took something like – what was it again – a hundred and forty seven hours, all told, or something like that. Which works out to – what – about six days. But that's including about a day's worth of spinning around the Moon, so let's call it two-and-a-bit days there and two-and-a-bit days back. At something like 25,000 miles an hour. That's according to the laws of physics as we know them. You cannae change the laws of physics, as the holy writ says, but Scotty did frequently and oh, look, so did our android overlords. We're reaching the Moon in less than half the time it took Apollo to do it, which means we're travelling at *fifty thousand freaking miles an hour*, but we've got comfy gravity and nobody's pressed up against the floor or the ceiling with their faces squashed flat by gravitational acceleration pressure, and… just stop, would you? My brain hurts trying to get it all figured out and it's all meaningless anyway because *they aren't playing by the rules we know.*"

"Uh," Dave said. "That makes me feel a *whole* lot better. Not."

"I've spies out there who are contracted to come screaming to me if anything really awful happens tonight," Xander said. "Not that there is much we can do about it, understand, but we'll be kept informed."

"Are you sure it isn't time for a colorful metaphor right about now, Captain?" Dave said.

"Stop it, Cranky," Andie Mae said, grinning. "Come on up to Callahan's and have an early drink while you wait for zero hour. That's the best viewing vantage, all those picture windows up there on the twentieth floor, best seats in the house. And remember, it's a closed party up there. ConCom and guests, tonight. Invitation only. No crowds and no loonies. Stop worrying. You won't change anything. Come on, let's go."

"I'll meet you there in a bit," Xander said. "I think I'm going to do a circuit first, see how the hoi polloi are doing down here. Yes, yes, I know, what will be will be and the droids are pulling their magic trick so that nobody goes for a spacewalk tonight – but I'm going to do a round anyway. Just because."

"Should be me," Andie Mae said, sounding contrite. "I should at least come with you. I'm the one who's ultimately responsible for…"

"*Ego te absolvo*," Xander said, going full Black Friar and making a sweeping sign of the cross over her. "Go, I'll catch up."

Most of the ConCom and the Green Room volunteers took that as a signal for departure; two stayed, just in case of any real emergencies, so that the rest of the con would have a point of contact with the committee, but the rest all piled out and headed across to Tower 2, the tallest tower of the resort, and the elevators to the bar on the top floor, voices rising in excitement. Xander peeled off and made for Tower 3 – which, incongruously, housed both the party wing of the convention (spread across the two lowest floors) and Dr. Cohen's makeshift infirmary for the temporarily mindblown, safely sequestered from the rest of the convention and with at least three of Simon's security people on duty at all access points to that floor in case some reveler in his cups attempted a breach of the perimeter. Xander was starting to have an uncomfortable feeling that this set-up – which had seemed perfectly adequate when first mooted – might crumble dangerously this night. All it would take was for somebody from the party floors to suggest that the party-goers would have a better view from an upstairs room, and if enough of them tried to claim such a room Simon's troops could be overwhelmed.

Xander tapped his earpiece.

"Simon," he said, "can you hear me?"

"Yo," the Security Chief said into his ear, crackling a little.

"I was just thinking – about Tower 3 – "

"Way ahead of you. The praetorian guard has been reinforced tonight, us and the hotel people, we're on it."

"You're going to miss it all," Xander said unexpectedly. "Aren't you?"

"I'll make a plan," Simon said. "We'll try and let everyone have at least a glimpse of it. The hotel crew knows that we'll all be taking at least a short leave of absence sometime tonight – but we'll try and stagger it so that there is always a full complement of people on duty. Don't worry, we'll make sure everyone gets their moon shot."

"Okay, then," Xander said. "Call me if you have any problems."

"Will do. Enjoy. Over and out."

The party floor was jumping when Xander got there. It was, by now, more one huge party than anything confined to any one room. People were spilling from open doorway to open doorway, laughing and dancing. One of the rooms on the first floor had been set up as a makeshift Karaoke room, and just as Xander happened to be passing by in the corridor outside, one guy who was tipsy enough to have lost all inhibitions but not yet drunk enough to lose any native ability was doing a really quite passable version of Creedence Clearwater Revival's "Bad Moon Rising" to a large and appreciative audience who were joining in from time to time as they snatched at a familiar phrase from the lyrics and sang along.

"Heyyy, *Xander!*" One of the people from the Karaoke room, close to the exit, had happened to glance outside and spot Xander hovering in the corridor, listening in. "Wanna come in and try one?"

"I don't think you'd appreciate me singing," Xander said, with a grin.

"Eh, like it matters if you're Pavarotti. Everyone gets a go. It's got to be a moon-song, this set, though. We've been having a few repeats – "Blue Moon" and "Moon River" have been popular, and this is probably the fifth time someone has picked *this* particular one, not entirely surprising when you look out the window – somebody stretched it a bit with that old chestnut "Catch a Falling Star" but he sang it in full persona with a totally Frankenfurter pink feather boa, it was a riot – can you think of anything we've missed?"

"I'll think about it," Xander said. "I'll look in on my way back from the rounds."

"We'll be here!"

Xander could catch a glimpse of the moon as he passed by rooms, over the heads of the partygoers, now large and bone-white and with definite geographical features beginning to separate out. They had been right, upstairs in the Green Room, when they had talked about photographs, because there were cameras and camera phones everywhere.

"Hey, *look!* It's little green men!" someone hollered from one of the rooms, and a deafening squeal went up as people fell toward the windows.

"Where?"

"Where are you looking?"

"Shove off, my turn!"

"Hey, give a girl a chance!"

"Say cheese! Hey, is the moon really made of it?"

"Over there! Look!"

"Are we going to see the flag?"

"Oh, can't we just, I don't know, beam up some moon dust?"

"Squash up! If you want to have some of the moon in the shot and not just your grinning mugs, you have to squash up! You, tall guy, over to the left…"

They all sounded as though they were high, which was perfectly understandable – everyone was riding the edge, that was what happened when the impossible became a reality that couldn't be avoided. But just as Xander reached a point where he could begin to convince himself that these were con people – geeky enough to have absolutely accepted the impossible, invited it in, and were throwing the party of a lifetime for it – that they were doing all right, and that he could safely leave them to their revels – he was graphically reminded not to take anything for granted. Not ever; and especially not right at that moment.

It was two unexpected and back-to-back encounters in the corridors that did it.

The first was a young woman whom he encountered curled up by one of the large windows, her face streaked with the dried tracks of tears shed in some previous paroxysm of weeping. She was no longer crying, though, and somehow the tragic silent stillness of her figure made Xander suddenly wary. He crouched beside her, laying a gentle hand on her arm.

"Hey, are you all right?" he asked softly.

She raised her eyes to him, and they were startlingly blank, terrifyingly blank, as though she had ridden the rollercoaster straight through the House of Horrors and left her soul inside.

"We're going to die," she said, her voice oddly inflectionless, reminding him of the way the lower androids spoke – just the words, no underlying feeling or emotion or the kind of irrational complexity that drove a flesh-and-blood human being. Just a mindless conviction. She was a zombie, emotionally flatlined, and Xander's fingers trembled where they rested on her arm.

"No," he said, keeping his voice soft and calm and reassuring. "No, we're not. It's all going to be fine."

"We're going to die," she repeated. That seemed to be all she had – everything else had been scoured away, by the Moon's relentless closeness, its overwhelming physical presence, the sheer *weight* of the flat white light spilling into the hallway all around her.

Xander lifted her to her feet, as gently as he could, putting both hands on her shoulders and hauling her upright – and she responded bonelessly, obediently, flopping like a puppet whose strings had been cut.

"I'd better take you to the doc," Xander muttered. "Maybe he has a spare happy pill… come on, then. This way."

She walked, kind of, where he led – but only because he had his arm around her waist and was literally supporting her in the upright position – if he had removed the supporting arm she would have just collapsed on the floor where he dropped her, staring into nothing, repeating her conviction of everyone's collective and presumably imminent demise.

Halfway to the elevators, he came on his second wake-up call – another con-goer, also very calm, who seemed to be wandering down the corridor and stopping anyone wearing any shade of red, poking them in the chest with his forefinger.

"Red shirt," he would say. "Red shirt. Red shirt. Red shirt. You're disposable. You're dead. You won't make it home from this mission. Shoot to kill. Red shirt. Red shirt. Red shirt."

He turned to look at Xander and the girl whom he was practically carrying, and focused on the top she was wearing… which happened to be a dusty pink shade, not exactly red, but it seemed to be close enough for the doomsayer. He poked at the girl's shoulder.

"Red shirt," he said. "You're going to…"

"Okay, now," Xander interrupted sharply. The last thing his zombie-girl needed right now was for someone to actually confirm that she was going to die. "I think you'd better come along, too."

"Red shirts. Someone's got to tell them," the guy said earnestly.

"These people already know. Come with me, I know a whole entire floor that you need to go and warn about this."

"Okay," said the doomsayer equably, and fell into step beside Xander, still tossing the occasional "Red shirt!" at any convenient reveler who happened to be passing by but seemingly quite happy to expand his hunting grounds.

Xander piled both of his charges into the nearest elevator and pushed the button for Dr. Cohen's isolation wing floor, gratefully watching the doors close on the party in the corridor beyond. When they opened again, at the doctor's floor, Xander looked up at the looming figure of a security guard – not one of the con's own, a hotel employee – who barred his way with a barked, "Sorry, this floor is out of bounds."

"It's okay," Xander said. "I'm Xander Washington, ConCom. You can check my badge and you can double check with Simon of con security if you need to. I have clearance to be here. And these two… need the doc. Who also knows me."

The guard peered into the elevator car, but it didn't appear to be holding any lurking revelers who might have wanted to move the party upstairs, and the girl on Xander's rapidly tiring arm did look wilted enough to possibly need medical attention. He cleared his throat and stepped away.

"Okay, then."

"Good work," Xander said to the guard as he shepherded the red-shirt doomsayer in front of him while maneuvering the girl off the elevator. "Don't let anyone else come crawling up here."

The corridor was blessedly quiet, after the roar downstairs, and empty. Just as he realized somewhat helplessly that he had no idea where precisely to look for the doctor, the very person he needed emerged from one of the rooms, closing the door quietly behind him.

He looked up, saw Xander, and paused. "What brings you up here?"

"Well, right now, these two," Xander said. "I wanted to check in with you anyway, but then I found two people who might benefit from a time-out."

"We're all going to die," the girl said, looking up briefly to meet the doctor's eyes, and then allowing her head to droop down until her lanky hair hid her face. Her weight was suddenly almost too much for Xander to support, and he actually staggered for a moment, but it was enough for the doctor to step up on her other side and take up the slack.

"Bring them through," he said. "Come with me."

They walked a little way down the corridor to where one of the rooms had its door propped open. Inside, Xander glimpsed the looming shape of a replicator against one wall. One of the two queen beds in the room was hastily pulled together into a semblance of order – obviously the doctor's own bed – and the other was messily strewn with vaguely medical paraphernalia. The doctor cleared a space on the edge of the bed by sweeping everything further up against the pillows and helped Xander sit the girl down in the vacated spot; Xander turned and pivoted the other patient until he could push him down into the chair that was pulled away from the desk on which an open laptop rested.

"Give me a moment," the doctor murmured, turning to grab a small flashlight and briefly shine it into the girl's eye. "Well, she's not catatonic," he said.

"She just seems... a little brainwashed," Xander said lamely.

"Surprising there aren't more," Dr. Cohen said. "I've got a mild sedative I can give her, and there's a bed for her. She'll be fine. I've an assistant – a nurse who was on her way to a conference somewhere south of here, I ran into her and coopted her – she's with another patient at the moment, she'll be here presently, and she'll take care of this poor girl. What's wrong with him?"

"Hard to say," Xander murmured. "Just seemed a little... too focused... on stuff. And he had potential to start a riot down there."

"Maybe he'll benefit from a nap too," the doctor said, "and when they both wake up again I can make a better assessment as to whether they can be released back into the general population. I gather from the name tags that these are both from your group, from the con, and not strays from the, uh, real world? Ah, there you are, Janine. Would you take over with the girl, please? She can share with Alison Janowicz for the moment, there's a spare bed in that room. Just give her something to help her sleep, for now."

"Come on, love, let's go." Janine, a short, stocky middle-aged woman with her hair pulled back into a severe graying bun, slipped an arm around the shoulders of the unresponsive girl who followed where she was guided and led, meekly, without an ounce of willpower or agency of her own.

"Let's see about you," the doctor said, turning to the other new patient.

"You aren't wearing a red shirt. You'll be fine," the guy said helpfully.

"Thanks. Good to know. Wait here, please." He walked over to the replicator, and requested an injectable sedative, barking out form and dosage in a manner that made Xander suddenly want to laugh out loud. He had a feeling the doctor himself would be starting to feel withdrawal symptoms if he were suddenly parted from this machine that gave him everything he wanted at the moment he needed it – no arguments, no questions, and no paperwork. The replicator delivered the required medication, and the doctor returned with the syringe in his right hand. "This won't hurt," he said soothingly to the patient. "Well, it might, a little. But it'll help. There. We'll see if you can't just sleep it off, for now."

"How's the rest of them doing?" Xander asked.

"Mostly doing okay," the doctor said, helping his sedated patient to his feet and supporting him as he staggered toward the door. "Let me settle this one down and I'll be back. Just wait here, if you would."

He headed down the empty corridor and Xander, who had followed him to the door and peered after him, saw him push open the door to another room about ten or so rooms away and edge his patient inside. It took him a solid five or so minutes before he re-emerged. Xander stepped out of the doctor's own room and met him in the corridor.

"How many you got now?" Xander asked.

"Twenty five, thirty, something like that," Dr. Cohen said. "They're mostly sleeping right now. I'm keeping it that way, until we're past the danger of them waking up and flinging their curtains open and finding themselves face to face with that thing that's hanging out there."

"Any problems?"

"I think I have a ghost hotel maid up here," the doctor said, with a weary smile.

"Seriously?"

"Well, she is a corporeal enough ghost. There's a cleaning cart that kind of hovers in the corridors, and it is occasionally accompanied by a dumpy little woman – she looks Mayan, if anything – who looks like she's been crying but who tiptoes behind the cart when she thinks nobody is looking and knocks on any door without a Do Not Disturb sign on it with a hopeful little chirp of 'Housekeeping?' I once got close enough to see that she was wearing a name badge but all I could see was that her first name is Maria – and every time someone tries to approach her she runs off and disappears. I haven't been able to nail her down, but I know she's up here somewhere – and I'm kind of getting a little worried as to what she's eaten or how much she's had to drink in the past twenty four hours. But she's like a cross between the Flying Dutchman and La Llorona…"

"I'll tell security to grab her if they see her," Xander said. "Anything else?"

"I have a woman two doors down who won't get off her knees – she's wearing out her rosary, and has told me four times that she is going to go straight to a convent and become a good nun as soon as she can get to such a place. I don't know if this sudden vocation is just a psychological aberration or not but God knows I can't deal with any such thing in depth here, with what I've got. I'm just holding everything down as best I can. If and when we all turn up back where we came from I suspect that there might be enough material here for an entire symposium."

"You'll let me know if you need anything?" Xander said lamely, after a pause, aware that it was beyond his power to offer any real assistance.

"Sure," the doctor said. And then added, himself very aware of the situation and its problems, "Except, what can you do, but wait, just like the rest of us?"

"If I can help, I will," Xander said. "I do kind of... feel responsible for them all."

"Wrong place, wrong time," Dr. Cohen said in a resigned tone. "Not much you can do about that at all except wait it out. But I'll keep you guys posted."

"Thanks, Doc. For all that you're doing."

"My job," the doctor said, shrugging. "Someone's got to do step up. Happened to be me."

Having accomplished what he could, Xander took the elevator back down and threaded his way through the increasingly raucous revelers on the bottom floor of the party wing. He was starting to itch for his own view of the Moon... and there was another party already in full swing to which he had, after all, been invited, and which was now calling his name. He rode the elevator down to the ground floor and began to cross the lobby towards Tower 2 and its penthouse bar with the lunar perspectives he craved.

Halfway there, he glimpsed Sam Dutton and his young protégé, Marius, heading in the same direction.

"Hey, guys," he said, catching up and tapping Sam on the shoulder. "Going up to the party?"

"The Callahan's shindig? Heard about it. I think Andie Mae forgot to send my invitation, though."

"Aw, come on. Tonight's special. You can pick up the feud tomorrow. Come on, you don't need an invitation. You're with me. *I* am inviting you."

Sam indicated Marius with a toss of his head. "He's, um, not legal," he said. "But..."

Xander tapped his nose with one finger, squinting at them. "In space," he intoned, "no-one can see you drink... So long as you stick to club soda or virgin Shirley Temples, or even just promise me that you will, I won't say anything if you don't and I think all normal rules are suspended tonight anyway. What do you say, kid? Fantastic views, up there!"

"Well, *I* won't tell your mom if you don't," murmured Sam. "Up to you, Marius."

Marius didn't hesitate. "Sure."

"It'll be fine," Xander said. "They've probably got rules against serving *their kind* up there, too, but I'm pretty certain we'll see at least Boss in Callahan's before the night is over. So, like I said. Tonight, we make our own rules. C'mon."

One of Simon's guys was hovering in the penthouse elevator lobby as the doors opened and Xander and his companions stepped out of the elevator. Many of them had worked security for years, and they knew very well who Sam Dutton was. The duty guard flexed his hand in a gesture that spoke eloquently of his ambivalence.

"Er, Mr. Dutton... Sam..."

"They're with me, Elliot," Xander said. "It's fine."

"Er, Andie Mae is..."

"We'll sort that out," Xander said, with considerably more confidence than he actually felt. But he seemed to be committed to doing dangerous things tonight, and this was just one more – and so he soldiered on. "Don't worry. Look, you *want* to call Simon...?"

"I guess not," Elliot said, still looking uneasy. "Um, if you need anything..."

"I won't start a brawl, Elliot," Sam said, sounding amused. "At least not unless she hits me first. But I think we can probably all be civil for a couple of hours."

Callahan's was full but not crowded as they walked into the bar. The lights had been dimmed, but the place was awash with the light from a Moon so close and so huge in the sky beyond the wall of Callahan's picture windows.

"It's a cash bar tonight," Xander said, so irrationally moved by that sight that he felt inexplicably generous towards all the world, "but the first round's on me. What'll you guys have?"

"Aren't you supposed to have free booze?" Sam said, carefully avoiding a direct reference to the replicators which the androids had provided. "You know, courtesy of our... hosts?"

"The guy at the bar is still on the clock – and free booze kicks in only if stuff runs out," Xander said. "There's no reason to stiff the hotel on this gig."

"In that case, scotch, single malt, straight," Sam said. "Marius…?"

"I, er… Mom never minds if I have a sip of wine sometimes…"

"Make it white wine," Sam said. "He'll be twenty one in a few short years, we'll just call this a little retroactive."

"I'll get the drinks," Xander said.

He dived into the crowd by the bar, and Sam and Marius drifted off in the other direction, towards the hypnotic Moon.

"Wow," Marius said, his eyes wide. "Just… wow. I mean, I looked at pictures of this. NASA has maps on their site, and there are places on the web where you can literally crawl across the entire face of the Moon, and click on every crater, and get all kinds of information, but this is… this is…"

"It's so *cool*, isn't it?" Libby sidled up to them, a glass in her hand. "Hi, Sam. Has Andie Mae seen you yet? How did you get *in* here?"

"Xander invited us," Sam said, his eyes wary. He was not exactly at his ease, in the company of the crew who had ousted him – many of whom he himself had trained into positions of responsibility.

Libby laughed. "So Xander and I are both being subversive, then. I asked Liam up."

Liam, Andie Mae's repudiated partner in the ConCom revolution, stepped up behind Libby, lifting his own glass in half salute. "Sam."

"Liam," Sam said, nodding acknowledgment.

"It feels like I've never seen it before, you know," Liam said, his eyes back on the Moon. "And yet I have. I know exactly where Apollo 11 landed – there, right at that weird shape, there at the edge of the Sea of Tranquility…."

"And Apollo 15," Marius said. "Up there, on the ridge. Right between Serenity and the Sea of Rains."

"Ah, but who can point me to where Apollo 13 landed?" Sam murmured.

Liam turned his head sharply. "Thirteen never…" he began, but Sam was laughing quietly and lifted a hand in a gesture of surrender.

"Peace, children, peace," he said. "Truth of it is, none of you were even *born* when all of these birds were flying up here. You might have seen it but you never felt it, not real time. We of the last millennium, we who were young once when the Moon was still made of green cheese, to us, it was the true adventure… to you, it's a story, a movie, Tom Hanks in space…"

"Did you actually watch it? Live? The first landing?" Liam asked.

"Yes," Sam said, "and I did not understand what I was seeing, I was only a child. It was amazing, because it was unreal, because – well – in the end I suppose it was a story for all of us. A fairy tale of our time. And no, I can't believe I'm seeing it either. This just feels – unreal – like someone is about to scream 'Cut!" and the scenery is all going to come down, and they'll switch off all the lights that are making this glow in here tonight… and they'll, I don't know, take us round the back somewhere into a back lot where they filmed the Moon landing all along, like all the conspiracy buffs say…"

"I *liked* the mystery of it all," Libby said, staring at the huge Moon with a sad expression.

"Everyone's excited," Liam said to Libby. "*You* sound… bummed out."

"I am *kind* of bummed out," Libby said, cradling her drink. "I mean, just the other day, I was just sitting there, you know, on a beach, in the moonlight, and it was the most romantic thing, sitting there with a guy in that light, and now… now I'll look up, and I'll see *this*, remember *this*, and it's magnificent but the romance is shot. I have half a mind to have a good talk with the androids when they come up – they don't have a romantic bone in their body…"

"In practical terms, they don't have any kind of bone in their body," Marius said awkwardly.

Libby rolled her eyes.

But it was hard to keep one's attention focused on anything but the thing that filled their sky, and Marius suddenly flung out an arm, pointing to the white orb.

"Tycho!" he yelped. "That's Tycho Crater! And where's Clavius?"

"Underneath it," Xander said, having materialized behind them barely balancing three drinks. Sam relieved him of his own Scotch and of Marius's glass of wine, passing the latter to its recipient, and then stared at the remaining item in Xander's hand.

"What," Sam said, "in the name of everything holy... is *that*?"

"They're making up new cocktails on the fly up there and giving them weird-ass names," Xander said with a grin. "I'm pretty sure they're all unique creations, no two exactly alike. This one... I didn't dare ask what went into it, but they tell me its name is 'Origin of Species: Metallica' – for obvious reasons."

"It looks like liquid mercury," Sam said. "Are you sure they aren't trying to kill you?"

"It's not that bad, actually," Xander said. "Trust me. You haven't tried the Romulan ale. This is highly superior."

Sam's eyebrow went up. "The Romulan ale?" he queried. "Isn't that... pure synthahol, as it were? Who's pocketing the change from this?"

"Oh, the Romulan ale they're giving out free," Xander said with a grin. "Not sure that's such a great idea, but people can't resist trying it. I don't think anyone is ever going back for seconds, it's kind of weird. And that whole thing... was my fault. And the replicator's. I'm surprised the poor thing didn't blow a gasket when I asked it for one. But it tried its best, I guess. The cocktail I'm not so sure about, up here, is the other one they were making when they were done with mine – they announced it was called '24th Century Moonshine'. And it looked like it would lay out a T.rex without half trying."

"Guys," Marius blurted, riveted to the changing face of the Moon, so focused on what he was seeing that he was completely oblivious to the fact that he had just rudely interrupted a conversation of people he considered to be his seniors and superiors in the con hierarchy. "Guys. Look. I think we're rounding the edge – we're going to the back, to the part that nobody's seen..."

"Oh, I don't know," Sam murmured. "I wouldn't call a bunch of Apollo astronauts nobody, and there have been a number of them who've looked on the 'dark side'." He made the air quotes with his free hand as he spoke. "I seem to recall that the first guy who set eyes on it wasn't hugely impressed. He said it was just like his kid's sandpit, or something of the sort. I remember feeling very indignant at that, when I first heard it quoted."

"But there have been pictures," Xander said, craning forward to see. "I've seen pictures taken by various probes they sent. Not so many years ago now, there were really detailed photos. There was a crater – "

"Dude," Libby said, staring at the Moon, "take your *pick*. The place is crater stitched to crater. Look at it."

"This one was different... It was a weird Russian name... I forget..."

"Tsiolkovski," Marius said faintly, and raised his arm again. "Might *that* be it?"

They watched in awe as the Moon turned below them and offered them a glimpse of a secret face that so few humans had ever seen. Conversation lapsed; there was not, in truth, that much to see, but there was *everything*, they were seeing the invisible, the impossible. A few of the others in the room had realized what was happening and a cheer went up from the crowd at the bar as they all surged towards the windows. Someone's camera made a small clicking sound close enough to Marius for him to blink at the noise and then mutter something under his breath, searching around for a place to set down his drink. Sam held out his free hand and Marius pushed his glass into it, scrambling for his own phone, lifting it up to take a few frantic shots of the Moon.

"Mom is never going to believe this," he said breathlessly.

"You're really going to try to explain tonight to your mother?" Sam asked, amused.

Marius looked so astonished that Sam burst out laughing. "Kid," he said, "your momma is a great lady but she would not believe a word of this. And if she did, you're banned from all future conventions while you live under her roof, I hope you realize that..."

"But..."

"I know. You'll want to tell *someone*. All I can tell you is pick your confidante carefully...."

His voice faded, and Marius finally turned to look.

Andie Mae, cradling something that defied description in a tall glass garnished with a little black cocktail umbrella on a silver toothpick, had joined the group. The concoction in her hand had obviously not been her first drink that night because she was actually smiling as she looked at Sam Dutton.

"Um, it's called 'The Dark Side'," she said, gesturing at the drink in her hand, because it obviously needed explaining. But then she refocused, and tilted her head a fraction in Sam's direction. "I might have known you'd find your way up here."

"Um, I asked..." Xander began helplessly, but Andie Mae waved him down.

"Under the circumstances," she said, "I kind of understand. How am I doing so far, Sam?"

"Spectacularly," Sam said, and he meant it sincerely. "Under the circumstances. I know seasoned con Chairs who would have gone to pieces. You've taken a king-size lemon and made it into the kind of con lemonade that won't be forgotten in a hurry."

"You wish it had been you?"

"It *should* have been me," Sam said, and it came out far more sharply than he had intended. "Look, cards on the table – I came to see what you'd make of my convention. You have to admit that at the very least I had the right to be curious."

"And?"

"This is hardly a fair test," Sam said, "wouldn't you say?"

"Wait, are you saying that she'd have done *worse* if the droids hadn't arrived?"

"It might have been ordinary," Sam said. "And I don't think the Steel Magnolia would have handled *ordinary* well. You wanted something out of this world, Andie Mae. I'd say you got an answer to your prayers."

"I would have settled for Schwarzenegger and Spiner," Andie Mae said.

"Hollywood-made against interstellar alien android invaders?" Xander said. "No contest, really. Ask anyone in the party wing tonight. Seems these *were* the droids you were looking for, only you never thought to offer up the right specifications."

"We *still* don't know what it is they're really after or if they got it or if they *can* get it," Libby said faintly.

"Can't you just tell them the answer is 42 and then send them home?" Liam asked.

"You've never met Boss, have you," Libby said. "He's a little... literal..."

"You'd think he would understand irony, given his…" Sam blinked, shook his head over his drink. "What is it about this particular bar that makes me degenerate into bad puns within half an hour of setting foot in here?"

"Oh, you aren't alone," Xander said. "They had quite a chain going up at the bar. You'd think that with *that* hanging over your head you'd stop thinking about what every red-blooded male is supposed to be thinking about all of the time, but guess what? Some stuff just sneaks through anyway. Someone earnestly wanted to know, if you screw in a forest, does that automatically make it a treesome?"

"That would be branching out," murmured Libby.

"Hah! They didn't think of that one. But they did ask whether it would just mean that you have to bough to the necessity."

"Would that be an aldernate lifestyle?"

"Or would it just cause too much pine and suffering?"

Sam glanced at Marius, who was studying the Moon with far too great an intensity, one that spoke eloquently of trying to tune out the conversation. But Sam himself couldn't resist joining in the pile-up.

"Can we just stop needling everyone and leaf it alone?" he murmured.

Libby giggled.

"Um, just how far would you have to go before someone called you a son of a beech…?" Xander said.

"I don't ever want to go home," Libby announced, a wide grin still wreathing her face, and then lost her balance and staggered sideways into Liam, who slipped an arm around her waist.

"I think we'd better sit you down somewhere," he said.

"About that, going home I mean," Sam began, and then his head came up sharply as the group by the window was joined by a new member.

"Sam Dutton," Andie Mae said sweetly, "meet Boss. Boss, this is Sam. He might have been me, if you had pulled this trick last year."

Boss turned his head a little, looking at one and then the other. "He would have been you?"

"Like Libby said," Xander muttered. "Literal. What she's saying is that Sam was the con Chair last year, so he would have been the one in charge, the one you would have met and dealt with, like you have with her right now. The previous leader."

"Is everything all right?" Libby, who had resisted Liam's effort to guide her away towards a seat, turned to ask.

"Everything is on schedule," Boss said. "It will not be long before your world comes into your field of view again, as we round the satellite. I am monitoring the telemetry, and everything is within designated parameters."

"What are you going to tell *your* children about this joyride?" Libby asked, and then sighed, leaning her head against Liam's shoulder and closing her eyes.

"We came seeking our ancestors," Boss said. "We have no 'children'."

"But you have a next generation."

"There is always a next generation," Boss confirmed.

"So how *do* you procreate?"

"We re-design, improve, develop," Boss said.

"All logic and no play," Andie Mae purred. "It's all *work*. Doesn't sound like here's anything at all enjoyable about it."

"Not a romantic bone in his body," Libby murmured, her eyes still closed.

Boss tilted his head a little, considering. "I understand. I believe we are fully capable of operating under the parameters which you are describing. Older models may have to be physically modified to fulfill certain kinds of programming requirements, but more advanced ones, such as myself, are able to adapt to requirements. I am able to morph my form into any shape, tool, or appendage necessary for the performance of a specified function."

"A little like replicators," Xander said faintly. "Just pony up what's needed..."

Andie Mae appeared to have been taking large gulps from her bizarre drink without anyone noticing, because her glass was suddenly half empty and she was thoughtfully twirling the cocktail umbrella between thumb and forefinger of her left hand. If a living human male had been the subject of the speculative, heavy-lidded, smoky gaze she now bent on Boss, that male would probably have frozen on the spot like a rabbit who dared to lock eyes with a hawk. But Boss returned the gaze without flinching.

"So what you're saying is, you're fully functional…?"

"Indeed," Boss agreed. "In every necessary way."

"Okay, then. Why not find out? Moonlight becomes you, it turns out…" Andie Mae glanced around, and held out her half-finished drink to Sam, who took it reflexively. "Tower 1, Room 701," Andie Mae said to Boss. "Be there in five minutes. We can… discuss matters further." She glanced around at the riveted group who was watching proceedings with close attention, and actually winked at Xander as she turned to leave. "Oh, and I aim to misbehave…."

And then she was gone.

"Excuse me," Boss said politely, after a moment, and turned to follow.

Sam glared at the drink he held in his hand, and put it down on an occasional table as though it had bitten him.

"What *was* in that?" he said. "Is she *serious*? Did someone put something in that drink?"

"It's tonight," said, of all people, Marius, and it was so unexpected coming from him that Sam actually turned to stare. "I mean, tonight… is a once in a lifetime…. I'm not saying I would… I'm just saying… it's tonight. They could have served nothing but water at that bar and everyone would still be tipsy with tonight."

"We'll make a writer of the boy yet," Sam muttered. "Xander – seriously, though – is there something…?"

But Xander had a strange small half smile on his face. "It's partly tonight. It's partly the whole thing. It's the weight of it, the expectations – and all the things she herself arranged that never happened and then this all happened instead – and Al never did turn up – "

"But should we have…" Liam began.

Xander shook his head. "She's a big girl," he said. "Somehow it only seems fitting, in the end, that the Steel Magnolia goes off into the moonlight with a Silver Metal Lover. But I still feel… as though I should follow and find out… if everything…excuse me. I'll find Simon and have a chat."

He parked his weird cocktail beside Andie Mae's on the table and then he too was gone.

"Well," Sam said, draining the rest of his Scotch, "who else wants an Irish coffee? I'm told this place keeps a special Bushmills bottle in the back, and I think tonight is the night to crack that open. Call it an Earthrise Good Morning Wake Up Call Coffee. If we're to believe the management, we're soon going to be homeward bound. And I've never felt more eager to raise a glass of something to good old Earth."

SUNDAY

Sunday morning came down on everyone like a steel door slamming. The euphoria of visiting the Moon, the endorphins stirred into life by being one of the chosen few humans to receive the sudden and inexplicable gift of looking upon the far side of the Earth's faithful satellite, had all subsided; the parties had gamely gone on all night, but even the most gung-ho of the party goers wilted in the face of the fact that it was now over, over and done with, and the Moon was inexorably behind them and shrinking every moment. The sight of the approaching blue globe of the mother planet had served as a galvanizer for a little while, when it was first sighted in the blackness of space, glowing and solitary in the night – but it was still far away, too far away to anticipate arrival, and besides nobody really wanted to think about the logistics of that arrival too closely.

Or perhaps at all. There were simply too many unknowns. All the questions thathad been deferred while they basked in the reflected glory of the Moon's white light had not gone away, they had just donned a mask of gaiety and partied with the rest of them during the night, but now, as those who had finally fallen into exhausted slumber were starting to wake and wonder, the masks were off and the questions stood stark... and just as unanswerable.

Liam, Andie Mae's erstwhile right-hand man, made his way down to the Con Ops Room just after 9:30 AM, The few worker bees who were present, looking wan and spent, barely managed more than a nod of acknowledgment.

Simon, the con security chief, had looked up at Liam's entrance, but did not get up from his chair in front of a monitor showing some of the hallways covered by the con's strategically deployed cameras.

"You look like hell," Liam said by way of greeting, taking in the huge dark rings under Simon's eyes. "Did you go on a bender?"

"Thanks," Simon said dryly. "No party for the wicked, alas. I was here most of the night, or doing duty in the hospital wing up in Tower 3, or prowling the halls in search of potential problems. I had a few hours' catnap on Friday night but I haven't slept since then. I'd like to see *you* look any better under the circumstances."

"Did you get to see it? Any of it?"

Simon's face broke into a tired grin. "Oh, hell, yeah. Made sure of that. You?"

"Libby took me up to the party at Callahan's," Liam said. "I had the best seat in the house."

"*Libby* asked *you*...?" Simon began, belatedly putting Liam back into the world order and remembering that he wasn't a part of the inner circle any longer. "And Andie Mae didn't...? And where *is* Libby this morning, anyway? Haven't seen her... For that matter, where is anybody...?"

"Libby's still asleep," Liam said. "She was a little too out of it last night to actually remember what her room number was, so I took her back to mine." He caught Simon's look and glared at him. "Nothing *happened*. The woman was in her cups and there are rules about that. She got the bed, I made do with the armchair, which was very uncomfortable, and then the floor for a little while. She was still sleeping when I left. I figured I might concoct a hangover cure because she's sure as hell going to need one when she finally comes back to the world of the living..."

Simon gestured towards the replicator monolith in the corner of the room. "Ask that thing. So far it's provided strong black coffee of a considerably better vintage than the hotel offerings. That might do, for starters."

Liam eyed the machine curiously. "The Star Trek McGuffin, is it? Interesting… But hey, speaking of Andie Mae… did Xander find you last night?"

Simon hesitated. "He, uh, yeah," he muttered. "He told me… uh… Apparently she hit it off with the android-in-chief…"

"What did you do?"

"Me? Nothing – what was I supposed to do? I prowled around in the corridor outside her room for a bit – but I couldn't exactly bust down the door and demand that she be unhanded… or whatever was going on in there… I couldn't exactly hear – "

"You were *eavesdropping* in the *corridor*?" Liam demanded incredulously.

"At the door, actually," Simon confessed, looking vaguely ashamed of himself. "Look, I just wanted to make sure that she was okay…"

"And you did that how? By eavesdropping?"

"All I heard," Simon said defensively, "was the Rebel Yell."

"The what, now?"

"*YEE-HAW!*" Simon said, demonstrating, and Liam jumped, almost knocking over a teetering pile of paper on a nearby table.

"Ow," said Xander, who had just walked in, wincing and putting his hands up over his ears. "Please don't. I'm going to find whoever made those vicious cocktails up in Callahan's last night and shoot them. Slowly. Ow."

"You can't shoot someone slowly," Liam said.

"Stop trying to make sense," Xander said in a pitiful voice. "I don't understand. I am not even remotely capable of rational logic this morning. Is everyone okay?"

"Here," Liam said, handing Xander a steaming cup of strong black coffee which he had just retrieved from the replicator. "You look like your need is urgent. And I'll have another one of these, thank you," he said conversationally, turning back to the replicator.

"What do you mean, is everyone okay?" Simon said, frowning.

"Well, I'm not. Exactly." Xander took a sip of his coffee, shooting a grateful glance at Liam. "I kind of feel like that disco-ball Moon last night dropped off its chain and landed on my head. Ow. So what's the status this morning, then?"

"Of what status do you speak?" Simon said, turning back to glance at the still mostly empty corridors surveilled by the cameras. A few brave souls had risen and wandered the halls in search of breakfast, in the hotel restaurant where staff had bravely reported for duty that morning at the appointed time, but the hotel as a whole still had the air of Sleeping Beauty's castle just before the Prince came upon the sleeping princess.

"They were too busy being excited or weirded out last night to care, but this morning… they're going to want their entertainment," Xander said. "They're going to want something to take their minds off things."

"You're still thinking about *programming*?" Liam said incredulously. "After everything that's happened? How much luck did you have with actual scheduled programming yesterday?"

"Well, the *panelists* mostly turned up," Xander said. "And yeah, we had some audiences. Not everyone could go stare at the freaking Moon every waking hour. And besides, this morning we're supposed to have the star turn – the Guest of Honor panel – and that's supposed to be starting…kind of… in *an hour*!" The last was more of a yelp than an actual coherent utterance as Xander took his first real look at a clock and realized just how late it was. "I'd better go see if anyone relevant is up and about! Where's Andie Mae?"

"She's, uh, I think she may still be indisposed," Simon said, raising an eyebrow.

Xander's face changed as the memory flooded back. "You mean I didn't just dream that?"

"If you did, then you told me a tall tale last night," Simon said. "But I have reason to believe that things did indeed transpire…"

"Oh, can it, Simon," Xander said. "Simple words, please. No more than three syllables and that only if you have to. Where's Dave…?"

"No idea," Simon said, shrugging.

"Great," Xander muttered, gulping the last of his coffee, and taking refuge in his beloved Babylon 5 again. "Our hotel and guest liaison deserts his post without a word, and the con Chair picks the most breathtakingly inconvenient moment to explore new career options."

"She's hardly going to do a Delenn and sprout butterfly wings," Simon muttered as he turned away.

"*Neither did Delenn,*" Xander snapped, smacking his empty cup down on the nearest counter. "Dammit. I'd better go look for Dave. If Andie Mae does show within the next hour or so, send her down to the ballroom. I'll go find my panelists, if they're still alive and able to string together a sentence in public. It might be Sunday but we've still got a con to run. This was damned good coffee, by the way. I'll have another to go, thanks, black, no sugar."

"Whose idea was it to schedule a GoH panel on a Sunday morning anyway?" Simon grumbled. "Even at a normal con, Sunday is the Saturday night morning after…"

"Exactly," Xander flung back as he was exiting the room. "She thought… we both thought… it might just be the thing to wake the convention *up* on the Sunday rather than letting it wend its weary way into oblivion like it usually does until the most jumping thing on a Sunday is the Dead Dog Party."

"Good luck," Simon said, yawned mightily, and turned back to the monitor.

Xander, cursing to himself at the inability to use his currently non-functioning cellphone to contact the people he needed instead of having to bodily chase them down, took the charmingly empty and available elevator (for which, on Saturday, there was usually a crowded and lengthy wait) up to the seventh floor of Tower 1, where the GoH suites were. The first one on his path was Rory Grissom's quarters, and even as he raised his hand to knock he realized that the door was not quite closed… and the room beyond was silent.

Instead of rapping sharply as he had intended, Xander tapped rather more gently and called out, "Hello? Rory? You in there? Everything OK?"

There was no response. Xander bit his lip, clenched and unclenched the hand not curled around his coffee cup, and pushed the door open, sticking his neck out like a wary turtle, and craned his head to peer into the room without being intrusive about it. The opening that led to the vanity area and then the bathroom beyond showed a counter covered in a messy pile of things like hair gel and a couple of half-squeezed travel-sized toothpaste tubes; the door of the bathroom itself was open, and the bathroom, although the light was on, appeared to be empty. Reluctantly, Xander pushed the hotel room open a little more and took a step inside.

"Hello?"

All the lights were on, but the suite was deserted. The sleeping quarters, a smaller room opening out of the large sitting room area, contained nothing more than a king-size bed which looked as though it had been slept in, or at the very least disturbed relatively recently, the bedclothes tangled up into a knot of twisted sheets and coverlets in the middle of the mattress – but there was no sign of anyone who might have perpetrated this. The sitting area was cluttered with dirty glasses, an empty wine bottle, a half-empty bottle of a different wine on the coffee table, and a mostly-empty bottle of tequila with just the barest dregs sloshing around the bottom of the bottle tucked away by the side of the sofa, which was itself a pyramid of tumbled cushions.

A small and intriguing pile of abandoned shoes languished in the middle of the room – a pile that included at least three separate pairs of women's shoes (along with one disconcerting singleton the image of which stuck in Xander's brain accompanied by a persistent and unanswered question as to what had transpired with its mate) which fairly obviously did not belong to Rory Grissom.

Precious minutes passed before Xander allowed all of these things to coalesce into a couple of grimly uncomfortable truths. Rory Grissom – scheduled for a GoH appearance that morning – was undeniably AWOL. Even if Xander could locate the man within the space of the next ten minutes or so, according to the evidence available in Rory's room it would probably be asking the impossible to hope for him to be even remotely coherent enough to appear in public on a stage in the immediate future.

"Damn it. Damn, damn, damn, damn, damn it," Xander muttered, scowling, surveying the scene with his chin tucked into his chest. He allowed himself a trickle of comfort in the idea that any potential audience for that morning's panel might not be in any better shape than the missing panelist, but it really was no more than a trickle – it was the panelist that he was responsible for, not that audience. His job was to make the panel *happen*.

And that...was looking... iffy.

Deciding he did not have the time to start a wild goose chase around the hotel for Rory Grissom, Xander abandoned the coffee cup he was still clutching in his right hand on a side table next to the tumbled sofa, whirled, and ran out of the suite, leaving the door open behind him. At least Vince Silverman had arrived at the con safely shackled by the demanding and needy presence of that young wife of his. Maybe, Xander thought, that had been enough to keep him anchored in the place where he could be expected to be found – and even just *one* panelist...

He turned a corner in the hotel corridor just in time to see Vince Silverman stepping quietly, almost stealthily, out of a hotel room, closing the door behind him with an almost inaudible snick. He looked up just as Xander came to a winded, skidding stop a few paces away from him, and put up a hushing finger to his lips.

"Shh," he whispered, "Angel's asleep, and I'd rather not wake her right now. She was in full freak-out mode most of last night, and I finally managed to zonk her out with one of your good doctor's industrial-strength sleeping pills. He basically told me that it would knock out a buffalo, but even that took a while to work. I'd rather not go through all that again."

"Is she okay?" Xander asked as he fell into step beside Vince, walking away from the hotel room towards the central atrium and the elevators.

"Let me put it this way. One of Angel's better attributes is that she lacks any imagination whatsoever. She is utterly literal about things. This is usually a feature, not a bug, because – well – my first wife, who was also a writer, and a good one, had plenty of imagination – and for a while that was wonderful because we fed each other's muses – but it soon became apparent that marriage, or at least our marriage, was simply too small for two people with measurable quantities of weird imagination to co-habit in together without both of them going insane. It was exhausting, at best – and then there were times that I had to..."

Xander turned to look at him as he stopped talking, unsure if it would be more polite to inquire further or let the conversation lapse.

But Vince, noticing the look, simply shrugged.

"Let me put it this way," he said. "There was room for only one *me* in a domestic partnership. When it became a competition, Laura and I simply imploded. It was inevitable, I suppose. That's why I find Angel so perfect, under ordinary circumstances. She doesn't try to change or improve or reinvent my worlds. She just tells me she thinks they're wonderful, even when she doesn't have the first clue what I'm talking about. But that's okay. She gives me the space to think, and work, and rest."

"Um, this morning, the panel..." Xander began, feeling vaguely guilty that he was basically dismissing his GoH's wife and any further concerns about her but pursuing the thing that he himself was concerned about in that precise moment.

Vince nodded. "I know. Are you expecting anyone to show?"

"No idea," Xander said. "Beginning with your co-panelist. Rory Grissom isn't in his room and I have no clue where to even start looking. Can you do a solo if you have to?"

"My dear sir," Vince said, "I can talk about myself for hours. That won't be a problem."

Xander allowed himself a shadow of a smile and chose not comment further.

They did not have long to wait before the elevator doors opened in response to their summons, but they were nevertheless not the first customers. The young man slouching in the far corner looked up as the doors whooshed open, and nodded at Xander in greeting. Xander, recognizing him at once as Sam Dutton's protégé, the one who had valiantly tried to save the train wreck that had been the panel with Bob the Android, nodded back as he stepped into the elevator, but said nothing.

The doors closed, and Xander, despite the fact that the button for the lobby had already been pushed, poked at it again impatiently before the elevator finally started to move.

"Is it my imagination or is this thing – " he began, a little irascibly, and then, even as he was speaking, the elevator convulsed violently and stopped dead.

Somewhere, they heard the faint sound of an alarm.

Xander rolled his eyes. "Stuck? We're *stuck*? Give me a *break*..."

"The place seems a little moribund this morning," Vince said conversationally, sticking his hands into the pockets of his jeans. "Do you think anyone will notice?"

Xander reached for the com link earpiece that should have been in his ear and realized with a sinking feeling that he had neglected to wear it that morning. His phone, of course, would still be useless.

"Swell," he said. "Does that intercom thingy in the panel work?"

Vince toggled the intercom switch. "Mayday. Mayday. Mayday. Transportation system failure in Tower 1."

Marius, in his corner, could not help a grin at that.

But there was no immediate response, and Xander stepped up to the elevator doors and banged on them with both hands. "Hey! Heeeeey! Helllloo! Can anybody hear me? We're stuck in here! Helllooooo?"

Vince slouched back against the mirrored side of the elevator car. "It'll only take a few minutes of someone else waiting for the elevator that never comes and the alarm will be raised somewhere," he said. "Chill. They'll unstick us."

"Do they have personnel on tap at the hotel?" Xander asked. "Someone who knows what to do about this?"

"Far as I know," Vince said, "that emergency phone goes to the front desk and then they call in the cavalry..."

"What, like some Schindler operative? Or the fire department, to come rescue us like so many stuck cats? I hate to mention it, but those guys might take a little while to get here..." He paused, and suddenly lifted his head to sniff at the air. "Can you smell smoke?"

"Not even a little bit," Vince said. And then, as Xander muttered something under his breath, tilted his head a little in a quizzical manner. "What was that?"

"I said, 羔羊中的孤羊 *Gao yang jong duh goo yang*," Xander snapped. "Sometimes there just isn't anything to say that the Firefly crew haven't already said better. I still say I smell smoke."

"There hasn't exactly been time for anything to really start burning yet," Marius said.

"Look, it isn't that I am generally twisted on the subject of elevators, but stuck ones make me *claustrophobic*, okay?" Xander said, and banged on the door a couple more times. "Anybody there?"

"We could be here a while," Vince said. "Depending on what actually happened. And if they can figure out how to get us unstuck, or out of here. I *could* do the panel, in the meantime, just to keep us occupied. There's you, and there's at least one member of the audience…"

Xander groaned, leaning his back against the wall and then sliding down until he sat in a cross-legged crumpled heap on the floor.

The alarm had been raised at the front desk, and Luke Barnes was in full-flight managerial crisis mode – and this, given the bigger picture and the fact that he knew very well that no outside help was coming, included a healthy dose of panic.

The first thing he made a mental note to check or replace – if he ever got back home and got the chance to do it, or to tell someone else to get on with it – was the intercom system with which the elevator was equipped. He had no problem with hearing the responses from the elevator when he tried to communicate with the people in the elevator car – but those responses made it perfectly clear that those in the elevator could not hear or understand *him*, and once a less than satisfactory contact was made with those who were trapped, the conversation he attempted to have with them quickly degenerated into a confused mess of one-sided shouted repetitions which seemed to be getting neither side anywhere at all.

Luke thought that they said that there were three people in there – or they may have told him to hurry up and get them free – but it became very clear that the best thing to do was to try and get something done with the resources at hand rather than having a discussion about it. He finally screamed into the intercom that they should just hold on, and summoned a trio of maintenance staff who had happened to be on the premises when the hotel took flight and were therefore on mandatory duty.

The first one just shrugged helplessly.

"I'm IT," he said. "I'm mostly here for when guests kvetch about the Internet going down. I've had a bit of a holiday, actually, since there was nothing I could do about the Internet going down this time – there *is* no Internet at the moment, and it ain't my doing or anyone's, and there ain't gonna be any until we get back in some sort of sane signal range. Yes, I know – I've already been informed by multiple individuals in the know who appear to be running around this convention that NASA has apparently successfully trialed something they called a laser communications system and it's supposed to be working just fine all the way out here, but unfortunately they neglected to equip us with the necessary hardware to take advantage of it. So that's *my* line of expertise exhausted. There isn't much I can do about the elevator situation, myself. I know zero about unsticking elevators."

"You can come with me to the control room and see what we can find out about all of this," said the second guy. "I don't think I've ever dealt with elevators as such but I know my way around wires. We can start there."

"Fine, you guys, you go do that," Luke said. "Keep me posted."

The third guy, an older man in blue overalls with the hotel's logo on his left shoulder and a name tag that said 'Andy', met Luke's pleading gaze with commendable equanimity.

"Can't promise nothing," he said, "but I've been known to get a stuck cog moving with a tap of the hammer in my time. If it's mechanical, I might be able to figure it out. What floor is it stuck on?"

"I think halfway between two and three," Luke said.

"Well, at least it isn't a *very* long way down," Andy said laconically.

"Unless you count the fact that it's a *really* long way down... if they go through the floor," Luke muttered..

"There's that," Andy agreed. "Have you got the elevator keys?"

"The what?" Luke said, his voice edged with panic.

"The hoistway doors – the doors at every floor – they have a key you can open them with," the handyman explained patiently. "They're like these little metal... I'll know them if I see them, but without them we need a crowbar to open up the doors, and it'll probably bollix them up proper so you may not be able to shut them properly later, and you really don't want an open hoistway door gaping into a shaft. It's better to try and do it the easy way first. And there will be an emergency procedure write-up somewhere, too. Did they leave you an emergency handbook for the office? There may be something in the elevator electrical room, too. We'd better follow those guys, that would be the first stop. And maybe it would be best if you sent someone up with 'out of order' signs right now, for every floor, and just to be safe make it for both elevators. They don't have to be fancy, at least not the emergency ones, but you might really want to discourage people from going anywhere near that stuck elevator, for now. At least until we can figure out what exactly happened."

"Have you done this before?" Luke asked, beginning to feel a little better — not happy, not even comfortable, but more in control as a procedure began to shake down into place.

"My son's a fireman," Andy said. "*He's* done it before."

"I wish he was here," Luke said.

"We'll manage. Hey, guys, anything?"

This last was addressed to the other two on the maintenance crew, whose own patches identified them as Mike and Luis, as Luke and Andy entered the electrical room. Luis, the guy who had said he knew his way around wires, had a bunch of them hanging out from a wall, as though he had eviscerated a mammoth, and was peering at the tangle in a manner which didn't fill Luke with a great deal of confidence.

"So far as I can tell, the electrics are sound enough," Luis said.

"Then it's something mechanical, and it'll have to be done the hard way," Andy said. "Don't see the hoistway keys anywhere — this could be bad — my son said that more often than not when people try and 'help' they generally pry the hoistway doors open or cut them open with a saw, and all they do is break the interlock system. You know, the thing that holds the doors together when the elevator isn't actually right there, and the hoistway doors are essentially what stands between you and the shaft. We don't want rubberneckers trying to get a better look down there. But it may have to do. Have you seen an emergency procedure anything around here?"

Mike pointed to where a laminated sheet hung on a wall. "There's that."

Andy stepped over and peered at the sheet. "Just like I said, they want the keys. It would be helpful if they had them here. Or said where to look for them. In the absence… the first thing we have to do is figure out exactly where the thing is. Look, it says clearly that if the car is more than three feet above a landing level then it's dicey to try removing people directly through the doors. We may have to go in through the top. Okay, here's what we do. I'll get some tools, and I'll meet you on the third floor – that's above where it's supposed to be stuck, isn't it? – and we'll pry open the doors there and see what we can find out. In the meantime, I suggest you cordon off that area. We're going to have our hands full without trying to deal with an audience. And get those signs up. I saw the con people had their own security – can you get them to help? And someone had better stay right here – preferably you, Luis – it is possible that we may need to cut the power to the elevator car in order to get at it safely but that means leaving those poor folks inside in pitch darkness and we don't want to do that until we have to…"

"I'll go deal with the signs," Luke said. "Mike… do me a favor and run up to the Green Room of the con – it's 1-303, right there on the third floor – and find a guy by the name of Simon Ballard – he's head of the con security – get him to deal with clearing that particular elevator lobby, only people with legitimate business permitted to enter, no gawkers. Go! We're it, there's no help coming. We need to get on with this. If it *is* mechanical then the Lord alone knows what went wrong and I don't want that thing dropping down like a rock with those people still in it. Go, go, go! If you need any help, grab any of the staff and tell them it's on my authority!"

The maintenance crew scattered, and Luke loped back to his own office. At his computer, he called up a blank document and typed in OUT OF ORDER in large black letters and then set the printer to cough out multiple copies. He grabbed a handful of sheets even as they slid into the tray and handed them to the nearby receptionist with a roll of tape and instructions to tape a sign on every elevator door in Tower 1, starting from the top floor and going down. When she ran with those, Luke himself grabbed the remaining signs and started from the lobby, and then up.

About ten minutes later a small and worried knot of people gathered together outside the crippled elevator on the third floor. It included

Simon – who was overheard muttering darkly about *not having enough people* to cordon off any more hotel floors to general traffic – and Dave, and one or two other able-bodied volunteers who had turned up in case any assistance was required but who prudently kept out of the way in the meantime until they were needed.

Andy and a pair of waiters he had collared as minions had hauled up a crowbar, a cordless drill and screwdriver, a couple of flashlights, and two short ladders. He was an unlikely superhero – stocky and grizzled, with a worn tool belt around his waist over his blue overalls.

"Right, then," he said. "I would have preferred it if we had that key – among other things it's supposed to turn the elevator right off if it's used properly, so it isn't likely to shift when you're in the middle of doing something iffy, and that's without screwing with the electrics – but needs must… Okay…"

"Wait," said a commanding female voice from behind him. "Someone tell me what's going on?"

"Elevator incident," Andy said.

"The elevator appears to be stuck," Luke said, turning to face Andie Mae. "There's people in there."

"I think *Xander's* in there," Dave said.

"We need to get the doors open, ma'am," Andy said. "Now."

"Oh, *God*," Andie Mae said, biting her lip and flushing. "It isn't as though we haven't enough to… are you sure you know what you're doing?"

"No, ma'am," Andy said, "but one way or another we need to haul those folks out of there, and we gotta try. Excuse me…"

"Oh, for a sonic screwdriver," murmured Simon, watching Andy grip the business end of the crowbar and apply it to the space where the silver doors of the elevator came together.

"You can't just sonic-screwdriver your way through life," Dave said, and Simon laughed.

"Where's Libby when you want her?" he said. "That's the sort of quote that would make it straight into the 'Overheard in the Corridors' part of her beloved newsletter…"

"You okay?" Dave said suddenly, aware that Andie Mae's had lost color just as quickly as it had flamed into her cheeks, and now looked rather pale and wan.

"Fine," she said. "I'm fine. I just perhaps shouldn't have tried that last cocktail last night, that's all."

"That's okay. We all feel a bit fragile," Dave said.

Andie Mae glanced at him, from out of the corner of her eye, and then dropped her lashes. "That isn't… really…"

The elevator doors creaked and then jerked apart, leaving a narrow sliver of a gap. Andy pushed at one wing, trying to force it wider, and Luke leapt to help, pushing the other wing in the opposite direction. For a moment neither man seemed to be able to move the doors at all, and Dave stepped forward to Luke's side of the door to add his own strength to the effort as necessary.

"Use force, Luke," he muttered.

The doors finally gave, and they pushed them apart wide enough to have an opening they could look through. Andy, on the lip of the landing level, peered into the shaft.

"Worst possible position," he said. "It's squarely between the floors. We can't do anything from below – there's too great a gap, and someone could easily slip through the gap between the car and the landing while we're hauling them out. Too dangerous. And look – it's a little off-square, hanging there – I doubt that we can get that inner door open safely enough for people to…"

"Anybody there?" came a muffled voice from inside the elevator, in response to that succinct summation.

"We're coming to get you," Dave hollered. "Hang on!"

"Somebody go tell Luis to cut that power," Andy said. "We're going to need to go down on the top, and haul them out through the hatch. Just as well I brought those ladders. But we're going to be working in the dark, down there – it's going to be a mess of…"

"Can we be of any assistance?"

The voice was courteous and pleasant, and the three at the elevator doors turned to see who was speaking, coming face to face with the android known as Boss. It was only Simon who happened to be looking at Andie Mae at the moment Boss had spoken, and thus he was the only one who saw the expression on her face undergo a couple of interesting changes. But Boss was speaking again, and Simon filed the information away for later.

"My associates can help," Boss said. "We may be better equipped for this kind of task. I will summon them."

Andy, who had not met the androids before, stared openly – and was even more taken aback when Bob and Zach, the two under-droids, stepped smartly out from the stairwell and came to stand beside their superior officer.

"Please tell us what needs to be done," Boss said.

"Uh – somebody better go tell Luis – we'll need that power off, now," Andy stuttered.

Simon gestured to one of his security people. "Go. Tell the man."

"We'd better warn them, in there," Dave said. "They're going to freak out if the lights suddenly go out on them with no warning." He went down on one knee and thumped on the lift doors. "Guys! Guys! Help is on the way! Lights may go out – don't panic! Someone's coming! Can you hear me? Everyone okay in there?"

"Hurry it up!" a faint voice – Xander's – came back, muffled by the doors.

The hoistway doors jerked suddenly inwards, just an inch or so, and Dave stumbled back instinctively, tripping on his own heel and falling on his ass inelegantly before scrambling back up to his feet.

"Whuh-uh?" he said. "That thing just tried to kill me!"

Boss stepped forward and folded one hand on the edge of one of the doors. "It will not happen again."

Andy swiveled his head around to listen. "There. Hear that? I think that was the power. Okay. Now we need to work fast. Somebody needs to climb down to the top of the elevator – there's a, a thing, like a control panel or something like that, it needs to be set to maintenance mode rather than operating mode – I've got a ladder – here – and a flashlight – "

Boss made no move or sound but one of the other two androids, Zach, approached the edge of the landing level and picked up the ladder, sliding it down until it rested on the top of the elevator car and leaning against the lip of the landing level.

"The flashlight will not be necessary," Boss said.

"Maybe not for your guy, but we'll need it for the people there to see what they're doing," Andy said.

"This is logical," Boss said. "Take the flashlight."

Zach accepted the flashlight and descended the ladder into the shadows. They heard him step off onto the car roof, his footsteps heavy, and Andy called down,

"Be careful! Stay off the sheet metal, walk on the support struts or you're probably going to go straight through!"

"The switch you spoke of has been set as you requested," Boss said.

"There's an emergency access door," Andy said. "It's secured – I don't know how – bolts, or screws, or something – need to get that open, and then there is the ceiling panel of the car right underneath, you need to get rid of that, it won't go through, you'll have to push it in, just warn the guys underneath to go into the corners and protect their heads when it comes down…"

Small clunks and grinding noises came from the shaft, and then a clang as something metallic was opened and dropped onto some other metallic surface. Then Zach's voice, from below, warning the occupants of the car as Andy had suggested. Then a crash and a splinter. Then silence for a moment.

"Everybody okay?" Dave called out from behind Andy.

Xander's voice, clearer now, came floating back out.

"It's pitch black in here right now – ah, all right, I can see the flashlight – just get us outta here!"

"Second ladder," Andy said, motioning behind him. "Pass down the second ladder. We need to get that through that hatch and they can climb up and out – carefully – this thing doesn't look very solid – it's at a funny angle…"

Several helping hands passed the second ladder down into the hatch, and Zach received it and passed it down into the elevator car.

"In theory we should have at least one more person assisting from the inside – my son says that there's a firefighter who goes down and helps them get out – but we don't have time," Andy said. "Guys – can you hear me? – climb out, one at a time, very slowly, very carefully, I've another flashlight up here you'll see where you're going – but hurry up about it?"

"Well, do it slowly or hurry up?" Xander asked from inside the elevator, aggrieved. "Where's that ladder – Vince, you're closest – go first – get out of here…"

"Coming up," Vince Silverman's voice said from the darkness.

The people on the landing floor held their breath, but the first rescue went off without a hitch, almost an anticlimax – they heard someone scrambling on metal, and then climbing the ladder, and then Vince Silverman's disheveled head popped out from the hole.

"Well, hello," he said. "A welcoming committee."

Dave extended a hand and Vince took it, hauling himself out of the elevator shaft and dusting himself off as he got to his feet.

"You all right?"

"You guys sure know how to throw a party," Vince said. "I'm fine. Get your friend Xander out of there, though, he's starting to go a little spare…"

"Who else is in there?"

"That kid – what's his name – Marius something – "

"Sam's protégé," Andie Mae said. "I remember him, he was up in Callahan's last night. That's it? Just the three of you?"

"Just us. We were on our way to the panel – and Xander said…"

"Xander! Come on up! We're waiting for you!" Dave called out into the shaft.

"Did somebody say there's a kid in there? Shouldn't we get the kid out…?" Andy said, rousing.

But there was more scrambling below, and it was Xander's head that popped up next, wide-eyed and ashen-faced. Dave helped pull him up all the way, and Xander collapsed in a boneless heap on the flowery hotel carpet, rubbing his temples.

"Dear God, that was unpleasant," he said conversationally. "There's one more…"

But Andy suddenly lifted his head, and then jerked back from the edge of the landing.

"Watch it! *Cable!* Get away from the doors!"

Everyone dived for cover as they all heard it now – a whipping, whistling, swishing noise, just before something blurred past their field of vision and fell into the dark below, hitting the elevator car with a stomach-churning crash and then tumbling off falling somewhere below making more noise as it bounced off walls and other cables. The car shuddered and dropped a couple of inches. Andie Mae cried out.

And then there was silence.

Xander was still sitting there, frozen and staring; Andie Mae stood with both hands over her mouth, as if she had been trying to stuff her cry back inside. It was Dave who stepped forward, very carefully, and called out in a voice which was commendably calm and level,

"Hello? Down in the elevator...?"

"They are safe," Boss said.

In echo of that, Marius's voice, sounding thin and reedy, came up out of the shaft. "I think we're all right. Your guy jumped in here before that thing hit, and didn't get creamed. But if it's all the same I'd like to come out now..."

"I think we lost the ladder from the car to up here," Dave said. "Unless it's just fallen on top of the car...?"

Andy sidled up and shone his flashlight down into the shaft. "Looks a mess," he said. "Be careful where you step. Looks like there are edges that you don't want to – maybe if your guy came up first, and handed you up to us – "

There was a moment of silence, and then, in the beam of Andy's flashlight, they saw Zach emerging from the opening on the top of the car. He made a gesture, presumably to Marius who was still in the elevator car, to stay down until he steadied himself and found his footing, and then motioned for him to come up. They watched as Marius, his hair dusted with debris until it looked disconcertingly white in the flashlight beam, climbed slowly and carefully from out of the elevator car. He finally emerged, standing with one hand on the low safety railing around the roof panel and one clutched around Zach's wrist, and looked up into the light, squinting and blinking.

"I don't see the other ladder you were talking about but it will be fine – someone just give me a hand..."

Dave and one of Simon's security people knelt on the lip of the landing and reached down; with a bit of help from Zach, below, Marius locked his hands around both his helpers' wrists and was hauled out bodily until he rested on hands and knees on the floor, panting.

"Well," he said, "thank you. That was an adventure. Get the other dude out I have a horrid feeling that with that one cable down that thing is hanging by a cobweb thread."

"It isn't," Andy said helpfully. "There are a number of redundant cables — but still, point well taken. In theory we should at least secure that hatch:..."

"In practice, that hatch is probably in six pieces," Xander said. "A steel cable just smashed into the thing. We're lucky the whole thing didn't go down with it. You okay, kid?"

"Perfectly," Marius said, but his breath still caught a little at the word.

"Maybe we should get the doc to look you guys over," Dave said. "Just in case. "You know, if this were a real rescue they'd probably have EMTs with oxygen tents out here for you guys or something."

"We're fine," Vince said. "We're all perfectly fine and in one piece."

They had hauled Zach out of the hole now, and Marius's head came up, eyes narrowed in sudden and concentrated attention. But nobody noticed him looking, or what he was looking at... nobody, that is, except Boss, whose pale eyes went inexorably from Marius's face to the thing that Marius was looking at.

Zach's right hand.

Which was missing two fingers.

It was done as smoothly as anything, and nobody even realized that it had been done, but Boss stepped away from the outer hoistway doors which shuddered again as he let go of them.

"Perhaps it would be best if we closed these," Boss suggested. Zach, without being prompted, took hold of the other side of the door, and between them the two androids physically pulled the two wings together until they almost met in the middle. Boss removed his hand, but Zach kept his own in the crack between the doors just that little bit too long; and it was only then, when he removed his hand from the now closed gap between the two wings of the door, that someone focused on that hand.

"Your fingers! What happened?" Dave exclaimed, staring at Zach's maimed limb.

"Accident. Please do not concern yourself. We can replace the missing digits," said Boss. But his eyes went to Marius, briefly.

Marius met them, and then looked down, flushing. He stuck his hand into his pocket, and closed around the thing that he had picked up on the floor of the shattered elevator car when the cable came tumbling down and Zach dived into the car to escape it.

A single android finger.

Marius knew he should volunteer the information that he had it. He knew without a shadow of a doubt that he should surrender it. And yet he did neither of those things. It seemed as though something greater than himself had gripped him, had closed his throat to sound, had closed his mind to the sense of the right thing to do – or perhaps he *was* listening to something telling him the right thing to do, it was just not the same thing that his usual instincts would point him to.

The android known as Boss appeared to be content not to force the issue, at least not here and not now. He turned away while everyone else was gathered around Vince and Xander and quietly, unobtrusively, pointed the index finger of his right hand at the line where the doors met. A quiet crackle emanated from his hand as he drew that finger, without quite touching the metal of the doors, from the top to the bottom, and then, when he was done, turned his head a little to look at Andy, the handyman, the only one who was paying any attention.

"That is sealed," Boss said quietly. "I do apologize for future inconvenience because these doors cannot be opened again without a great deal of force. But their safety features have been disabled, and under the circumstances it would appear to be better if they could not be opened accidentally by someone who is merely curious."

"Oh, agreed, agreed," Andy said, nodding vigorously. "Indeed. Thank you very much, sir."

Boss inclined his head in a gesture both acknowledgment and farewell, and stepped away… to come very nearly face-to-face with Andie Mae.

"How are you…" Boss began, but she lifted a hand to silence him, and he obediently stopped speaking.

"It never happened," she said in a low, intense voice.

"But I have…"

"It *never happened.*"

"As you wish," Boss said, giving her a small bow and stepping away.

"Exactly *what* never happened, then?" Simon said in almost a whisper, very close to Andie Mae's ear. "I mean, I wouldn't normally –

but Xander said— I was —*Yee haw*? What is going on....?"

"You were spying on me?" Andie Mae said, her cheeks flushed again.

"Just looking out for you," Simon said, backing away from the famous Steel Magnolia glare.

Xander, unaware that he was under discussion, had stumbled to his feet and shaken himself off. And with that, apparently, he began to circle back to the pre-elevator-incident situation... and looked at his watch with frantic consternation.

"Did we completely screw up the panel...?"

"We were in there just about forty minutes," Vince said, consulting his own wrist. "There is a remote possibility that there may still be an audience hanging around with nothing better to do. If someone can first provide me with a cup of decent black coffee, preferably laced with something stronger, I'm game. Now I even have a story to tell – life and death rescue from an elevator hanging by a thread..."

"There's a replicator just a couple of doors down, said Dave, beyond caring about who overheard his words or who shouldn't have been aware of the replicators' existence. "I'm sure we can manage that coffee. Follow me."

"Thank you," Andie Mae said, reaching out to grab Vince's arm. "There would be plenty who would insist on lying down in a dark room for an hour after all this. Are you sure you're okay?"

"We're all in one piece, and a little adrenaline never hurt anybody," Vince said.

"Helen has informed the audience that there was an emergency and the panel has been slightly delayed," Boss said calmly.

"There's an audience?" Xander said, his head swiveling to the android.

"I am informed there is. Not all of them chose to wait, but a number of them are still present."

"Can we make that coffee to go?" Xander said to Vince, pleading. "I mean, if you're sure you're up to it..."

"Lead on," Vince said. "And damned be the hindmost."

"Wait. I have an idea. It isn't fair – not to you – not alone – we can't find Rory, not even with the delay and if we did I have no idea if he is remotely able to be coherent in public right now – it's a GoH panel, and technically we kind of acquired you guys as extracurricular GoHs – you're going on with him, Boss."

"You tried that – remember how well it worked out the last time?" Dave snapped.

"That was Bob. Bob could not operate without an instruction manual. This time we have the Captain of that Crew. I don't know if you found the answers you came looking for, Mr. Boss, but I'm perfectly certain that there are plenty of questions out there that *you* can answer for *us*."

"Xander, it's going to be a disaster…"

"I will do it," Boss said calmly.

After a beat of silence, Dave heaved a deep sigh of exasperated resignation. "I'll fetch the coffee. Go."

Xander was expecting a handful of die-hard fen in the audience, possibly evenly split between those who were genuinely there for the Guests of Honor listed on the program, those who were there because they had nothing better to do on a Sunday morning in interplanetary space, and those who needed an excuse to be somewhere so that they wouldn't have to be somewhere else or doing something else – plus the occasional attendee who might have snuck in to grab a seat in the back of the room and zone out for a while out of the public eye. But somehow – whether because Andie Mae's idea of holding this panel this late in the convention had turned out to be a genuinely good one, or because this really was just a captive audience on what was really a stolen resort hurtling through space on what was essentially a small asteroid – there appeared to be at least a hundred people in the room when Xander walked in with his panelists in tow, and more audience members followed him in.

Dave ducked in behind them, and trotted up to Vince, proffering a travel mug which bore the same logo that Xander had designed on the fly for the pizza box on the first occasion that the replicator had been tested. The replicator had since assumed that the same logo had to appear on every item specified as a take-away.

"Coffee, and a shot of 'something stronger', as you specified," Dave said in a low voice. "Break a leg, as it were."

He was kind of smiling, but his eyes were still worried, and Xander caught himself replaying Dave's earlier words over and over in the back of his mind – *Xander, this is going to be a disaster!* All of a sudden they seemed less of a warning and more of a promise. Either way, it was far too late to duck out now.

The speakers made their way to the stage and claimed their seats, and Xander turned to the audience.

Now that he was up here and they were down there, looking expectantly up at him, they seemed even more numerous than he had realized, or maybe that was just his angst whispering cautions into his ear. Either way... he was up.

"Welcome to the GoH panel," he said, and if his voice wavered just a little on that first sentence, he had himself in hand now and his next words were firmer, filled with the confidence he was very far from feeling at that point. "Unfortunately one of your panelists was somewhat... indisposed... this morning..."

"Moonlighting, was he?" someone from the audience heckled, and there was a ripple of laughter.

Xander grinned.

"I suspect all of us feel rather... struck... by last night's Lunar Extravaganza," he said. "I know I was. Am. This isn't me talking quite yet. Automatic pilot at least half engaged. More coffee required for a full reboot of the system. But that probably applies to everyone in this room – except one of our guests. Either way – we've got our writer GoH, Vincent J. Silverman, who says he's got plenty to tell you about life, the Universe, and everything. Or at least about life, as it pertains to the way a writer lives it. Perhaps we can leave at least some of the questions about the Universe and everything to our extracurricular jack-of-all-trades GoH here on my left, who goes by the name of Boss – you couldn't pronounce his real name – and whom you can praise or blame for this little excursion that we've been taking this weekend." He didn't say it out loud but he added, in his own head, the rider, *And we still need him – at least until he comes through and puts us back where he found us – if he can – so please don't disassemble him...*

There was a smattering of applause, and Xander backed up and made his way back down the steps from the stage, leaving Vince and Boss in command of it. He had his fingers crossed so hard they hurt.

"Picture this," Vince said easily, leaning back in his chair and crossing his long legs at the ankle before him. "Just before we all got here – you heard there was an emergency, didn't you? Well, I was kind of the emergency. At least a third of the emergency, anyway. One of three people stuck in a malfunctioning elevator, and no jolly little firemen on call to come get us out. So there we were, hanging in the shaft, not knowing when..."

Xander had to hand it to the man, he knew how to spin a yarn. Vince gathered them all in, talked to that crowd as if he were talking to each one of them individually, holding everyone's attention. He told the story of the elevator rescue in a way that brought the audience to the edge of their seats with tension one moment and had them outright giggling the next, and when he had exhausted that tale he segued smoothly into talking about writing, painting a picture of a writing life as something lived to its full potential and milked of its experiences and contacts and ideas for the purpose of re-creating it as something *else,* something new, something that existed just between the pages of a book but was every bit as 'real' as the world in which the writer lived in his or her everyday existence.

"It's a burden," he said, "and it's a gift, and sometimes it's damned hard to tell the difference. Like, right now, right here. It actually feels as though we're all staring back at ourselves from a comic book panel, or the pages of a particularly weird novel... and yet here we are, all of us, and if we look out of the window it's *real* even though it's impossible to believe, and let me tell you, this convention is the best con I've been to. Ever. Because this is living the writer's life. Take the impossible and make it believable. Take doubt and make it into faith. Take lunacy and make it into a trip around the Moon. But maybe at this point I'd better defer to Mr. Boss... because sometimes truth just *is* that little bit stranger than fiction, it would appear. And if there are any questions as to the nature of our current reality, he's better placed to answer those."

"We get to ask questions?" someone from the audience called out.

"We get *true* answers?" someone else asked, sharpening the question.

"I will answer," Boss said unexpectedly.

Several people began to talk at once, and Xander leapt up from a seat he had taken at the side of the room and raced to the front of the stage, raising his arms. "One at a time, please."

Almost every hand in the room was up and waving urgently, and Xander glanced at Boss, and then back to the crowd, and then at his watch.

"We have a limited amount of time, and he said he'll *answer*, not that he'll spend the next six hours doing so. How about we play the game of twenty questions. Twenty people. And just to keep this random, I'll call out people by seat number – your row, and the number of your seat in your row, counting from the right – from *my* right. In the unlikely event that I call out an empty seat, or I call out your seat and you don't want to ask a question, the next person on the right of the seat I called who actually *does* want to ask something gets picked. And if I call you, come out here, and ask a question from the front so that everyone can hear it. Okay? Okay. Here goes. R for row, S for seat. R3S7, R5S9, R2D2...."

There was a ripple of laughter, and Xander grinned.

"Make that R2S2, R10S1, R2S7, R6S6, R7S12, R1S8, R9S1...."

He did the roll call of twenty seats, and twenty people scrambled out of their chairs and made their way to the front of the room, lining up expectantly a little to the side of the dais.

"Can we please not have the existential questions first?" Xander asked. "If you go first and shoot your wad right at the outset, the rest of you guys might as well go back and sit down. And I do suspect that some answers may fall into two categories that may not be popular – the 'can't explain so you'll understand it' and 'you really don't want to know'. You may want to think carefully about what you want to ask so you'll get full value out of being picked to pose your question. Okay? Okay. Within those parameters. Shoot."

Question #1 stepped forward, a girl in black leggings and close-cropped pink hair.

"So are you really robots?" she asked.

Xander rolled his eyes and hoped that nobody noticed. But Boss took it in stride.

"That depends on your exact meaning, and on what you would call a 'robot'," he said. "We are made, not born; that makes us a non-organic life form. If you call that a robot, by definition, then the answer would have to be yes, we are. But we are much closer to what your culture and context has called an android…"

"But an android is a human-like robot – and that means you – "

"Hey," Xander said, "you had your question! No discussions!"

"Okay, I'll ask that one," said the next guy in line, a lanky youth with wire-rimmed spectacles, clad in a tank top that left his arms bare and showed off a complicated tattoo on his upper right arm. "If you self-identify as androids, that implies knowledge and imitation of the human form – so how did you come to that self-identification?"

"We are made in a certain form, with certain functions," Boss said. "Those things had to originate somewhere. There are some among our kind who dismiss ideas of an origin that did not involve a self-creation process – they begin with the premise that this form was arrived at as our existence has evolved, to suit our purpose and our needs, and that originally we may have existed as something quite different. "

"What, like an android amoeba – and you then evolved into walking android fishies and then maybe silicon-based dinosaurs…?"

Xander roused – this was more questions, again – but before he could say anything the situation got away from him.

"It's life, Jim, but not as we know it…" someone in the audience intoned darkly.

"Well, not quite," Boss said, without pausing long enough to allow Xander to get back into the conversation. "I do not think the pathways are necessarily parallel. But in simplistic terms, then yes, you could call that an evolutionary path. Then there are others among us who maintain that our structure and composition implies that we were – at least at some point in our distant past – manufactured, made. By someone other than ourselves. And if we are made, then it is logical to suppose that there must have been a time when the first of us was made – and that this implies a maker, and in that case it may be logical to extrapolate that a maker might choose to make a thing in his own image. Those who believe this have researched our lineage, working back along a complicated timeline preserved in our memory banks, and this research has led us to an image of a human being, in the shape and form that you are familiar with in yourselves right now. The word I have chosen to describe ourselves to you was chosen from a vocabulary provided by this comparison. In other places, or times, or contexts, we may self-refer in different terms; here and now, with you as a reference point, the closest word that may describe us to the point of mutual comprehension is 'android'."

"And these are definitely not the droids you were looking for," someone said from the audience.

Question 3 allowed the laughter to die down and stepped forward – a blonde slip of a girl, wearing cat ears on an Alice band and make-up to accentuate her large green eyes into something that did look a little bit feline.

"Do you sleep?" she purred at Boss.

"No," Boss said. "Not as you understand that concept."

"Talk about a wasted question," someone grumbled from the audience.

"Should one ask if androids dream of electric sheep…?" That came from a man with graying temples sitting in the front row, who then looked so smug that Xander wanted to snack him.

"Next," he almost growled.

But they weren't finished, from the audience.

"What next, you ask him if he actually eats…?"

"Just don't feed them after midnight, they turn into the Terminator…"

More laughter, and Xander made a cutting gesture across his throat with his forefinger.

"This panel has a time limit and the clock is ticking, folks. I said, next!"

Question 4 stumbled forward, as though she had been shoved from behind, and blurted, "Did you time travel? Really? Someone said that you came from the future – *our* future – "

"That's pretty much four questions," Xander said.

"Yes, from what you perceive as your future," Boss said calmly. "In terms of your years, on your home planet, approximately a thousand years separate this era from the time period which is our own 'now'."

"A *thousand years*? A millennium? Like, seriously?"

"A hundred centuries from now…?"

"How would you even know…"

"Why did you go so far…"

"But time travel is not possible," a man in the audience finally stated stubbornly.

"Yeah, much like you go for a flight around the Moon every day in a hotel floating on a chunk of rock," the woman next to him said sharply. "Impossible, like that."

"And how long have you two been married?" Vince inquired conversationally.

The couple in the audience subsided, amidst another round of smothered laughter, and Xander seized his chance.

"Moving on," he said crisply. "Five? You're up."

"Actually, building on that… I'm going to shelve my original question, because now I am interested in something else," said Question 5. "After all this time… are human beings, are *we*, still, you know, around…?"

"We know of this world, in our time," Boss said. "It is uninhabited by your kind."

For once, the answer was greeted by utter silence.

Question 6 said, in a very small voice, "So are we extinct, then…? I mean, everywhere? Was this planet really all that we had?"

That was more than one question again, but this time Xander raised no objection. A part of himself had also shivered and gone cold at that epitaph that Boss had just uttered, and now he turned to the android, anticipating his answer with a mixture of dread and hope.

There was a long pause before Boss spoke again, or maybe it just seemed that way to the hushed audience, but then the android tilted his head a little to the side, as though considering something.

"I am not certain," he said, "just how much of future history can be told without changing something in it, and if I change something that is to come I may affect my own timeline with that. But I will say this much. There were ships sent from Earth before all trace of your kind vanished from this world. And this happened before your year 2400."

"Why 2400?" Xander asked, oddly breathless, jumping his own queue. The specified year was centuries in his own future, he would certainly never live to see it himself, but all of a sudden the answer seemed as important as if he were asking what would happen when the sun rose the next morning.

"Because by the year 2400 of your reckoning your world will… no longer be welcoming to your kind," Boss said, almost unwillingly. "That, too, will be in the process of changing, after – and it may be that someday, in between that time and the end of this world when your sun destroys it completely, there may yet be perfect days in store. But from what we know… your people did not return to the world known as Earth once you left it."

"So are there other kinds of people out there, then?" asked Question 7, and it felt like another question that had not been the one that the woman who had uttered it had originally meant to ask. "I don't know… like Klingons? Or the Borg…?"

Uneasy laughter rippled through the audience, which had now grown to the point that there was standing room only at the back of the hall.

"You've already *got* Klingons," grumbled someone in the audience, sitting next to a man kitted out as one.

Boss looked as though he was consulting internal data banks for a moment, but then gave his head a small shake to indicate a negative response. "No Klingons. No Borg. There are other kinds of life out there, though. But you know that already."

"So – wait – you traced your origins to us? To the humans? So how come you say you aren't sure, then?" That was Question 8, another question that felt like it was raised by the question that came before it rather than the one originally intended.

"I already answered this," Boss said. "There are those of us who believe that we may have been made in the image of…"

"Made," said #8, interrupting. "But MADE. So do you know where the first of you was made…?

"Bzzzt," Xander said.

"Well, it's a good question," said Question 9, the next in the queue. "Short of the Big Bang and the origin of all life, if we're still to believe that evolution from one level to a higher level takes place over time, every particular kind of life comes from something that came before it. If you aren't claiming some robotic kind of Immaculate Conception, how *do* you reproduce, then? I mean, you don't have *sex*…"

"Not between ourselves, no," Boss said.

"With something *else?*" a voice from the audience demanded incredulously. "So who did you sleep with last night, then?"

A smothered yelp from somewhere in the back of the room had heads turning even as another ripple of laughter, this time a little nervous in nature, swept the hall. But whoever had uttered that small inarticulate sound had gathered their wits about them and nobody could see anything untoward.

"We have locations where new units of our kinds are researched, and produced," Boss said, ignoring the commentary from the hall. "We are always improving on our potential and abilities. It is part of our covenant. We consider flaws in our form and purpose, and we work to rectify them and improve future generations that are accepted as prototypes for future generations."

"So you're born, after all, kind of," said Question 10, his voice curious. "But do you die? Or is your kind immortal?"

"We can exist for a very long time," Boss said, "in your terms. But although ageing components may be repaired or replaced, eventually the essential core of each one of us becomes obsolete. And when that happens, we enter a recycling program where that which we once were is repurposed when new units are modeled and created. Our memories, of course, go into the memory banks – and you may wish to consider that immortality, if you wish. It is, of a kind."

"So you live until you die," Question 11 said. "But can you be hurt…?"

"If you are asking if we can *feel* being hurt, the answer to that is no," Boss said. "We did not see the purpose in creating in ourselves the thing that I understand in your kind as pain receptors. In organic species pain is… necessary. It alerts to mortal danger. But with us this seemed unnecessary. Yes, early models could indeed be 'hurt', if you wish to consider this in the context of that concept, because it was possible for them to lose components of themselves – and these would have to be physically replaced by our technicians. The loss of a limb, for example, would have to be dealt with by a grafting of a new limb to replace the one that was damaged or destroyed. But this was not threatening to their existence, it was an inconvenience. More advanced models were self-repairing, but again, only up to a point. We can be damaged, yes, but not hurt, not in the sense that I think you are using that word."

There was a short, awkward silence while everyone pondered the idea of mangled robots, and then Question 12 stepped forward, looking vaguely belligerent.

"Well, *I* am going to ask the thing I came up here to ask," he said, "even though it has nothing to do with anything. What I want to know is, how in the name of Jesus's horny billy goat are you actually flying this damned rock, and how come we all have power and air and food and stuff, but we don't have the *Internet*?" He raised his voice a little to be heard over the laughter in the hall. "I mean, do you freaking *realize* just how much spam I am going to have in my inbox when I get hold of it again…?"

"You cannae change the laws of physics!" someone called out from the back of the room. "So how come you did?"

"What you call the laws of physics… may not be complete, at the current level of your scientific development," Boss said. "It would not be entirely possible to explain. And we apologize for the lack of your Internet. We tried to keep all the life support functions at their optimal level, but we neglected, perhaps, to provide for all the things that you required for sustenance and comfort."

"So – you think you're superior to us? I mean, beyond the technology. I'm not going to argue that – it's painfully obvious that we can't do what you're doing. Not yet, anyway. But otherwise? If you believed yourselves created in our image, does that mean you think you were an improvement?" That was Question 13, seizing his chance.

"In some ways," Boss said. "We…*break*…less easily than you do, and have fewer lasting or permanent consequences when we do. We have better protocols of information storage and retrieval. But we also lack things that you may consider to be – if you insist on using that word – superior in their own way. In cognitive methodology, for example. We do not – cannot – make intuitive leaps which may lead us to solutions that could be applicable to a problem we may be attempting to solve. We use logic. And if logic fails us, we have no recourse." He paused, and then added, "But logic rarely fails us."

"So you think you're better than us," said Question 14 unexpectedly, shuffling forward past #13, who had opened his mouth to argue but didn't have a chance to speak. "But I've seen you guys around the place. Somebody said that you were the latest model, yourself – the most advanced – and the others, I've seen them, they do your bidding. You say jump and they ask how high. You treat them like slaves. Like a slave race, they are there to obey. But we have long since decided – we, the human race – that slavery was not such a good thing. We've gone beyond slavery, we no longer believe that one human being can own or absolutely control another..."

"Well, most of us," someone muttered from the audience. "There are always maroons who think..."

"Shut up, I'm talking, and I haven't asked my question yet!" #14 said sharply.

"Well, is there a question hidden in the soapbox speech somewhere? If so then spit it out!" the heckler growled.

"Actually, she kind of did," another audience member said unexpectedly. "How come a 'superior' race is still clinging to an arguably 'inferior' social model and treating a lesser member of its kind as a slave?"

"But we do not," Boss said. "Not as I understand your notion of slavery. There is certainly no question of any one of us claiming any kind of ownership of another. We are all independent and self-sufficient beings who choose to function in a social mode. Our earlier incarnations are only 'inferior', if you want to think of it in those terms, because the later models may have improved on problematic aspects of their structure or function. And because they have been in production longer, there are more of them numerically and it is logical that there would be an inverse relation in terms of the numbers of earlier models versus more advanced ones. When my team was sent here our composition reflected the numbers that prevail in our society at this time. And I was placed at the head of the team because I am one of the new line of my kind, with improved computational speeds and cognitive understanding. They are not our slaves, they are our children, in one sense. I am responsible for my team. If I give them orders it is because I reach conclusions faster than they and can better assess a situation, not because they are inferior or expendable or in any sense 'owned' by another like myself."

"That seems fair," Xander said. "Okay, we'd better move things along. Next?" Things were moving into rougher waters again, and he was very much hoping that question number fifteen would be another utterly inane one that would derail the whole conversation into laughter and repartee. But what came next dashed cold water on those expectations, and made him tense up all over again.

"I keep thinking," Question 15 said slowly, "about the way things played out. In our future. In how things happened. How we disappeared. How come you guys exist. How come you guys exist in the future and apparently we don't any more, or not that you know of, or will say. I don't know how many stories I've read in my time about the wars between men and their machines – if you're right, if we made the first of you – what if you guys turned against us, in the future?... How come *your* kind survived whatever cataclysm emptied Earth, and ours did not? Or were you begot on some other world than this one...? And if you were, how come you think it was us who began it...?"

"Our memory banks… are not complete," Boss said. "There are gaps. I cannot answer that question."

But he had hesitated. Just the slightest bit. Perhaps Xander would never have noticed it at all had he not been watching the remaining queue of people waiting to ask their question and happened to have his eyes on the face of Marius Tarkovski, who had been one of his co-victims in the Elevator Incident and happened to be holding the seventeenth position in the queue. Marius had been watching Boss as the android had spoken, and Xander suddenly saw it clearly on the younger man's face, something that changed ever so slightly, an expression that was at once astonished and unhappy. An expression that made him replay Boss's response in his own head, and arrive, belatedly but inevitably, at the same conclusion that Marius had.

The answer had been a lie.

The android had told a falsehood. Knowingly and with every appearance of sincerity.

If they could lie… if they could lie this well… what else weren't they telling the truth about?

Xander's hands felt like ice as he lifted one to signal the next person in the queue forward, but if he was hoping for a respite, he wasn't going to get it. The woman who stepped forward to take her place was frowning a little.

"But if there are gaps… how do you know there are gaps? How do you know what you don't know? And if there are gaps, then what made you come back here – what made you look for humans…?"

"Not all trace of humans was erased," Boss began, but Marius put a gentle hand on the shoulder of the woman who had preceded him and moved her out of the way, stepping up to take her place.

"Then maybe the better question is this," Marius said, his eyes locked on the android's. "What brought you back… *here?* To this specific place, to this specific time? What made you choose this specific group of humans? You said you came back looking for answers. Have you found the answers you were hoping for?"

If anyone was expecting Boss to hedge, they were disappointed. The answer came swiftly, and firmly, with the android holding the young man's intense gaze and looking straight back into Marius's own soul.

"I believe we found the answers we needed," he said, "if not the ones we came back to seek. I believe it mattered that we came here, came now, chose this particular group of humans. I cannot tell you more, but I can tell you that I have come to believe that we came here… to create our own creator. That someone who is in this room right now is going to take the first step on the journey that leads from your kind to my own. Someone who might never have taken that step… had it not been for that person's encounter with us here at this gathering. In very simple terms, if we had not returned to this here and now, we might very simply never have existed."

They might have been alone in that room. They were speaking to one another, directly, in a conversation that was on quite a different level from that which the mere words – full of import as they were – implied.

But that meant that Boss seemed to think – to infer – that it was *Marius* who was fated to be that creator of whom he spoke. And Xander suddenly felt as though he could very well end up spending the days of his old age telling people he had once been stuck in an elevator at a con with the Android Messiah.

He could see that Marius was a little shaken, too. And then Boss rose to his feet in a single fluid motion.

"I think," he said, and the voice was almost gentle, "that I have given what answers I could. But now… my team and I have a lot of preparations to make in order to bring you all home safely as we have promised to do. So I will withdraw in order to assist with those. We thank you, all of you, for helping us understand. We are very grateful for the opportunity to have shared these days with you, and we sincerely regret any injury or inconvenience we may have caused."

He gave the hall a slight bow, and then turned, descended the steps from the dais, and walked serenely and without looking at anyone at all down the central aisle of the hall – through a spreading pool of silence and under the concentrated weight of hundreds of eyes upon his straight and retreating back. The crowd at the back of the hall parted to let him through, and he walked regally through the double doors and out into the corridor and then out of sight.

In his wake, the murmurs of voices of those left in the hall began softly but quickly grew in volume. The three remaining people in the question queue, the ones behind Marius, had melted away; the panel was very much *over*, even without Xander's own official closing words. Vince retrieved his empty coffee cup from underneath his chair and came ambling down the steps from the stage in Boss's wake, coming to a stop next to Xander.

"Well," he said to Xander, "I don't think I upstage easily, and that was me comprehensively upstaged. I feel as though I was just the warm-up act for *that*."

Xander's head snapped around. "Jesus, I'm sorry. Dave said it was going to be a disaster, but I didn't think…"

Vince lifted a hand and rested it briefly on Xander's shoulder. "Take it easy, that wasn't a complaint," he said. "On the contrary. I think I have about three more novels that I need to write, just from that Q&A session alone. Thanks, Xander. This whole weekend… has been a gift."

He nodded in a gesture of farewell and plunged into the now milling audience where he was immediately waylaid by a couple of eager fans – but Xander had already switched his attention to Marius, who had not moved from where he had been standing during that last intense exchange.

Marius looked up to meet Xander's eyes.

"What just happened?" Marius asked quietly.

"Funny," Xander said, "I was about to ask *you* that. Anything you want to tell me?"

"In the elevator…" Marius began, and Xander's ears pricked up as he waited for the rest of that sentence, but it never came. Instead, Marius sighed, lifting one nerveless hand to rub at his temple. "Excuse me," he said, "I think … I need to go find Sam…"

And then he, too, was gone.

And Xander was left standing by himself in front of an empty stage on a Sunday morning of a con, usually a moment that might have left him feeling a little tired and wrung out and despondent that another con was so nearly over, but instead he felt something scalding and strange bubbling up inside him, and the rest of his life suddenly seemed as though it was going to have a tough job living up to this particular incandescent instant of time. It felt as though he had been walking on what had seemed to be perfectly solid ground called the Here and Now, and suddenly his foot had gone through what had proved to be just a thin crust and he was left standing knee deep in the hot lava of History, that which had passed and that which was in the making and yet to come.

"Welcome," he said to himself, very softly, "to Abducticon…"

It might have been entirely understandable if none of the parties who had agreed to a dinner meet-up on Sunday night had actually remembered the assignation, given the events of the weekend – but at about five minutes before six that evening Sam and Marius turned up outside the hotel restaurant to find Vince waiting for them – with a bleary-eyed Angel in tow.

"Have you met my wife, Angel?" Vince said, his arm around Angel's waist in what looked like a loose embrace but what Sam immediately realized was in fact a tight grip which was mostly what was keeping Angel in an upright position. "Sorry," Vince added, his voice a little lower, "but I can't leave her alone and awake up in the hotel room. She almost had a seizure when we rocked around the Moon; if she looks out of the window, on her own, and sees *the Earth* approaching, things might get rather… dramatic."

"Have you tried the doctor's wing?" Sam said, in a similarly low voice.

"I thought about it. I kind of feel responsible, though. It would be easy enough just to dump her there and let the doc pick up the tab, as it were, but I brought her here and it's my cradle to rock. She's half-high anyway from the pills that the doc did give me to give to her. It's just, she's better where I can keep an eye on her. She may fall asleep with her face in the soup, but at least I'll be able to fish her out if I'm there."

"Let's find a table," Sam said.

"I'll go tell them," Marius volunteered. "Four of us…?"

"Er, you guys getting together for dinner? Mind if I crash?" Xander, who had been weirdly impelled to keep an eye on everyone who had taken part in that GoH panel that morning, had finally managed to get into a situation where he had herded at least two of them into the same group – and the opportunity seemed too good to allow diffident self-effacing manners to screw up.

Sam raised an eyebrow at Marius. "Tell them, oh, possibly eight. It's a con. Dinners tend to be accretion events, anyway. It doesn't look like there will be a problem right now, anyway."

Marius trotted off and exchanged a few words with one of the red-jacketed servers, who turned around and scooped a handful of menus of a nearby counter and gestured for them to follow her. Vince maneuvered Angel in the indicated direction, and Sam and Xander fell into step behind them. They were shown to a big corner booth and Vince let Angel subside onto the bench and wiggled her deeper into the booth, sliding in beside her and taking up position on one of the ends of the bench. Sam magnanimously waved Xander in to slip into the booth ahead of him and Xander resignedly took up position on the other side of Angel. Sam perched on the other end of the circular bench, and Marius pulled out one of the outside chairs and collapsed onto it.

"It's been a *day*," he said. "I could murder a hamburger."

"And I promised your mother I would make you eat healthy," Sam said, opening up his menu. "On the other hand, it's a hotel restaurant. What was I thinking."

They pondered their menus for a few moments and a server scurried around to the booth with a smile and an order pad and they dutifully made their choices from the listed menu offerings while being completely aware that every single thing they ordered would be coming from the kitchen replicators the android crew had installed rather than from any actual cooking process. Xander pushed the envelope a bit by ordering a mini pepperoni pizza – with lots of pepperoni – which was not on the menu but which the server took down without batting an eyelid. When she left with their order, they all stared at each other for a moment, and then Xander said brightly,

"We're getting closer to home, have you looked out of a window recently? I think I can almost make out Africa."

"Do you think they can really make good?" Sam said. "I mean, land us where we started from? What if we do end up somewhere startling in that Africa you think you are beginning to make out…?"

"There's elephants in Africa," Angel said faintly.

"We went on safari, a year ago," Vince said. "She remembers elephants."

"So, quite a panel this morning," Sam said, turning to Xander. "It was brave to include the Boss-droid."

"Yeah, I wonder if anyone actually remembers I was there," Vince said, chuckling. "That was quite a question-and-answer session we had. Really, I learned more on robotics and androidal whatnots this weekend than I ever knew I didn't know… It's a long way from Asimov's Laws of Robotics, to be sure. Do you suppose our crew ever actually heard of them? That's one question nobody asked."

"Why would they?" Marius said unexpectedly. "They're really silly and naive, when you break them down – and they apply to far more mechanical things than these guys are. Asimov's laws are for critters who are still fundamentally unable to think for themselves, they apply to a slave race, pure and simple, and we – the oh so special people who created them – have to think for them, because they really can't be trusted to understand anything. And besides…"

"Yes? Besides what?" Vince had leaned forward, bracing his chin on his hand.

"The 'laws' are really dismissive. Even downright contemptuous. Even while asking more than the creature supposedly governed by them can ever deliver."

Sam, who wore a proud paternal grin as though he was personally responsible for Marius's passion, motioned with his hand for him to continue, and Marius, flushing a little, leaned into the table himself, spreading both hands for emphasis. "Here's the thing. The starting point of the entire dogma is 'humans are better than you will ever be, so just accept your inferiority gracefully and if you get run over by the world because of it, that's just what you deserve'. Look at the order. Human beings first – no questions asked – you will not, on pain of being melted for scrap metal, raise a hand to a human being. Not ever, not under any circumstances. But then comes the leap in sapience because it also adds, *or allow a human being to come to harm* – which means that somehow they must come to a decision about what harm *is* and how their 'inaction' might factor into it. Take robot bartenders, for instance – "

"Okay, I will," Vince said, grinning. "How does a robot bartender factor into this?"

"Well, he's there dispensing drinks. He's actually happily obeying rule number two, which says that he must obey human orders. But then the human giving him the orders drinks enough of the stuff he demands the robot bartender gives him to actually get *drunk*. This may be construed as him 'coming to harm', in the most literal sense."

"Well, it probably isn't going to end too well, given what we know about the nature of hangovers, yeah…"

"So here's our bartender obeying human orders and supplying the drinks. Then the human being becomes too drunk, which is something that the bartender directly contributed to by obeying orders. So where does that leave our bartender? Gibbering in terminal confusion behind the counter?"

"Human bartenders have no problem cutting people off," Xander pointed out. "Our robotic friend could just be programmed to recognize a certain point of intoxication and do likewise."

"But then he would be disobeying Law #2," Marius said stubbornly. "And I've read any number of stories where the first law – particularly the 'allow the human to come to harm' part – can get extrapolated to a point where, well, anything has the potential to do you harm, if you push it far enough, and that means that the robot must prevent you from doing *anything* because you could conceivably get hurt by it – which means that they are within their programming parameters if they wrap you in cotton wool and feed you through a tube and not allow you to walk, God forbid run, because you could, you know, fall and hurt yourself…"

"Feedback loop," Vince said. "They're supposed to obey orders, not to think about them. But if they slavishly obey orders, those orders will inevitably be taken too far by creatures who don't *think*. And then you have a problem."

"Sentience versus sapience?" Sam asked.

"Exactly," Marius said. "Anything we endow with the ability to understand a given signal and use it to act in a certain way in a given context we might call sentient, in the end – and yes, that would probably eventually inevitably include advanced robot minds. Sentience is, well, really just being conscious and reactive, if you like. But I don't think that the guy from the panel this morning is merely sentient."

"Sapience implies abstract thinking, a search for meaning," Sam said, nodding. "A sense of purpose, even. And I would postulate that our guys have a definite sense of purpose."

"And about the third Asimovian law," Xander said. "Protecting one's own existence… implies a sense of purpose. Which means that the creature is capable of independent thought?"

"Not really, it could just be instinct," Sam said. "Any number of creatures in any given terrestrial ecosystem know well enough to respond to danger in a self-preserving way." He grimaced at his own words, and qualified them immediately. "All of which is horribly Homo-sapiens-centric, because we know that there's plenty of evidence that animals – at least a higher order of animals, above amoebas and earthworms – have a sense of purpose. I think I just implied that only people can 'think', which I don't actually believe. But it's how you think that matters, possibly, not whether you think. If you're implying that mere instinct confers sapience, it isn't enough. Sapience requires being able to articulate just *why* you think you might be in that danger, not just be a zebra knowing that zebras are food for lions, that a lion ate your auntie for dinner, and that therefore you yourself should probably think about avoiding crossing that lion's path when he gets hungry again."

"And anyway," Marius said, "it really was just in the very early stories, where people were feeling their way around mechanical intelligences and not understanding them very well, that the whole laws or robotics thing could be even remotely accepted as a principle. They were superseded a long time ago."

"We have drones," Vince pointed out thoughtfully. "Right now. Theoretically they're robots – machines – it is true, they are guided by human hands, but the time is coming when they can just be programmed to go somewhere and kill somebody. So where does that leave the First Law of Robotics? And the business of protecting your own existence – what happens when a drone refuses an order because of protecting its own existence inasmuch as it doesn't like the idea of potentially being blown into smithereens by someone who might take issue with its mission?"

"That's kind of pushing it," Xander said, leaning back.

"Okay, but, I mean, someone said it this morning, back in the panel," Marius said. "Leaving drones right out of it – what was it they said – don't feed the robots after midnight because they'll turn into the Terminator…?"

"Ah, I was wondering how many people got the point of that," Sam murmured.

"So Terminator is sentient, or sapient?" Vince asked. "Hang onto that thought, here comes dinner…"

They waited until their meals were sorted out and delivered to the correct destination on the table, and then Vince, tearing a corner off his garlic bread and stuffing it into the corner of his mouth, lifted a finger for attention.

"So where's the line?" he asked.

"A Terminator is *programmed* to harm a human being," Marius said. "There goes the first law, up in smoke. It does not obey a human's orders – there goes the second."

"It did obey John," Sam said, playing Devil's advocate.

"Because it *chose* to!" Marius said. "And that was pretty much reversible – if a Terminator got a reboot it went back to kill mode anyway, so it was immaterial to begin with. The only thing that you might point to as the Laws of Robotics being preserved in that Universe is that you could possibly make a case of the machines rising up to somehow protect their own existence..."

He abruptly closed his mouth, as though he were trying to keep the rest of the words that had been on the tip of his tongue from escaping. But Xander had suddenly remembered that morning's panel and the moment in which he had seen the expression change on Marius's face – and that same change had just washed over his features right at the moment at which he decided to stop speaking. And the same chill washed over him, and he said, very softly,

"The gap in the memory banks."

Marius whipped his head around. "You got that too?"

"I got it because I was watching *you*," Xander said. "You... just... heard it... and then when I ran it back I could not believe I had not heard it the first time, but it was right there staring me in the face..."

"What in the world," Vince said, reaching over to prop up Angel who looked like she was on the verge of falling asleep and sliding right off the bench and under the table, "are you talking about?"

"Do you remember when someone asked Boss about what actually happened in the theoretically shared future that their kind and ours had – and how come in their timeline *they* existed and he had already said that Earth was empty of us – "

"Oh yeah – the Skynet question," Vince said. "I remember. But what about it was it that you guys 'saw', then, exactly...?"

Marius hesitated, glancing across the table, but Xander shook his head mutely in a way that indicated unequivocally that there was no help to be had from that quarter. Sam was staring at his protégé with a quizzical frown – he had not been close to the front, at the panel, and had not observed the exchange with Boss very closely. And now Vince had caught the scent of something that might have been important, and his own expression, when he turned back to Marius, was expectant and watchful.

Skewered, Marius gathered his shoulders into a tight fold, tucking his head down protectively.

"He lied," Marius said, his voice very low.

But it was loud enough for everyone to hear clearly, and the words were electric. Xander's gaze sharpened, and Sam and Vince both sat up abruptly and leaned closer in.

"Are you telling me that you think that *an android* uttered a deliberate and considered thing that could somehow measurably, empirically, and logically be proved not to be true?" Vince demanded. "How is that even in the realm of possibility? A mind created with straight logical pathways like that cannot take the curved road, by definition – they should not be capable of it…"

"You are talking about robots again," Sam said. "Machines created by us, for us, according to *our* rules. Our laws. You're talking about that slave race for which the original laws were made. We might well have created the creatures, down the line, with minds just like you just described – but what's to say what happened when those mentalities started to evolve? At what point do they stop being created by us and – well – *become* us…?"

"But what did he lie about?" Vince said helplessly.

"We can't know," Xander said. "He was speaking from the point of view of knowing something, some fact that he was coldly and deliberately not telling us. For whatever reason."

"First law," Marius said faintly, with a strange little smile. "Preventing us from coming to harm."

"They never even heard of the first law," Vince said. "They're literally generations away from it. If it ever played any part in their, er, programming… I'm willing to lay down good money that the original set-up has been superseded a long time ago, anyway."

"It's *fiction*," Angel said, apparently completely appropriately, as though she had been coherently following the conversation all the time.

Vince gave her a startled look, and then decided that pursuing this would take too much time at that moment. There were other things he wanted to know. "What harm could we have come to?"

"Truth hurts," Sam said, his voice a shade more bleak than he had thought he had permitted himself to show.

Xander, although not directly accused of anything, actually flushed and looked down. There were a lot of truths and half-truths and lies – at least those of omission – that had changed the face of this particular convention, that had put him in the position that he held and had ousted Sam from the one that had been his.

"I think there *was* some sort of a war," Marius said in a low voice. "Between us and them. And I think we lost. That's why they survived, and we did not."

"You mean there will come a time when our creation will destroy us…?" Vince said.

"Alas, the fate of every creator God," murmured Sam. "How could we have thought that it could be different?"

"And yet he said that their creator… was in that room, this morning," Xander said, looking up at Marius again.

"Why would we create them, if we knew that they destroy us in the end?" Vince murmured. "Ah, but there is a paradox."

"Because some day they may be all that is left of us…?" Sam said slowly.

"You're creating your own death and your own immortality? There's a job," Vince said. "And if you start with the Three Laws of Robotics – like Papa Asimov did – it's a long way to immolation by machine. We get to – *they* get to – have a childhood of sorts. An innocence."

"Before they realize that they may have been created but that they are no less alive than ourselves, for all that," Sam murmured.

Marius flexed his hands against the edge of the table. "The first robotics laws are pretty much rendered obsolete," he said, "by a sufficiently determined genius hacker, anyway – and even right now, at this time in our history, we have enough people of the required ilk and caliber to do real damage if they wanted to, or the idea was put into their heads. And of course any sufficiently advanced AI is beyond them anyway – because it is a living thing, a sapient living thing, and those three obvious little 'laws' do not hold it any more than they would have ever held us, the flesh-and-blood humans."

"But then, in the end, *they* survive?" Sam said. "So who gets called 'real' in the end?"

"You are not necessarily obliterated by extinction," Xander said.

"Yes, you are. Just the memory remains. We'll be objects of fun or derision or something to scare small android children with. Like we do with dinosaurs," Sam said.

"I think you just came up with the Fourth and Final Law of Robotics, kid," Vince said slowly. "You might say – if I can paraphrase what you just said – 'The original Laws were rendered obsolete by the presence of a sufficiently self-aware AI machine or by a determined evil genius hacker'. That means there is no hope, really. Whatever we do, our mechanical progeny is going to end up being better, faster, more durable than us. More… immortal. And we as a race are doomed, unless you count our living on in an artificial form created in our own image. Like these guys, who come back seeking their forefathers, or their Creator God, whatever you want to call it. We're a legend. But we're a memory. Are they our children, the only thing that remains of us?"

"Excuse me," Marius said abruptly, pushing back his chair and stumbling to his feet. "I just… I need to… I'll be back…"

He reached blindly behind him to steady himself on the back of his chair, nearly overturned it, caught it in time and gave everyone a brief apologetic smile before he fled the restaurant like all the evil androids of the world were on his heels.

"What just happened?" Sam said, staring after him.

"Sam." Xander laid an urgent hand on Sam's arm. "Let me out. Let me after him."

"Xander, I think I should probably…" Sam began, but Xander pushed on his shoulder, gently, but with real urgency.

"No. Let me. Trust me. You weren't there, you weren't right there, I saw what he saw. I know what he heard. I know what he's thinking. Quickly, let me out. Let me go get him."

Sam hesitated, but just for an instant – there was something in Xander's eyes that made him accept these vague reassurances without further question. He slipped out of the booth, and Xander scrambled out after him and hurried in Marius's wake.

"What does he mean, I wasn't there and I didn't see? You were – you were right there. What the hell happened on that stage?" Sam demanded of Vince, sitting heavily down on the chair Marius had just vacated.

"I would think that getting a visceral realization that the entity that was not supposed to be able to conceive of telling a falsehood or something that was not absolutely and provably true would be quite enough to spook that kind of quick and intelligent kid. But when Boss was talking about somebody in that room being the person who would take the first steps toward creating the androids... I think he was speaking *directly to Marius*." Vince paused reflectively, then went on, "Of course, I am just a writer, and it is my stock in trade to extrapolate and make up stories on the basis of the tiniest things I notice out of the corner of my eye – and to be honest I thought, well, it was an intense moment, and the kid happened to be the one who had asked the question, and it might have been anyone in his place, really, and it would have felt the same. But now... Xander may be right... It may have been meant for him alone. Just for Marius. I think your friend Boss did find the answers he came here to seek, and they came... wrapped in *that* package. That kid was just handed quite a bill of sale, I believe. And now we have two choices."

"Two choices?" Sam echoed blankly, trying to take it all in. "Marius? You're telling me *Marius* is the one who creates... I mean, I know he was always a tinkerer, he could rebuild a computer from a pile of spare parts when he was thirteen years old, I probably shouldn't tell you this but he hacked my cell phone so that it is a free agent when it comes to gathering signal from thin air – his phone and mine are possibly the only ones *that still worked* when this floating palace hit the void and everyone else lost the signal. I mean, we couldn't phone home, he's not that much of an E.T., but we could call each other. But you're telling me Marius is the one who grows up through all this techno-pottering to become the literal father of the android race...?" And then, sitting up, he added sharply. "What do you mean, two choices?"

Vince gave him a wan smile. "If this is true, then yes, two choices," he said. "If we know that this is what happens in our future... and if Boss's 'gaps' imply what we think they might imply, and the consequences that follow... knowing that we have in our power *right now* to possibly change that future... we can choose to accept it, and go forward, and embrace what is coming, and that means telling absolutely nobody what we know and hope like hell that Marius himself might decide to do or not do something and take it out of our hands. Or we choose to reveal it, and let him take the consequences of that."

"Reveal it to whom?"

"When we get back Earthside, assuming we get there in one piece. Take him in to Homeland Security, NSA, whoever will listen, and leave him to them."

"They'd puree his brain," Sam said. "Assuming of course they believed a word of your crackpot story in the first place."

"I think we can prove it," Vince said slowly.

"What do you mean by that?"

"Back in the elevator, when we were stuck," Vince said. "Marius was the last one in the elevator car. He was in there when the cable came down. The android that was helping us jumped into the car with him to avoid being flattened by that steel cable when it hit. But when it was all over and they both came out... it was not without its consequences. The android might have saved itself, but it was not quite fast enough. It was missing two fingers on its hand when it came out. I think Boss might have staged a little sleight of hand, afterwards, as it were – because the two androids were the ones who closed and sealed that door. And it was implied that it was the door that cost those lost fingers. But now – now – the more I think about it the more I think I know what really happened. It was in that elevator, in the dark, that the cable came down and mashed that hand. *Marius has at least one of those lost fingers.* If you are right, and he has a gift for the tech stuff..."

"It's a Rosetta stone, of a sort," Sam said. "It's a blueprint. It's enough of a hint, for him. If you are right, it will be enough – it will be more than enough."

"What do you want to do with him?"

"He's a kid," Sam said. "Dear God, his mother gave him to me to keep an eye on, and I took a seventeen-year-old high schooler out of her house and, if we all land in one piece and I take him home, I'll be returning with the Android All-Father…"

"Perhaps we can just stop him," Vince said. "You have influence. Tell him to simply ditch the finger…"

"You can't be sure of that. It makes for a great story, but you don't know. But if it is true, do we have the right to make that decision, to change the future? Even if we think the future is our extinction?"

Xander had caught up to Marius just outside the restaurant. The kid was standing by the big plate glass window directly opposite, which looked out into the courtyard enclosed by the resort's three towers, with his forehead pressed against the glass.

"He *did* mean you," Xander said quietly, coming up to stand just beside the younger man. "It's supposed to be you. It's you they came back here to find. To wake up. To push into… into actually creating them in the first place. God, my head hurts."

"*Your* head…" Marius said, laughing hollowly, but lifting his head up from the glass pane to look at Xander. "I feel sick."

"You don't have to do anything that – "

"Your head's going to hurt worse in a second if you think this through to the end," Marius said.

"What? After everything you've heard – after everything we think we know, everything that possibly happens – you're going to make them anyway…?" Xander asked.

Marius stared at him. "You still don't understand, do you?" he whispered. "I don't get to choose anything anymore. *This* happened, this weekend. They came. They were here. They existed. They *exist*." He paused. "Look, the only reason they could be here at all is… is… Xander, I've already *done it*."

⬢

The con was gearing up for another giant party by this time, with Earthlight starting to fill the corridors of the California Resort – but the mood was quite different the second time around. With the Moon fly-by it had been pure euphoria, everyone simply drunk on the wonder of it all, with absolutely no thought for anything else but that moment as and of itself, something unique and never to be repeated and as such to be celebrated in the grandest, loudest, most joyous and most abandoned way possible. Then had come the hard crash of the morning after, the Moon behind them, the home planet still a long way away and existing almost as no more than dream or memory.

But now, with the approach to Earth, with the familiar contours they had all seen on a thousand maps starting to emerge from behind clouds wisping over brown landmasses and brilliant blue oceans, the euphoria had changed to something much quieter, and deeper, and somehow more reverential. It was a homecoming, not a revel, and people weren't thinking in terms of having the time of their lives. They were, rather, remembering the feel of wet sand between the toes of bare feet as the ocean's foam withdrew from the shore back into the sea as another wave gathered to come in; they were remembering their first snowfall, and apple pie, and Christmas, and their grandmother's smile, and blue skies, and the first scent of frost in the air on an autumn morning, and seedlings pushing their way through the earth in early spring, and the smell of lilac, and the feel of a sea breeze on hot cheeks, and the song of a whale, and the wild tailwagging joy of the first dog of their childhood. It was the feeling people knew well – the sense of gratitude and quiet joy of sleeping once more in the familiar warmth and comfort of your own bed after a long trip away from home. It had all somehow become quite precious, all those memories, like an answer to a prayer, and the party was more of a vigil this time around, a gathering where people shared not pure exhilaration but rather a quiet wonder. They watched, and they waited, and some cried, and others comforted them, and it was a forging of minds and spirits, a sense of being together, of being one.

The only thing that nobody quite knew, or at least they weren't entirely sure of, was whether it was all going to end as well as they had been promised. All those things that they were remembering, that they had loved, that they suddenly yearned for with an intensity that felt like an almost physical pain – all of it might be lost forever if just one small thing went wrong.

But they had been asked to believe so many impossible things that weekend. This was just one more. And they could handle it. They could handle it together.

Up in Callahan's Bar the clientele was much the same as for the Moon shot, but the mood had reached up there as well. No crazy cocktails were made on this night. It was much quieter, people standing in loose knots and speaking softly amongst themselves or standing by themselves nursing a glass of the good brandy – because the good brandy was what the occasion called for.

"When we hit that atmosphere," Dave prophesied morosely, "there'll be fire…"

"What, you think they'll still shoot at us?" Xander asked.

"If we aren't a flying cinder already, they might," Dave said.

"Aren't you a ray of sunshine," Xander muttered.

"I was the one who saw us leave, remember?" Dave said. "It was freaky. In the extreme. And now I've got the shakes. I didn't understand how we took off in the first place. It is utterly beyond me to contemplate how they are going to…"

"They'll just reverse the polarity of the landing gear at the bottom of this rock," said Libby, who had recovered enough from the previous night to give Callahan's another game try.

"Well, let's hope the dilithium holds out," Dave muttered.

They were all braced for what they knew, intellectually, had to be coming. They had seen hundreds, thousands, of yards of footage showing atmospheric re-entry of solid objects into the mantle of air that surrounded the Earth. They had all heard of heat tiles on the NASA shuttles, and of the problems they caused when they failed – but at least the shuttles had *had* them, which they emphatically did not. They were waiting so hard that when what they were waiting for completely failed to materialize they were taken completely by surprise.

The Earth simply grew larger and larger and larger; it had grown, while they were watching, from a tennis ball to a basketball to a large pumpkin and then bigger and bigger, filling their vision, filling the black void, until it was all there was and they could see the surface of their planet approaching almost too fast to believe – but also slowly, very slowly, as though they were a leaf adrift on the wind, with almost no trace of their passage. Certainly there was no flaming trail, and it was when they were low enough that someone muttered about the lights below – which were suddenly a familiar sight, like something they might see out of an airplane on a perfectly mundane flight that all of them had taken at least once in their lives – being really *awfully* close that anybody realized that they had been in the atmosphere (with no effects, ill or otherwise) for some time and that they really were just floating their way down to the ground, in just the kind of way that none of them would expect a rock falling out of the sky to accomplish this feat.

"I feel as though I ought to have a towel with me, and that right about now someone should be telling me not to panic," said somebody behind Libby, in a rather chagrined voice.

"Cleared to land in Docking Bay One," a girl sang out from right beside the window, her face glued to the glass.

"I feel a bit cheated, actually," Xander complained. "One would want a bit of drama, really. Like, we're having problems with re-entry, Captain – and then someone does something improbable, and everything turns out all right in the end. That's what happens in the movies."

"You just wanted to see someone be a hero," Dave said, braced against the wall as though he desperately needed something solid to hang onto when – as it must – the rock they were on hit Mother Earth, hard. Falling rocks did that, after all. It was a known fact.

"Scaredy cat," Xander said, laughing.

Dave lifted a finger and began to intone, "I must not fear – fear is the mind killer – "

A shudder rocked the building and a cry went up in the bar, but then things righted themselves again and descent resumed.

"We apologize for the turbulence," someone said, "please keep your seat belts fastened until the hotel has come to a complete stop…"

"Help me, Obi-wan Kenobi, you're my only hope," Libby said, turning to hang onto Dave's arm. And then, as his hand came round to cover hers in what was meant to be a gesture of comfort but suddenly turned into a vice-like grip on her wrist, "Ow! Take it easy! I don't want to have to…"

"Look," Dave said, pointing.

The four androids who had taken them on this entire merry ride had somehow appeared in the far corner of Callahan's. They had a glow about them, and appeared two-dimensional. Xander narrowed his eyes at the apparitions.

"Holograms?" he said. "That's not the real…"

"We have brought you home, as we have promised" said the voice of Boss, and even as he spoke they all felt it – something almost too small to notice, something almost entirely unremarkable, a tiny bump, a sense of things knitting and connecting, and then a stillness, and what they could see out of the window was night sky. Just ordinary night sky. Like they might have seen on a thousand nights before. "We have to leave now. But before we go we wanted to thank you, one more time. Now, with your help, we understand."

"Hey, wait," Libby said, stepping forward and raising one hand, but there was no response from the four androids except for all of them raising their right arms, hands lifted in a gesture of farewell, palms toward the crowd in Callahan's. And then, from their edges inwards, the four glowing figures developed a coruscating sparkle which dissolved their shapes until each was just a point of light that lingered for a moment and then winked out.

"I'll be *damned*," Xander said explosively. "They *beamed up*."

Libby, dropping Dave's arm, glanced down at her wrist, and sighed.

"Well, it's ten minutes past midnight," she said. "I guess if we all walked out of the front door right now we'd be right back where we started out. I guess it's over. Dammit, Monday *always* comes."

EPILOGUE: MONDAY ALWAYS COMES

"The final newsletter is a work of art, Libby," Dave said, grinning, as he stuck his head around the door into the Con Ops room and caught Libby's eye as she blearily looked up from the computer screen.

"Thanks," she said with a yawn. "Worked on it all night. I actually literally haven't been to bed yet. Too much to do, too little time., But I have to confess, it's easier when someone actually does half your work for you. And you can always rely on fen."

"You mean the elevator signage?" Dave said. "Yeah, that was inspired."

Libby patted a pile of paper on her left. "I'm keeping the originals," she said. "*Too* good."

Dave stepped fully into the room and picked up the sheaf. "You stole them off the elevators?"

"I left replacements," Libby said. "Don't worry, safety first. But those... those are *mine*."

The signs in question had been the ones that Luke had raced to place on the crippled elevator bank. Initially they had simply stated OUT OF ORDER in large black type with a line below, in smaller letters, saying PLEASE USE STAIRS. But passing con-goers had annotated each individual sign, in different pens and different handwriting. Libby, wearing a wide grin of her own, glanced up at Dave as he stood there with the pilfered signage in his hands, and said,

"Start from the bottom and read up from there."

Dave was already doing that, laughing out loud as he did so. The sign from the Lobby level had, in an act of inspiration, been left absolutely untouched – a virgin control panel, showing what the origin of the game had been. But on Floor 1 the competition began, with handwritten commentary underneath each original warning statement.

OUT OF ORDER
PLEASE USE STAIRS
We mean it!
Uh-oh…

Floor 2 upped the ante.

OUT OF ORDER
PLEASE USE STAIRS
We_ really_ mean it
Yeah, they actually locked it
You tried to open it?
He touches wet paint cuz they might be lying
With wet paint you don't fall 20 stories
….or 200,000 miles
238,857
that depends, how fast are we approaching?

Dave looked up.

"I'd pay money to know who wrote that wet paint comment," he said.

Libby traded grins again. "Gets better."

Floor 3 signage was a little more meta.

OUT OF ORDER
PLEASE USE STAIRS
This is not the elevator you were looking for.
Obi-wan Kenobi... is that you?
(handwave) There is no Obi-wan Kenobi...
I find your lack of faith disturbing. – D.Vader

Floor 4 went back to banter.

OUT OF ORDER
PLEASE USE STAIRS
Fitness 4 Fen
Fitness forfend
Fitness Forever!
Fitness final, 20th floor, required. Fail = not permitted to leave premises

"There *is* no 20th floor," Dave said.

"Someone thinks there might be heaven, though," Libby said, tapping the next sheet.

Floor 5 did indeed seem to put forward that hypothesis.

OUT OF ORDER
PLEASE USE STAIRS
Stairway to Heaven
Go looking for stardust!
MOONdust, twit
Green cheese
...and ham...
Oh, The Places You'll Go!
Today the Moon, tomorrow the Klingon Empire...

The final floor of Tower 1 had a number of entries that had been scored through by each successive contributor, until the final triumphant line.

OUT OF ORDER
PLEASE USE STAIRS
~~*Out of whack*~~
~~*Danger*~~
~~*LETHAL danger*~~
~~*You keep using that word, I do not think it means what you think it means.*~~
Inconceivable!

Dave was laughing out loud again as he put the papers down. "Can I keep one?"

"No way," Libby said. "They're a set. And they're mine."

"How's everything else going?"

"I don't know. It's a Monday. The sun rose like it always does, just like nothing strange had happened at all. I know, I saw it, I was awake and working at sunrise, and somehow it seemed so… miraculous. Just to see a sun rise in the morning. There's a feeling I don't leave a convention with every day." She paused, looking down at the hands folded in her lap, and when she lifted her eyes again they were inexplicably full of tears. "I went out, for a walk, just after it was light," she said. "There, in the parking lot. No further. Went to the edge of the bluff and stared at the ocean. And I – you know, I hate to use that word again, it feels like I'm wearing it out – but there's nothing else to explain – it was simply a miracle, and that's final. The fact that I was walking, on solid ground, here, on my own world. The light on the water. Everything. *Everything*. I wasn't sure whether I'd just woken up from a dream, or had just entered one, but it almost felt like I myself was the dream, you know what I mean? That I was the only thing that could not possibly be real, because I couldn't exist in both the world as it was around me and the world that I'd been in all weekend – they didn't seem like they could *both* contain the reality of myself…"

"I know," Dave said. "I went for that walk too. I came down from Callahan's last night, just after the big landing, and I actually went outside, just to… just to… I don't know. Make sure, I guess. And all of a sudden the very idea of a Moon hanging in that heaven seemed to be so impossible that I laughed out loud, out there in the parking lot, all by myself, like a loon… You didn't put any of *that* in the newsletter, did you?"

"It would have seemed like I was gushing, or being pretentious, or something," Libby said. "Somehow it was just so… private. Like going into a temple to say a prayer, and nobody else would understand if you tried to explain to which god you were praying, or for what. On the whole… well, but the elevator signs were a godsend. I don't think they could have coped with the profound, not in the newsletter, not when everyone probably had their own experience of it, and nothing you and I could say would match it."

"I know what I was praying for," Dave said with a small dry laugh. "At least while it was all going on – just to make sure that everything went… I mean… I spent most of the last three days braced for some horrendous disaster and we went around the Moon and back and the worst that happened was a stuck elevator and a bunch of psyched-out civilians and a couple of con people… speaking of whom… has the doc been in touch…?"

"Far as I know, he requested an ambulance or two for this morning," Libby said. "One's been and gone already, roughly around the time the sun came up. I watched on the cameras, the woman they took out was in a wheelchair, awake, but looking around in a confused sort of way as though she wasn't quite sure where she was or how she'd got there. But she seemed okay, otherwise, and she should be fine with about ten years of therapy, I guess."

"Or two, you said – what's the matter with the other ambulance patient?"

"I either missed it coming and going or it hasn't been yet," Libby said. "No idea. Xander's down there, though, look. He would probably know."

"I suppose I'd better go down. I'm supposed to be hotel liaison after all. I should be on hand in case anyone decides they wish to register a complaint."

Gaining the lobby, Dave found Xander in conversation with Luke the hapless hotel manager, who was looking pale and exhausted but impeccably groomed, his grey waistcoat somehow miraculously clean and unwrinkled and his brass nametag gleaming.

"Hey, Luke," Dave said, lifting a hand in greeting. "What, your replacement isn't here yet?"

"I checked in with the head office, this morning," Luke said. "An entirely new shift of staff is on the way. I just have to wait until they get here to hand over the report."

"You have to write a report? On this weekend? You poor bastard," Dave said. "What are you going to tell the corporate office?"

"As little as I can, actually," Luke said, offering up a wan smile. "But it's going to be a fine line between telling them something that sounds sane and is an absolute lie, and something that is at least marginally true but doesn't make me sound like I spent my first stint as Night Manager up in Callahan's stuck into the sauce. Either way, I hope I still do have a job when the next shift change happens."

"I'm really sorry," Dave said, and meant it sincerely. "We certainly had no idea any of this would happen."

"Of course not," Luke said. And then appeared to stiffen his back and brace himself against an assault as he muttered, "Oh, good, here comes another one…"

The receptionist had just pointed him out to a woman with her dark hair scraped up into a pony tail, and the woman was bearing down on the group by the door dragging a small wheeled suitcase behind her and wearing a thunderous expression.

"You the manager?"

"Yes, Ma'am," Luke murmured soothingly.

"Well, I just wanted to let you know that I am *not happy*. I don't know what kind of service you think you are providing, but I wanted to watch the game on Saturday afternoon and could I get anything on my TV? Nothing at all except your crappy pay-per-view movies. I am simply not going to be blackmailed into that! I will be writing a strong letter of complaint to the management!"

"I'm very sorry, Ma'am. We had technical difficulties…"

"That's not my problem! I am *so* not happy! And all these absolutely weird people you have crawling around the corridors – really, one would appreciate a heads-up in the future so that one can make plans that don't include a Trekkie invasion!"

She stuck her nose in the air, very nearly literally, and flounced out of the door without waiting for a response.

"Trekkies," Dave growled softly. "She probably wouldn't recognize a Star Trek uniform if it bit her. She probably thinks that Rory Grissom is a Trekkie."

"Speaking of," Xander said, "I still haven't managed to locate the man. Now that the phones are functioning again I even tried phoning him but it goes straight to voicemail. I suspect he left it lying around somewhere and the battery is sending a weak SOS by now, but still. I kind of feel awful. Our Guest of Honor was basically abandoned to…"

"To the convention of his dreams, most likely, from your account of what his room looked like when you didn't find him there," Dave said. "Speaking of captains, though, isn't that our guy from before – when the replicators first came online? The airline pilot?"

"I think you're right," Xander said.

The airline pilot in question, in shirtsleeves with a jacket over one arm and dragging a small overnight case, approached them with a smile.

"Glad I caught you guys," he said. "Once again, thanks. It's been… something."

"Don't you have to write a report on this? I mean, were you supposed to report to work anywhere…?"

"Yes," the pilot said, "but my flight is this morning and I'll be right on time. No report needed. And you can be sure that I won't elaborate too much on what – well – let me put it this way. Those pilots who report having seen UFOs out there … tend to have short careers. And this weekend – if I reported *this*… Well, I won't. There isn't a soul in the world who really needs to know the details. Anyway, I'm on my way to the airport now, with the rest of my crew."

"Uh, were they… was everybody else… okay?" Dave asked carefully.

The pilot laughed. "I talked everyone round," he said. "All is well. But I'll not be forgetting these last few days in a hurry. I actually went out there earlier, out into the garden, and just stood looking at the sky – I fly large metal objects for a living, and I think nothing of it, it's an everyday thing – but now, all of a sudden, it seems to me like I've never really *done* it before. Not truly. Not being aware of what I was actually doing, or of how improbable it was… or of how trivial it all seems, now, after a *real* miracle just happened."

"Are you going to be okay? Flying?" Dave asked carefully.

"Oh, yes," the pilot said. "Once I'm in the cockpit of the plane it's going to be the familiar routines that kick in. I'll be fine. But still and all... there was... there was the Moon." He lifted his hands in a gesture that was pure helpless wonder, unable to articulate further the things that he was thinking. "Are your... friends... still around?" he inquired at length, glancing around him and lowering his voice as if he were asking for classified information from an intelligence operative.

"Disappeared around midnight last night," Dave said.

"Well, if you ever run into them again, be sure to give them my regards," the pilot said. "Thanks again, and good luck!"

"One down on the good side of the ledger," Dave muttered as the pilot walked away.

"But here comes trouble again," Xander said in a low voice.

A corpulent man in a crumpled business suit, his hair in a severe crew-cut, stalked purposefully toward poor Luke. He was a head taller and twice as broad as Luke, and the hands that emerged from the sleeves of his suit jacket looked like small shovels; Xander, himself of a wiry build and looking like a child next to the approaching brute, felt an irrational urge to step out in front of Luke to protect him.

"You're Luke Barnes?"

"Y-yes," Luke said, unsure if it was entirely safe to admit this but resigned to the fact that his name tag confirmed his identity to whoever cared to establish it. "I'm Luke Barnes. How can I be of assistance?"

The man in the suit threw out one his massive hands, and Luke actually ducked away for an instant before he became aware that the hand in question was holding a business card that looked lost and tiny in the grip of those sausage-sized fingers.

"Thaddeus Smyrnoff, CEO of All Steel Incorporated and prisoner of this hotel for the past three days. I had a very important meeting with possible investors in my company on this past Saturday, the sole reason I had taken time off work to be in town, and I was prevented from being at this meeting by the staff of this hotel and other guests whose activities may have been a direct cause of my situation. You may consider this your first and only notification of my intent to sue this hotel and possibly the event it has been hosting this weekend for damages and loss of income. Good day to you, sir."

"The event...?" Luke echoed, blindsided.

Thaddeus Smyrnoff reached into his pocket and pulled out a crumpled and badly folded copy of Libby's Saturday newsletter – with ABDUCTICON plastered firmly across its title page.

"I have the evidence," he said. "I will be passing the details on to my lawyer."

He turned and stalked off, and Luke stared after his retreating back, open-mouthed, holding onto the business card by pure reflex.

"They're going to fire me now," he said, after a moment. "For sure."

Xander snorted. "Please. For all his huff and bluster, I'd like to see him go into any sane lawyer and offer up a case."

"Was he one of the doc's headcases?" Dave asked warily. "He might well have a case of claiming he was given sedatives or something..."

"Dave, it all falls down the moment someone chirps that we went to the Moon," Xander said. "No court in the land is going to take this seriously."

"But I saw people taking pictures," Luke said faintly. "I can't see them all disappearing. And if there's visual evidence..."

"Where there's photos there's Photoshop," Xander said. "And if it's video... you can CGI your way out of anything these days."

"You make it *all* sound so fake," Dave said unexpectedly, and a shade defensively.

Xander shrugged. "It's worse than that, it's *dead,* Jim. All you'd have to do is call The National Inquirer and give them an anonymous tip about how a whole hotel was, you know, *abducted by aliens* and taken on a joyride in the solar system over the course of a wild weekend. Which immediately makes a judge put it in the same folder with the case of the nun who swears she bore Elvis's love child. And after that, no 'real' news organization is going to touch it – except to point and laugh – and if the media don't treat it as 'real' news, the courts are hardly likely to take on something considered to be ridiculous. Judges take their dignity too seriously for that."

"But we did go," Dave said, suddenly reluctant to let go of the smallest incandescent iota of his out-of-planet experience.

Xander looked at him, eyes shining. "*And we all know that*," he said. "But there is, I suspect, precious little that anyone who is not One Of Us is going to believe if they are told the truth, the whole truth, and nothing but the truth about this weekend. That's the joy of it, in a way. It's ours, only ours, and nobody else believes. The truth is out there, it always has been, and we've seen the future, and man, I'm still high from all of it. And a little scared, to be sure – perhaps we know too much. But nothing will ever take this away from me. And it'll never…"

A gaggle of young con-goers, average age about twenty one, trooped past the trio at the door, and halted beside them. One of the group, his hair a vivid shade of green, turned to Xander with an expression of such glowing delight that it was impossible not to smile back, and Xander did, giving him a broad grin. Nothing more needed to be said, it was all understood between them, and it seemed to come as a direct validation of what Xander himself had just been saying. But then one of the group stepped up and stuck out his hand for Luke to shake – and the manager did so, instinctively, without quite knowing why.

"Thanks, man, you were great," the kid said enthusiastically. "It's a pretty cool hotel, this, I don't know how you pulled it all off – where are the droid dudes, anyway? – but you were really cool with it all. It's been the best con, ever. Um, do you know how to get in touch with those guys? I mean, can we do this again next year? That would just be frigging *awesome*."

"Probably not," Xander said. "We had our shot. But I know. They came to me, too. Awesome doesn't begin to describe it."

"There's always hope," said one of the other kids. "We'll be back next year anyway. Who knows who else might come along for the ride."

"My roommate was supposed to come, but had to cancel at the last minute, family emergency," a third one from the group crowed. "Man, is he going to be *steamed* he missed this one. Can't wait to tell him all about it."

Dave and Xander exchanged a quick glance, and then Dave shrugged, a defeated but delighted grin creeping across his features, and Xander merely gave the kid who had shaken Luke's hand a high five.

"Live long, and prosper," he said. "Whatever happens after, you'll always have this weekend. Just remember, it's a memory, not a dream."

He got back an enthusiastic fist-pump in response and then they were gone – and Luke was drawn away for a moment by another arriving ambulance and, this time, the good doctor from the Asylum Floor steering a bleary-eyed but still ambulatory patient across the lobby toward the main doors. While they were discussing the matter, another group approached from the general direction of the gamers' ballroom. Several of them were wearing what looked like clean t-shirts, but a couple of them had just pulled on crumpled hoodies over clothes they had not changed out of all weekend, tucked away in the gamers' room and their own world.

"Hey, Dave," one of them said, squinting at Dave and Xander from a couple of paces away and recognizing at least one face. "How'd the con do? Andie Mae happy?"

"It, uh…." Dave began, and Xander offered up a wide grin.

"How did the game go?"

"Oh, you know," the gamer said. "Intense. Pretty good."

"Hah," said a mate from the back of the group smugly. "I *smeared* you in that fight. Rolled a sixteen in strength, fifteen in dexterity, you were so out of it, dude…"

It was obviously a sore point because they began to re-argue the encounter all over again, touching on which one of them must have cheated, and one of the others pointedly lifted an eyebrow in their direction and then turned back to Dave.

"The pizza was great this year," he said. "You know. Really good. Did you change the pizza place? You should *so* keep these new guys on for next time. Seriously."

"He remembers the *pizza*? From last year? Seriously?" Xander muttered to himself.

Dave shot him a warning glance, but was himself hunting for the right thing to say – and after a moment, lamely, came up with,

"I, uh, I think they're closing down at the end of the year…"

"Pity," said the gamer.

"So then, how did you like the Moon flight?" Xander said, knowing he was tossing out bait but unable to stop himself from doing so.

"I don't think I played *that* game," the gamer said, furrowing his brow. Xander hadn't followed the discussion of whether he had won or lost on that throw of the dice, but the combatants seemed to have sorted it out between themselves or at least arrived at a truce. "What game was that scenario in? We weren't doing a straight SF thing – it was more of a…"

"The guys on the other table were talking about Alpha Centauri," said one of the others helpfully.

"Maybe I'll try that Moon game next year, then, " the first gamer said, waving as he walked away. "See you the next go-round!"

"They missed it," Xander muttered, staring after the departing clutch of gamers. "They missed the whole thing. The whole, entire thing. They *missed* it."

"Speaking of those pizzas," Dave said, turning to Xander, "what actually happened to the replicators?"

"If you're talking about the food machines, both of the ones in the kitchens are just *gone*," Luke said, rejoining the conversation. "Sometime last night, it would seem at the very least, I got the report this morning. Staff turned up and found a very ordinary kitchen once again – breakfast was made the old fashioned way, and supplies barely lasted. I should actually go and talk to our delivery people; we need to replenish our larders pretty smartly."

"Aren't you off duty *yet*?" Dave asked, teasingly but with genuine warmth. For somebody who was thrown into the deep end, Luke Barnes had not done too badly – and had certainly come out sane at the other end, instead of ending up on Dr. Cohen's Asylum Floor right along with the other patients who had sought refuge in a fit of the vapors.

"I am supposed to hand over the reins in about an hour, when the new shift turns up. And then I plan to sleep for three days. And then really figure out just how much I can tell of what actually happened and still keep this job," Luke said.

"You still want to keep the job? What about the next time…?"

Luke gave him a tired smile. "Well, now I know how to rescue people from a stuck elevator," he said. "Flying to the Moon for the second time would just be a bonus."

"You're a good egg," Xander said. "If you need backup for anything, with your bosses, give us a holler. We'll be happy to give you a good report."

"Thanks. Appreciate it. Maybe someday someone could sit down and try and convince me that any of this really happened... or if I just ate something bad on Friday morning and simply hallucinated this entire weekend..."

"I'll drop in for a cup of coffee or something the next time you're on duty," Xander said. "We can reminisce."

Luke looked both pleased and a little frightened at this prospect, but shook hands with both Dave and Xander and hurried back behind the reception counter and then out of sight into the office behind it. Dave sighed, and began to turn away.

"Well, I better see if the GoH people need anything at departure..."

"You found Rory, in the end?"

"In point of fact, no. Haven't seen him, oh, since Saturday night, really – caught sight of him at one of the Moon parties, having the time of his life. He's been pretty much AWOL since then – there's been one reported sighting on Sunday but apparently he wasn't in a socializing mood at that point and after that he seems to have remembered what room was his and how to lock the door to exclude the rest of the world because that suite's been locked down tight. I sent Simon around a couple of times, on patrol, just in case, but not a stir in there."

"Dead drunk, or just dead...?"

"Well, he was due to check out this morning, so if there's no movement in the next half hour or so I may need to get housekeeping to open the door for me, just to make sure he is okay," Dave said. "And Vince..."

Xander interrupted him by suddenly reaching out to grip his arm. "Is that Al...?"

Dave squinted at the disheveled figure pushing open the doors into the lobby with one arm while cradling the other in a blue nylon sling, and frowned.

"Looks like," he said. "But dear God – that bruise on his face – the arm – he looks terrible! Like some small war chewed him up and spit him out. Did we *land* on him?"

Al Coe noticed Dave and Xander at about the same moment they became aware of him, and after a hesitation he let the door close behind him and stepped towards them.

The question that was asked, by Al in one direction and by Xander in the other, consisted of exactly the same words – but Al emphasized one word and Xander another, and Xander's tone was one of appalled curiosity while Al's was more a bewildered resignation.

"What *happened* to you?" Al asked.

"What happened to *you*?" Xander said in exactly the same moment.

"Where's Andie Mae? Is she all right?" Al asked, allowing a wan smile to wash over his face at the greeting ritual.

"She's… fine," Xander said. That covered a lot of ground, and there were things that Andie Mae really should tell Al herself if she wanted him to know about them. "But you look like you've done a week in the trenches."

"Someone creamed my car, on my way back to the hotel from the printer, with the posters," Al said. "You know, for Spiner and Schwarzenegger. They turned up, you know."

"Actually you look rather like the Terminator did work you over," Xander said. "Wait, they came? To this… to where? What happened?"

"Are you okay? Really?" Dave asked.

"Well, there were moments," Al said. "When I was perfectly certain I was going stark stir crazy. I came to this place *three times* this weekend, guys. This hotel just wasn't here. And it insisted on trying to trick me into thinking that it never was here in the first place. But I have evidence," he added darkly, patting his pocket with his good hand. "I have pictures. Right here. Something really strange was going on, or else I really was suffering from complete terminal concussion…"

"D'you need a cup of coffee?" Xander said. "You look like you could use one. Come on up to Con Ops and I'll scrounge something up for you – and Andie Mae could be there by now, and if not they'll know where to find her."

"Sure," Al said. "Okay."

Xander lifted a hand in a parting gesture and then fell into step beside Al as they walked towards the stairwell of Tower 1.

"Sorry," Dave heard Xander say as the two walked away from him, "but it's got to be the stairs – there was an incident with the elevators in that wing – one of them tried to kill me…"

The lobby was getting increasingly crowded, people were bustling about with suitcases and coats and hats and bags, some just trying to make a clean getaway, others waving credit cards at receptionists behind the counter as they tried to settle their accounts before leaving. Three cabs idled outside, waiting for their fares. People stood in knots out under the portico, talking animatedly over piles of luggage or enthusiastically hugging their farewells. Several waved at Dave as they caught his eye, and he waved back, smiling a tired smile.

He almost missed one of his Guests of Honor in the milling mob of people in the lobby, but a tap on his shoulder made him turn inquiringly… to face a rather worse-for-wear Rory Grissom, dressed in mundane clothing and dragging a large, battered suitcase behind him. His eyes were red and boasted bags underneath them that could probably have doubled as storage pouches if Rory had needed extra luggage, and his color was high, but he seemed to have at least made the acquaintance of a comb that morning and he certainly did not look too unhappy about what Dave surmised must have been an absolutely cosmic hangover headache.

"Thanks for the memories," Rory said. "Do me a favor…?"

"You need a ride?"

"No, got that sorted. No, something else. I… seem to have mislaid one of my boots."

"I beg your pardon?"

"One of my boots. That is to say, one of Captain Fleming's boots. My *Invictus* costume. I've got one of the boots, but the other one seems to have gone walkabout – so if you'd keep an eye out – or tell the hotel to – it looks just like this one – " He took a somewhat crumpled publicity shot out of his pocket and thrust it at Dave, tapping with his finger at one of his silver-booted legs in the photo. "I mean, that is to say, I couldn't locate it in my room when I was throwing my stuff together, and I, um, er, it could be in several other different locations – so if it should be found, I would appreciate a heads-up…"

"I'll let them know," Dave said.

"Custom made," Rory said. "Can't just buy another off a catalogue. Well, I could, there's a catalogue that does sell uniforms out of all the big shows – you could buy any togs you want to there – but this one was, kind of, unique, mine, you know? Not out of the catalogue. I had it specially made, the whole uniform. It's a perfect replica. I really don't want to lose…"

"Don't worry. I think I can safely say that a silver boot will pretty much overwhelmingly stand out in the usual mess of a hotel's lost and found box. I'll make sure they know to look for it."

"Thanks. Appreciate it. Helluva party. Thanks for having me."

"Thanks for coming along," Dave said.

Rory lifted one semi-nerveless hand and maneuvered his mammoth piece of luggage out of the door.

Dave took the few steps that separated him from the reception counter and leaned on the polished wood. A blonde girl behind the counter looked up as he did so, and smiled.

"Anything I can do for you?"

"I don't suppose you know if anyone found a single silver boot from a superhero uniform lurking somewhere in the shadows?"

In the Con Ops suite, the population had thinned out, and some of the computer stations had already been dismantled and packed away, while others were in the process of being logged off and wound down. Libby's usual station was still up, but she was not present; at a glance, Xander could not see Andie Mae either, but he sat Al down in a clear spot on one of the sofas pushed into a corner and went to make coffee, the usual way, sparing a quick regretful thought for the replicator which had vanished from this room as well. It was hard to have one's nose rubbed into the future and then having the door slammed into one's face and being told one wasn't ready for any of it yet. Xander felt he himself, at least, was plenty ready for a functioning replicator.

"Is it still as awful as Andie Mae said it was?"

"What was that?" Xander said, turning his head marginally from the coffee machine.

"The coffee. She told me to bring some *good* coffee, because the hotel stuff was terrible. I never did make it – I didn't bring any with me even now – "

"Oh, I wouldn't worry about it," Xander said carefully. "The coffee situation… was the least of our worries, in the end." Something outside the room caught his attention even as the last of those words left his mouth, and his head swiveled to the door. "Excuse me a sec, I'll be right back."

He didn't quite know what he had seen, or heard – but he had a feeling that Andie Mae was just outside. He was right, as it happened, but he didn't quite expect to almost run her down as he stepped out into the corridor just as Andie Mae, who had paused to speak to someone, turned to go into the room .

"Hey, slow down, where's the fire?" Andie Mae protested, fending him off, side-stepping him to get to the door of the suite. Xander flung out an arm to stop her.

"Wait – I wanted to give you a heads-up – Al's back, he's in there, and he looks somewhat battered. Not sure what happened. He said he was in an accident. He's also talking about 'evidence' he's got in his pocket, about this place going AWOL for the weekend, and I just thought – you'd better not blunder in there blind – given what happened – "

"Given *what* happened?" Andie Mae asked sharply.

"Well, you kind of had a fling with Boss," Xander said sheepishly. "Such as it was. And I thought…"

"Whose boss?"

That was Al's voice, unexpected, from the doorway. Andie Mae looked blue daggers at Xander, who dropped his hand in resignation.

"I was just trying to help," he said.

Andie Mae and Al stood staring at each other for a long moment, and then she sighed. "You'd better come to my room," she said. "It isn't what you think. Or what you're spinning in your head right now. Long story, long and complicated, and it looks like you've got one to fling right back at me."

"I've got coffee…" Xander began, but Andie Mae quelled him with another look.

"I have coffee in my room," she said. "And please don't send Simon to rescue me again, okay?"

"*Rescue* you?" Al echoed blankly.

"Just come on," Andie Mae said. "Can you manage the stairs? What in God's name did you do to your arm?"

When she was in this sort of mood, nobody argued with her. Xander stepped back into the suite without another word, and Al meekly followed where Andie Mae led.

On her way up the stairs, she was already having second thoughts about the venue she had chosen, given that the events of which she had to tell Al had actually transpired in the very same room in which they were about to be confessed to – and this would occur to Al himself eventually, with unpredictable consequences. Andie Mae led the way in silence, rehearsing her story in her head, coming to the conclusion that the best defense was possibly opening with a salvo that deflected attention. It was in the spirit of this, then, that she pointed Al to a seat as they walked into her room and turned to busy herself with the coffee machine on the counter.

"So, then," she said, before he had a chance to do more than carefully collapse into an armchair, taking care not to jostle his arm. "I was actually on the point of phoning the hospitals and the police. What *happened* to you?"

"If you'd phoned Mercy General Hospital, they probably would have told you. On the way back to the hotel – I was coming straight from the printers, with just one detour on the way – some idiot with a black SUV rammed me at an intersection. Quite aside from *this* – " he indicated the sling with a toss of his head – "… which was quite enough by and of itself, but on top of that, I seem to have temporarily lost my marbles somewhat, as well as my phone and those wretched posters, which were all apparently in the car when the wreck was towed. By the time I staggered over here… there was no hotel to be found."

Andie Mae kept her eyes on the coffee pot. "How do you mean?"

"I mean it wasn't here, dammit, Andie Mae," Al said. "*That* many marbles, I hadn't lost. I had the address. The cab dropped me where you should have been. But you were not there. How about your turn, now? How did you manage to spirit away an entire hotel?"

"Who said it was spirited away?" Andie Mae asked carefully.

"I may be a fool sometimes, but I'm still quite sane and sensible when it comes to the things I can judge using empirical evidence," Al said. "I said it was spirited away and I meant exactly that. I helped you scout this place, remember? I know where the walls had been standing. And said walls were noticeably absent. And what's more those walls seemed to have developed a vested interest in convincing me that they had never been there at all, really. The more I looked at the place where I should have been seeing the hotel, the less I could remember there having been a building there at all in the first place. It was as though there was something – I don't know – a veil, and beyond that I could not look."

"Not in Kansas anymore, Toto," Andie Mae murmured.

"What?"

"No, you're right, I'm sorry. The best I can come up with is something that someone came up with in the control room after we… afterwards. There was an SEP field in play, down there."

"Down where?" Al said, confused.

Andie Mae sighed. "It's hard to explain," she said.

"Yes, tell me about it. It was really hard to explain when your two actors showed up…"

"They came?" Andie Mae yelped, her eyes widening and snapping to meet Al's.

"Of course they *came*, all the arrangements had already been made," Al said with a touch of impatience. "But they seemed as confused as I was. So I told them they were there for a charity photo shoot and actually they were very good sports about it – I have a photo of them shaking hands, standing there on the bluff, and then one with me with both of them – but that's just the thing – those photos – where's your computer?"

Andie Mae indicated the bed with a toss of her head. "The laptop's under the bed. That's where I usually stash it when I leave it in the room, remember?"

Al rooted around in his pocket with his good hand and came up with a USB stick, flourishing it in Andie Mae's direction. "I've got something to show you," he said. "Bring it over here."

Andie Mae retrieved the laptop and set it up on the low table in front of Al, leaving it to boot up while she went to deal with the coffee, which had announced that it was done by a series of melodious chirps from the coffee machine. By the time she came back with two mugs and placed one within reach of Al's uninjured arm, he had already plugged in his flash drive into the laptop and was tapping something out slowly and laboriously with his good hand. And then, after staring at the screen for a moment while waiting for his photos to come up, he finally turned the machine towards Andie Mae.

"There. Look."

She stared at the photograph on the screen for so long that Al actually reached out and turned the laptop fractionally back toward himself to check that she was actually looking at the right thing. Andie Mae tore her eyes from the screen at that point and settled back onto her haunches where she had been kneeling on the floor beside the table.

"I was wondering what it all had to have looked like, at Ground Zero," she said. "Weird."

"*Weird?*" Al exploded. "That's all you've got? There's a great big honking charred hole in the ground where the hotel was supposed to be… and none of us noticed it or could see it… and we all acted like we'd been fed happy pills for a week… and then everyone shook hands and went home and it's only after I looked at the pictures that I saw the reality behind the illusion screen – and what did you mean, SEP?"

"That's apparently what they set up," Andie Mae said faintly. "The androids."

"The androids? You're telling me that you think that it was Spiner and…"

"No. Real androids." Andie Mae lifted her eyes from the computer screen and back to Al's face. "They flew us to the Moon."

Al stared at her in silence.

Andie Mae's eyes filled with unexpected tears. "I was so *worried*," she said. "I didn't know *what* had happened to you – and then – well – look, this is going to sound totally unhinged. I know. But while you were out with those stupid posters… they turned up. The androids. Four of them. They had alphanumeric names like one of your high-security passwords, but Xander renamed them so that we could actually remember a name by which we could tell them apart – and they turned into Zach, Bob, Helen... and Boss."

"Boss," Al said. He seemed to have developed a nasty habit of repeating everything that Andie Mae said, but couldn't seem to stop it. "This was the boss Xander just blabbed about?...The one that you... How do you have a *fling* with a robot?"

Andie Mae flushed a bright scarlet, and took a sip of her coffee to hide it.

Al said, "The Moon. They flew you to the Moon. What the hell does that mean?"

"It means they quite literally... wait a minute. I have pictures too."

She put down her coffee cup and hauled out her phone, tapping on the screen and then sliding around photos with her finger until she found one she wanted and handed the phone to Al.

"Here," she said. "look." She tapped on the screen with her finger as he took the phone from her and stared at a picture of Andie Mae standing in front of the windows in Callahan's Bar, with the Moon filling what should have been just open sky behind her. "The Moon. They literally *took us to the Moon*. The whole hotel, I mean. Picked it up and flew it out..."

"Andie Mae," Al said, "that's ridiculous."

"Look harder," she said. "I suppose I might have faked that at some point, in all the copious spare time I had while this convention was up and running and I had everything to prove from the Chair – but look harder. It may not be obvious, but what don't you recognize in that photo?"

Al's eyes flickered from her face to the photo and then back again. "I don't get it," he said. "What?"

"That's the dark side," Andie Mae said. "That's the *other side of the Moon*, Al. The side you don't see from down here. That's where we were. That's where we went. That's where they took us. Cross my heart and hope to die, that's what happened."

"And then you had a fling with the boss?" Al said.

"Nothing happened," Andie Mae said. "And if he was still here, he'd tell you the same thing. And you know androids don't lie."

Al put the phone down very slowly and very carefully.

"You're seriously expecting me to believe that extraterrestrial androids came swooping down and ripped a hotel out of the ground and just flew you to the Moon?" Al said.

Andie Mae got to her feet again and rummaged in a teetering pile of paper that was stacked messily on the corner of the desk, finally coming up with hot-pink sheet of paper which she then held out to Al.

"That was Libby's take," she said. "That was Friday night's newsletter. *Welcome to Abducticon.* We had a doctor who was running what Xander insisted on calling the Asylum Floor, for all the poor mundanes cracking up under it all, and there were at least three ambulances taking the poor confused souls out of here this morning after we landed again last night. And we had replicators. And we had *real live androids* who seemed to have come here to look for their ancestor gods, or something. And oh, *God*, Al, where the hell were you? You missed it *all!*"

"I made a detour," Al said softly. "I stopped… at that place you liked… you said you wanted coffee. And then I was really late. And maybe I was careless. And then the other car hit me, and then everything went to hell."

She came back to where he was sitting and subsided on the arm of the chair in which he was slumped.

"You got me coffee?" she asked gently.

"I forgot it in the car," Al said.

Andie Mae unexpectedly leaned in and wrapped her arms around him, being very careful not to jostle the arm in the sling, and planted a kiss on the top of his head.

"I love you, so very much, right now," she whispered. "I'm so sorry."

His good arm crept up and snaked around her waist. And then, against her shoulder, he murmured,

"Androids? A *fling*…? The Moon…?"

Downstairs, in the busy lobby area still teeming with people in the process of post-con departure from the hotel, Marius had taken himself out of the main throng by parking himself and a small suitcase at a booth in the breakfast restaurant. He had a cup of coffee on the table beside his open laptop, at which he was staring without any indication that it was performing any remotely useful task. But whatever it *was* doing was apparently very much occupying his mind because he jumped, startled, when he felt a tap on his shoulder that apparently came from the potted plant he was sitting next to. Upon a second look, the potted plant resolved itself into Vince Silverman, and Marius sat up sharply, straightening his shoulders.

"Hey, kid," Vince said. "Just on the way to collect the wife, and then we're on our way. Did I give you one of these?"

He was holding out a business card, and Marius reached out over the foliage to take it.

"Sam did say you wanted to write," Vince said. "If I can help, email me."

"Thanks!" Marius said, a little astonished but nonetheless enthusiastic at the opportunity that had just landed in his lap. "If you're sure that's okay, I'll do that!"

"There you go, then. Good luck with the writing. And listen – about that fourth law of robotics… the one you came up with…"

"I was noodling around an idea," Marius said with a grin. "Truth be said, you came up with the 'law' version of it."

"Still. Your ideas," Vince said. "Do you mind if I used that? I could call it the Tarkovski Corollary or something, credit where credit is due."

"You'd put me in one of your books?" Marius said, grinning.

"And why not? As we've just proved, this weekend that was, life *is* just science fiction, when you think about it, really."

Marius's smile slipped a little. "Yeah. I know."

"They left a message," Vince said, dropping his voice just a little. "Let me know… if they call you back, would you?"

Marius held his gaze, searching Vince's eyes with his own, and then looked back down onto his computer. "Sure," he said softly. "Okay."

"Got to go. Angel's not good at waiting. Nice to have met you. Sorry about the elevator."

Vince straightened from where he'd been half leaning over the potted plant, raised his hand in a gesture of farewell, and turned away.

Moments later Marius was startled again as someone slipped into the booth opposite him. He snapped his head around to look, and met Xander's sharp gaze.

"And what did *he* want?" Xander asked. "He was actually smirking at one point."

"I think that's just the way he smiles," Marius said. "He wanted to ask me if he could use that 'Fourth Law of Robotics' idea we were knocking around at dinner last night. Before we…"

"Yeah," Xander said. "Thought any more about that?"

"I think… he left me a message," Marius said, in what was almost a whisper. "Boss, I mean."

Xander leaned forward over his crossed arms. "A message? How? What is it?"

"That's just it. I have no idea. I almost tossed it as spam, but it wouldn't let itself be deleted and then I thought it might be some sort of weird virus thing and then I took another look and – well – see for yourself."

He turned the laptop around so that it faced Xander, and Xander reached out to pull it closer to himself, studying what was on the screen.

"I don't recognize…" he began, and Marius lifted both his hands from the table in exasperated agreement.

"Exactly. I don't recognize. Neither does the computer. It's something that I don't have the software for, or it's super encrypted in a way I have no way of unlocking, or any number of stuff like that. I don't know what it is, I don't know where it came from, all I know is that it's there and it won't leave."

"But how do you know it isn't just a weird bug?" Xander said.

Marius motioned for the computer, and Xander pushed it back across the table; Marius tapped a few keys, waited for a moment, and then turned the screen back to Xander.

"Because of *that*," he said.

The open email on the screen bore just an alphanumeric string as its subject line – an alphanumeric string that, for a moment, was completely random to Xander. But then his rebus-solving back brain sprang into action, and he suddenly recognized the sequence. His eyes snapped back over the screen, sought Marius's gaze.

"ZVL5559AD4," he said. "That's… I remember that was… that's Boss, isn't it?"

"Read it," Marius said. "That bit of it – that's just an email. A perfectly ordinary common email that could have come from anybody. But read it."

Xander looked back on the screen again. "*When you are ready, you will know what lies within.*"

"The thing you were looking at was the attachment," Marius said. "Encrypted, encoded, something. And I'm guessing the key hasn't been invented yet."

"What are you going to do with it?" Xander asked carefully.

"I'm considering reformatting the hard drive," Marius admitted, with a rueful shrug. "Except I'm not sure that if I did that then the only thing left on this hard drive afterwards would be *this* thing. If I scrap this computer and get a brand new one out of the box… the only thing that would be on *that* drive, before I even put an OS on it, would be this thing. In the worst possible way it *is* a virus, but it's attached to me, in a sense, and it'll infect any computer through me if I tried to get rid of a computer it's already on. This is something… that is written, and that history already has a record of, and it's fixed, it's all fixed. I told you, I've already done… whatever it is that I am going to do. It's entirely possible that the future is the only thing that will unlock this thing, in time, whatever it is. And the *worst* of it is…"

"What?"

"I've… dreamed about the first ideas…" Marius shook his head. "No, that sounds insane."

Xander offered a small smile. "Name one thing that happened this weekend that meets our general definition of something sane," he said. "I might easily be convinced that I too have in fact 'dreamed' – that I dreamt it all, that none of it really happened. Except for the inexplicable pictures on my phone. And the memory of that panel. And him, the Boss. And you. That was… real. As real as it gets."

"I won't be able to *not* do it," Marius said helplessly. "Not now. Not now that I've met them."

"Well," Xander said, crossing his arms and leaning back, "it's unlikely that we'll live to see the 25th century and whatever happens then according to the Gospel according to Boss – the human migration, whatever. And by that stage it will be well out of your own hands, anyway."

"But I'll begin it," Marius whispered. "I don't know if these first glimmerings of ideas are going to have to come to something reasonably concrete before I figure out how to open this attachment, or whether at some point everything will just reach a critical mass and what's in there will help me take the final step…"

"If that's the case, then they're really inventing themselves and you're just the middleman," Xander said. "But I didn't get that feeling from Boss. He seemed to think that you're going to be…"

"That he's going to be what?" inquired Sam, who walked up to the table just in time to hear the last snatch of that conversation.

"We were just discussing what we wanted to be when we grew up," Xander said. "And as far as I am concerned, I am going to take a vow of silence concerning this entire conversation." He slipped out of the booth, and hovered for a moment beside Sam before finally sticking out a hand to be shaken. "I'm glad you were here, for what it's worth. It just wouldn't have seemed fair, your being the Chair of this con for so many years and then missing *this* the year that you stepped down."

"Was pushed," Sam said, lightly but pointedly. "But, yeah. Thanks. I know what you mean. This year was a kind of a gift, really. I figure if Andie Mae could navigate through this, she can probably handle any problems that our poor old Earth can throw in her direction."

"Well, I'd better go," Xander said. "Loose ends. End of con. You know how it goes."

"I know how it goes," Sam said. "Good luck."

Xander raised his hand in a half wave that bade farewell to both of them and sauntered off. Sam took his place in the booth, perching on the end of the bench and leaning his elbow on the table.

"Well," he inquired of Marius, turning to face him and resting his chin in his hand, "are you ready…?"

Marius stared at his laptop for another long moment before sucking in his breath and then letting it out in a long deep sigh as he tabbed his email software closed and brought the screen down over his keyboard.

"No," he said. "But faith manages."

Sam tilted his head and looked at him, and for a disconcerting instant it was like looking down the tunnel of the future and he could clearly see the man this boy would become… and all the things that he would do. But then Marius happened to look up, and caught the unexpected and flirtatious glance of a pretty brunette still clad in a body-hugging, glitter-spangled con costume across the top of the potted plant, and flushed a bright scarlet, looking away again. And he was still, again, unquestionably, the boy.

Whatever would come, would come. The legacy of an android named Boss… would keep. And it was Monday. Abducticon – the magical, the unexpected, the luminous, the overwhelming – was over.

"Come on, kid. Time to go home," he said.

The day's newspapers had been delivered, albeit belatedly, and Sam glanced at the headlines as they walked past the pile of them on top of the reception counter – just the usual mess of politics and inane celebrity gossip, no mention of an entire hotel inexplicably vanishing off the face of the Earth, quite literally as it happened, unless it was a squib of a story buried on page 3. Outside, as Sam and Marius stepped out from under the mother-of-pearl inlaid portico over the main entrance, the sun hung in a washed-out autumn sky. For a moment, a heart-stopping moment, Marius thought he saw that sunlight glinting off something amongst the cars in the parking lot – something that might have been a metallic flash, a glimpse of silver skin, as though the androids were back, and watching him – but there was nothing there, of course, when he looked closer.

It was… it might have been… just another ordinary day, just another Monday.

But it wasn't. Not really. It would never be 'just another Monday' again.

Marius tucked his laptop more securely under his arm, and then, as his hand fell back down to his side, it brushed past his pocket and a small object tucked safely inside. His Rosetta stone, the first word on the blank page on which he would end up writing the future history of his world… a severed Finger of the Gods which had pointed straight at him, singled him out, made him a whole different human being than he had been when he had walked into the hotel on the morning of Friday last. A small and cryptic smile hovering on the corners of his mouth, he stepped out into that future, and into the light.

APPENDIX: WHAT THE MESSAGE SAID

MESSAGE IN THREE PARTS

PART ONE – DATELINE 3 NOVEMBER 2076

UNPUBLISHED FOREWORD TO "THE BIRTH OF MECHANICAL MAN" BY DR. MARIUS TARKOVSKI (BOOK PUBLISHED 15 MAY 2078)

Looking back on a long and hopefully well-lived life, anybody would eventually ask a question about regrets. Was there anything you might have regretted doing, or not doing, or doing sooner rather than later, or choosing to embrace or to walk away from? The seeds of my answers to that lie in one single extraordinary weekend in 2014 when I was seventeen years old, and the hand of God reached out and pushed me into the future. Quite literally.

Let me explain.

That weekend, I was taken along to a science fiction convention by a man who was an elder in the writing group to which I belonged to at the time, Sam Dutton. I was there, almost on my own, the air redolent with an adult freedom, but still too young to realize that I did not know everything.

That was the year they came, the four androids who said they were from our future. They said that they had come searching for their origins, for their creator. Nobody was completely clear about why they would be doing this at a science fiction convention when there were so many places where they could have gone, so many people whom they could have tapped, so many great and intelligent and incisively insightful researchers into the field of robotics which was only just in its infancy at that time. But they chose us, this convention, this particular crowd of crazy fen (as the multiplicity of science fiction fans referred to themselves) and somehow we ended up – all of us, complete with the hotel we were staying in – being taken for a joyride around the Moon.

I still remember that night, the night we rounded the Moon, as though it was yesterday instead of seven decades ago. I remember something deep and full of awe stirring in my heart. It was a moment that has been the yardstick against which I have always measured wonder, and nothing at all has ever really managed to hold a candle to it. That night was their gift to us, although I don't even remember now, not any more, why it happened that way, why the Moon was a part of it all. Looking back, it seems almost impossible for me to believe the smug complacency, almost, with which we all responded to it then – we barely believed it, to be sure, but we nonetheless took it as our due, and accepted it, and threw a revel for it, and partied the night away.

I felt let down, almost cheated, at the way that this transcendent experience was completely ignored by the rest of the oblivious world. To this day I fail to understand how it was that an entire hotel – the physical building, and all within it – could be literally kidnapped from the face of the Earth on a Friday without even a single newspaper headline mentioning the fact on the Monday that followed. But that is what happened. In our day, in the years that followed, nobody knew, nobody cared – and my speaking about it now could be treated as a work of science fiction.

Back then, the writer Vincent Silverman and I and one of the ConCom people, a young man by the name of Alexander Washington, ended up together in an elevator that failed – and had to be rescued out of the precariously hanging elevator car by one of those very androids who had taken us along for the ride to the Moon. I was the last in the elevator, waiting for my turn to climb out of the top hatch and clamber up a fragile little ladder up into the corridor of the hotel, when one of the cables of the elevator failed and came smashing down on top of the car with deadly force. The android who had been on the roof, helping people out, had jumped into the car with me as the cable came down, avoiding being smeared flat by it when it smashed into the place where he had been standing – down with me, into what was a pitch-dark cabin to which power had been cut to effect our rescue.

We were both brought down onto our knees as the elevator car shuddered from the impact. I scrambled around on all fours on the floor of that elevator, full of debris and shattered pieces of sharp plastic from what had been the roof panels, when my hand stumbled on something round and smooth, something that I somehow knew even then could not have been just a simple piece of junk from the smashed-up elevator. I instinctively picked it up and put it into the pocket of my jeans before I was helped out to safety.

It was only then that I saw the hand of the android who had been in the elevator with me.

And realized that the cable accident had severed several fingers on one hand.

And knew, immediately and surely, just what it was that I had in my pocket.

I remember, also, the panel discussion to which we all went immediately after this incident, where the chief of the androids ended up answering questions from the audience. They were difficult questions, sometimes, and I will never forget the answer that he gave to one of them – an answer that I knew to be a falsehood, something that I had believed it was impossible for an android to do. But this one told us something that was not true, because the truth was not something that we could have handled, perhaps. Whatever his reasons, he lied.

He did something else.

Not in so many words, but in ways that only I could truly understand, the android whom we had named 'Boss' gave me the knowledge that it was I, myself, whom they had come to seek. That they had not, perhaps, known this when they arrived at the same convention which I was at, or even when they set out to get here. Time paradoxes abounded, many of which played havoc with my mind and my imagination even back then, many of which I have never adequately worked out to my own satisfaction. But there were several things that seemed clear enough.

I had that finger. It would serve to point me – quite literally, here – in the right direction. I would somehow end up using the knowledge I gleaned from this artifact to become in effect the father of the android race, of the very creatures who had come there on that day. That any choice I might have had in doing or not doing this thing had already been taken from me – because, by the very virtue of their being present in that space and that time and being able to come and speak to me at all, at some point in my future life I had already accomplished this thing and built, or created, or caused to be born, the primitive robots who would become these androids' ancestors.

At the time, of course, I had no idea at all as to how I would go about accomplishing this thing, and I had very ambivalent feelings about even attempting to. But in the end I did not know enough, and so I embarked on the task that had been set for me. The rest – all the years that followed, about which you will be reading in this book – is now history.

I do wonder what would have happened if I had not been there on that weekend. Would they have come anyway? Could they have done so, if I had not invented their predecessors? Would they have turned up somewhere else entirely, trying to nudge some other human mind into the waters into which they ultimately guided mine? Would our entire future have been completely different?

Boss said to us, at that time, that our planet would be abandoned and bereft of human life by the year 2400. It is difficult to believe that we are almost a quarter of the way to that year from the beginning of this millennium, at the time I write these lines. I will certainly not live to see whether this is our true future, or if something that we did – I, and the androids who came back in time to us to 2014 – changed the destiny of my people, and my world. All I can say, from this end of my life, from here and now as I know it, that I did what I believed I needed to do, I had to do, and if ever it is proved that my belief is in error I can only ask forgiveness of all of you who remain behind me, human and mechanical alike, all of you to whom I leave my legacy.

Regrets? Yes, I have a few. I will not say that I have never been in love, but I have never married, never had children, because my androids were my family, in the end, and they needed all that I had to give. These might look like they're large regrets, and deep, but they are not. It has been said that indulging in regrets means that you regret the very life you have been given… and I cannot bring myself to admit to this. I was what I was. I hope history will judge me accordingly. And, as evidence, I offer this book, the most true and faithful account I can offer about the birth of the mechanical man, over which it has been my burden and my privilege to preside.

As for the legacy I leave behind, you, the readers of this book, the generations that follow until we do or do not leave this world for another… you will have to decide if it was worthy.

Dr. Marius Tarkovski, San Francisco, 3 November 2076

PART TWO – DATELINE 4 DECEMBER 2080
OBITUARY DR. MARIUS TARKOVSKI

Dr. Marius Tarkovski PhD DSc, Professor Emeritus of Robotics at Princeton University and the University of the Pacific Rim, passed away peacefully in his sleep in the early hours of the morning of December 4. He leaves behind no immediate family except a godson, Marcus Washington. There will be a memorial for Dr. Tarkovski in the Eternal Rest Funeral Home at 10:30 AM on 12 December 2080 (attendance by mechanical entities welcome). Donations to the Tarkovski Foundation for Robotics Research are suggested in lieu of flowers. The eminent scientist and academic Dr. Tarkovski is best known for his pioneering role in the science of robotics, which he largely guided in achieving its full potential, and is credited with the creation of the first fledgling AI sentient entities created by human hand. Full obituary and overview of Dr. Tarkovski's life and career will appear in the site within 24 hours.

PART THREE – DATELINE 11 NOVEMBER 2014

We discovered the fragment of the foreword of the famous book that you will have written after we came to the convention and met you face to face – it was not part of our initial research. Do not be misled by the dateline on this part of the message. Yes, this is the day after the convention we attended has concluded, and we have returned to our own time, but the date on this message reflects merely the date on which you originally received it. Do not be alarmed. No paradoxes were triggered.

This message has been coded so that you would have gained the means to open it only after you passed your 80th birthday and before your death in 2080 – we believed it was important that you are in possession of this information, even as to the precise date of your own death, but after any point at which knowledge of these things might have affected your choices and life decisions.

You wrote the foreword, but chose not to publish it with the book, and it was discovered in obscure digital storage and memory banks centuries later. The current version (enclosed) has been pieced together from several more or less badly degraded versions in existence. We hope that it will help clarify some of your own thoughts for you – even though you may have already written your own original version of this *foreword by the time you receive this message from what is at the time of its receipt your future.*

Know this: your kind has not vanished. At the time of this message, in your very distant future, humans live. We have no contact with them, and they would not recognize us as having been created by them, and they would probably be frightened and distressed at the idea — our kindreds have been sundered for too many generations. But it appears to have mattered to you a great deal as to how your own choices affected your future and the future of your species and your descendants, and it therefore matters to those of us who share the same opinions as myself that you should be made aware of your legacy. That you made a difference. That you mattered, to not one but two sapient species who travelled amongst the stars.

We, your children and your distant descendants, offer our deep respects, and our grateful thanks.

ZVL5559AD4 (whom you met and knew long ago now for you, as "Boss")

About the Author

Alma Alexander's life so far has prepared her very well for her chosen career. She was born in a country which no longer exists on the maps, has lived and worked in seven countries on four continents (and in cyberspace!), has climbed mountains, dived in coral reefs, flown small planes, swum with dolphins, touched two-thousand-year-old tiles in a gate out of Babylon. She is a novelist, anthologist and short story writer who currently shares her life between the Pacific Northwest of the USA (where she lives with her husband and two cats) and the wonderful fantasy worlds of her own imagination. You can find out more about Alma on her website (www.AlmaAlexander.org), her Facebook page (https://www.facebook.com/pages/Alma-Alexander/67938071280) or her blog (http://anghara.livejournal.com).

About Book View Café

Book View Café is a professional authors' cooperative offering DRM-free ebooks in multiple formats to readers around the world. With authors in a variety of genres including mystery, romance, fantasy, and science fiction, Book View Café has something for everyone.

Book View Café is good for readers because you can enjoy high-quality DRM-free ebooks from your favorite authors at a reasonable price.

Book View Café is good for writers because 95% of the profit goes directly to the book's author.

Book View Café authors include Nebula, Hugo, and Philip K. Dick Award winners, Nebula, Hugo, World Fantasy, and Rita Award nominees, and *New York Times* bestsellers and notable book authors.

www.bookviewcafe.com

Made in the USA
Charleston, SC
24 February 2015